SPECIAL MESSAGE TO READERS

This book is published by

THE ULVERSCROFT FOUNDATION,

a registered charity in the U.K., No. 264873

The Foundation was established in 1974 to provide funds to help towards research, diagnosis and treatment of eye diseases. Below are a few examples of contributions made by THE ULVERSCROFT FOUNDATION:

★ A new Children's Assessment Unit at Moorfield's Hospital, London.

★ Twin operating theatres at the Western Ophthalmic Hospital, London.

★ The Frederick Thorpe Ulverscroft Chair of Ophthalmology at the University of Leicester.

★ Eye Laser equipment to various eye hospitals.

If you would like to help further the work of the Foundation by making a donation or leaving a legacy, every contribution, no matter how small, is received with gratitude. Please write for details to:

THE ULVERSCROFT FOUNDATION,
The Green, Bradgate Road, Anstey,
Leicestershire, LE7 7FU. England.
Telephone: (0533) 364325

Love is
a time of enchantment:
in it all days are fair and all fields
green. Youth is blest by it,
old age made benign: the eyes of love see
roses blooming in December,
and sunshine through rain. Verily
is the time of true-love
a time of enchantment—and
Oh! how eager is woman
to be bewitched!

TO MAKE A LIGHT

The saga of the indomitable Irish beauty, Katie O'Neill who falls tempestuously in love with a visiting South African, Paul Van Riebeck. But their love is so overwhelming that they fight and part. Katie goes to Africa, is twice widowed and bears seven children. At last she meets Van Riebeck again and is free to marry him. The sorrows of their past quarrels and separations have brought them both wisdom.

HELGA MORAY

TO MAKE A LIGHT.

Complete and Unabridged

ULVERSCROFT
Leicester

First published in Great Britain in 1978

First Large Print Edition
published February 1989

Copyright © 1978 by Helga Moray

British Library CIP Data

Moray, Helga
To make a light.—Large print ed.—
Ulverscroft large print series: romance
I. Title
823′.914[F]

ISBN 0-7089-1947-2

Published by
F. A. Thorpe (Publishing) Ltd.
Anstey, Leicestershire
Set by Rowland Phototypesetting Ltd.
Bury St. Edmunds, Suffolk
Printed and bound in Great Britain by
T. J. Press (Padstow) Ltd., Padstow, Cornwall

1

INSIDE the large circular hut with thatched roof the walls were lined by black warriors wearing nothing but monkey tails between their legs. With spears held upright before them, they stood looking disdainfully proud, for they were the Matabele honour guard of King Lobengula—meaning "he who drives like the wind".

The King's naked haunches were squeezed into a wooden armchair draped with leopard skins, a beaded cloth between his legs, his stomach was the size of a bag of maize, his thighs immense, his melon-shaped head was decorated with white ostrich plumes. Through heavily lidded eyes he gazed down at a prisoner cringing at his feet.

"Speak!" Lobengula ordered and one of two warriors guarding the prisoner said, "Great King, this Moshana slave has dared to drink beer from your royal jar."

"Dog! Your lips have tasted the King's

beer." Lobengula's voice was a bull's bellow. "Cut off his lips," he instructed the guard.

A long knife flashed, the prisoner screamed, then his lips lay like worms at the king's feet.

Blood streaming from his grotesque mouth, the slave implored the King for mercy. "Mercy!"

"Your filthy nose has smelt the King's beer!" Lobengula cried to the guards. "Cut off his nose!"

With a downward slice of a short spear a warrior severed the man's nose from his face and the victim screamed in agony.

"Your eyes have seen the King's beer! Guard, cover his eyes!"

The warriors caught hold of the culprit and a knife point sliced neatly along the prisoner's hairline. Whilst the man screamed and writhed, they flayed his skin, dragging it down his forehead to cover his eyes with it like a bloodied curtain.

Lobengula laughed. "Feed him to my crocodiles in the River of White Stones."

As the screaming demented man was dragged away, the King turned his head around to look at the four white men, a Boer contingent led by one of the most famous Kaffir fighters, Commandant Paul Van Riebeck, who had been waiting to parley with Lobengula.

Disgusted by the King's cruelty, Van Riebeck muttered to his three friends, "Cruel bastard! I'd like to send *him* to the crocodiles."

Standing six foot four and of magnificent physique Van Riebeck had killed his first Kaffir when trekking from the Cape to the North, at the age of seven. God alone knew how many he had killed in battle since then, but Lobengula's cruelty revolted him. Now he stepped up to the King. His deep voice matched the strength of his personality.

"Is the great King done with his petty affairs?" He spoke the Matabele language. "Because the emissaries of the South African Republic do not like to be kept waiting."

Fierce pride in the Dutchman's blue eyes, like the blue that surrounds a flame, burned into the Kaffir's smoky eyes. "You have heard how we went to war with the English and how our Republic won

3

freedom back from the English? You have heard of our victory at Majuba Hill? Speak Lobengula."

Disgust and anger burned in Van Riebeck's eyes, his face was strong as a stone carving and the Matabele king forced a friendly expression to his own face, though hate for white men raced in his blood stream.

"*Aieu* . . . I have heard glorious tales of Dutch bravery, how with a few hundred men they beat off thousands of English."

"It is so," Van Riebeck solemnly declared, "and now once more our flag, the Vierkleur, floats high in Pretoria and over all the Dutch Republic. But let us talk of why we have come to Matabeleland. As friends we wish to warn you against the greed of the English, and in particular of one man—Cecil Rhodes. He is a vulture, that eats the victim before it is dead!"

Lobengula's heavily lidded eyes almost closed with slyness. "What could the English want of me?"

"Every fool knows they want grants to dig for gold in your country. Do you treat

4

me like a woman? If so, we shall leave— our time is valuable."

"Be patient—be patient," Lobengula said swiftly and, not wishing his parley to be overheard by his guard of honour, he manoeuvred his huge body from his throne. "Let us talk of these things in the cooler air."

"As the King wishes."

Van Riebeck threw a significant glance to the three Boers. They all considered it wise to help Lobengula keep face before his people and followed the savage out of the evil-smelling hut, relieved to escape the stench of Kaffir sweat and the rancid fat which they rubbed over their bodies.

The Matabele royal quarters were made up of two brick houses, built years ago by some English missionary. Behind them were rows of beehive thatched huts occupied by the King's wives. A circle of tall reeds enclosed the royal women's quarters. A distance away, covering miles of earth, were thousands of huts of Lobengula's subjects. Distant mountains stretched out to ring Matabeleland and pierce the sun in the scorched sky.

The royal yard which Lobengula led the

Boers over was scattered with heads and skins of oxen recently eaten at 60 royal feasts. Black clouds of flies hung almost immovable over the carcasses as savage dogs fought each other for the remains of rotting flesh. There was the added stench of goat's sour milk and sweating bodies of warriors sprawled around the yard sharpening spears and polishing long shields. They sprang up respectfully as Lobengula made his way to his ceremonial tree and squatted on a lionskin on the earth, as young, naked, beautiful black girls spread out lion and leopard skins for the Boers to sit on, then others came with platters of roasted meat and jars of Kaffir beer to set on mats before the men.

The girls exaggeratedly swayed their naked buttocks before the white men, and their perfectly formed breasts with large dark nipples made no movement as they walked. Their glowing black eyes were pools of lascivious invitation, but the Boers were too conscious of a white man's superiority to be tempted by black women.

Wearing moleskin trousers and faded shirts that clung to them with sweat the Boers sat cross-legged on the animal skins.

Their wide-brimmed hats gave some protection from the blazing sun. Their guns lay at hand on the ground before them. They took their long knives from their waists, chose portions of half-raw meat and cutting it up began to eat, whilst overhead vultures circled continuously, scrawny hairless necks stretched out awaiting prey.

"Now, my friends," Lobengula addressed the Boers, "our nations have been like brothers to each other for a long time starting from the lifetime of my father."

"Yes, Lobengula, even though at one time your father, Moselikatze, was our great enemy," Piet de Vries nodded encouragingly, "he became our great friend before he died."

"And have I not followed in my father's footsteps?" Lobengula demanded. "Do you fear that I shall take my friendship from the South African Republic to give it to the English?"

"No, no—you are too wise for such foolishness, Lobengula," Van Riebeck laughed, "for you know the Dutch rule the Transvaal. You know that in all the wars we fought with Zulus or Matabeles we have always been victorious. The South African Republic is once more a separate nation, no longer subject to the English."

"True, true, Commandant Van Riebeck, but the English who visit me here at the Place of Slaughter," he waved around the yard, "tell me how powerful is their White Queen."

"How do you know that they do not lie?" Van Breda leaned over the platters of meat to challenge the king. "*Who* amongst your people have ever seen her? How do you know that she even lives? That she is not a creature the English have invented to put fear into you?"

Lobengula's smoky eyes went bloodshot, and he was silent for several seconds as the thought took hold. "Yes, yes. Have any of your people seen or met this White Queen?"

"None of us have!" It was a lie, for Van Riebeck once on a mission to England had seen the small black-gowned Queen Victoria ride by in a carriage. "We do not know whether she lives or not. What man has proof?"

It was important for the Boers to remove

8

Lobengula's fears of the English to stop him selling them digging concessions.

"I do not deal with the lying English," Lobengula assured the four Boers.

"Yet we have learned that you have spoken to Englishmen coming from Cecil Rhodes, who want to buy rights to dig for gold in Matabeleland." Van Riebeck spoke warningly. "Do not be foolish and agree, for if you let them in to dig you will lose your power!"

"*Ja! Ja!*" De Vries went on. "And lose your *country*. You know well how the English have conquered the mighty Zulu nation."

"Only because some jackals betrayed King Cetewayo to the English," Lobengula barked angrily. "Before then the Zulu impis' spears drank of the blood of thousands of English. Think of the battle of Isandhlwana. Not a man, horse or dog was left alive."

"Yes, yes, terrible slaughter," the black-bearded Houton agreed unwillingly, for no white man liked the blacks to triumph even over the English. "But in the end the English were victorious. Do not forget

9

that, Lobengula, and they broke up the Zulu nation."

"You think they could do that with the Matabeles?" Lobengula angrily challenged in a bull's voice. "Never! We are the offspring of the Zulus! Our spears would drink the blood of every Englishman."

Van Riebeck said ominously, "It would be wiser not to let the English in to Matabeleland. Take our advice. We are Afrikaners—white men, it is true—but like you we are men of Africa, so beware and do not give the English rights to dig for gold in Matabeleland."

"*Ja, Ja*—no rights, Lobengula. Cecil Rhodes is *baif skelm*—no good for the Dutch or the Kaffirs," De Vries warned. "Ach, he is sick-making—never does he lie with a woman; his kraal is filled with pretty young boys. He is not a man like you or us, with wives and many children." De Vries waved his long knife around to include his companions and went on, "Already he tries to buy all the diamonds in Kimberley. He loves power—he thinks with diamonds and gold he can rule all Africa—Boers and Kaffir tribes. He would make slaves of your people. He believes the English should rule all men."

"*Aie-ee.*" Lobengula belched with satisfaction of his food. His strong teeth tore into a lump of meat and blood ran down from both sides of his mouth over his rows of chins to rest on his great oiled belly where flies were already feasting upon it. "And what do the Dutch advise that Lobengula shall do?" he asked slyly.

"Refuse any grants at all!" Van Riebeck snapped. "If you wish to remain king of your country."

"But tell me, big white one—why do you Dutch care so much for the welfare of me and the Matabeles?"

"One reason is because we have lived for years in friendship with you; the other reason is that we wish to stop the English coming up here, for Matabeleland borders our South African Republic. We have found gold in the Transvaal, but we sell no concessions to the English, rather let the gold lie in the earth."

De Vries took up the theme. "What use is gold? Can you eat or drink it, lie with it like a woman? Can it bear children? No! Man's riches are counted by the size of his land, by his number of cattle, his wives, his children."

"*Aie—aie*," Lobengula grunted "but my life as King of the Matabeles is not easy. My warriors want to dig their spears into human flesh. How much longer can I keep them like dogs on the leash? They want to kill men and if the English come here to dig, later my warriors can make war on them. This may be a good answer to my problem."

The Boers simultaneously burst out laughing at the cunning of the savage and it flashed to Van Riebeck's mind that a couple of deep knife thrusts over Lobengula's disgusting belly and into his heart, then a swift war with the Matabeles and the country would become part of the South African Republic. But today they were only four Boers here.

"Once more I say to you—do not sell concessions," Van Riebeck said. "Think about Kimberley. It belonged to the Orange Free State until diamonds were found, then the English annexed it. This will happen to Matebeleland if you let them in."

By the expression on Lobengula's heavy

face, the Boers felt they had at last penetrated to the savage's brain. There followed a few moments of silence whilst Lobengula ponderously thought of all that had been said. He was regretting having fed his favourite sister to the crocodiles last week for she could have advised him, but the witch doctors had smelt her out and accused her of evil thoughts and so causing his twelve-year-old wife of bearing a still-born son. At last Lobengula spoke.

"If my friends the Dutch worry about the safety of me and my people then I place myself and country under your protection."

Van Riebeck silently cursed the rotten agreement, the Pretoria Convention, which his people had made with the English Government at the recent Boer victory of Majuba; whilst it restored their freedom to them, it forbade them to annex any Kaffir tribes. His comrades also knew this well and now glanced at him, waiting for him to give a tactful answer.

"This thing we could do, Lobengula," Van Riebeck lied, "and to begin with we shall send one of our best men here with his wife and family to live at your Court.

He will advise on the best way of dealing with the English when they come begging for digging rights."

"Ah, that is well," the King nodded slowly, "that might solve my problems, and I shall promise my younger warriors to let them fight some tribes near the Zambesi—we are in need of slaves."

"That is as you wish, Lobengula. So it is agreed between us as allies that you will await our Ambassador to live with you and not give any digging rights to the English or to anyone else?"

"It is agreed between us, big white one. To your President, Paul Kruger, give my greetings and oaths of friendship."

The Boers finished off their Kaffir beers, wiped their knives bloodied from the meat on the lion and leopard skins, returned them to the sheaths on their belts and picking up their guns they stood up, but Lobengula had eaten and drunk too much to move.

"A good journey homeward and come soon again to eat meat with Lobengula who awaits your Ambassador. Oh, and in friendship, I hope your Ambassador will bring me a present of some cattle?"

"Two hundred head of our finest beasts," Van Riebeck said, slinging his long gun over his back. "Now we must go."

"*Aiee*, and, Commandant, if ever you meet a man who has seen the great White English Queen, *send* him to me and I will give him many presents of fine lionskins to hear him tell about her."

"Ah that is *if* she really lives—I think she and her power are all English lies," De Vries said.

The four Boers patted their stomachs as a sign of thanks for the meat and beer then walked to where their horses were tethered. They swung into the saddle and turned the horses' heads around and jogging out of the royal courtyard, they reined in for a second to watch a savage fight between the half wild dogs with *assvogels* which had swooped down on an ox's carcass. The dogs' huge pointed teeth tried for a grip on the terrible evil-looking birds whose claws tore at them whilst the Matabeles stood around cheering and laughing.

"*Maetie!*" Houton swore. "It's barbaric here. Let's go, let's ride out before these bastards forget we have signed a peace treaty with them."

The Dutchmen dug their heels into their horses and rode swiftly out of the kraal.

Once out in the bush Van Riebeck said, "Lobengula is so cunning that I'm not sure if we really succeeded with him or not."

"*Ja*, we must send a man of ours to live at his elbow as soon as possible. By God! I hope I'm not chosen for the job." De Vries spat out his disgust onto the dusty stony earth.

2

HEARING horses' hooves come thundering over the hard baked earth toward the house, Katie Van Riebeck sensed it was her husband. No other man rode like that. Excitedly she bundled some papers off her lap on to a nearby table and rushed over the lionskin floor-covering, out of the living room to the stoep.

Already Van Riebeck was reining in. He jumped to the ground and a Kaffir boy sprang forward to take his horse. Then the big man took the steps to the stoep two at a time and Katie was wrapped in his arms.

"Oh darling—darling. Thank God you're home!" She held her face up for his kiss. Then a few moments later she broke away saying, "The two weeks seemed an eternity. I was terrified of you being in Matabeleland. That swine, Lobengula, could so easily have turned treacherous and murdered you."

He chuckled. "*Ach*, Katje my love—

17

you will never lose your Irish sense of drama. The Matabele now fear us because we've beaten them so often in battle."

He had always called her "Katje" from their first meeting in Ireland, when she was a seventeen-year-old beauty and he about twenty-one, in Ireland to buy thoroughbred horses to mix with African stock. They had immediately fallen in love, but he had feared to take her to Africa. She was too delicately born and raised to endure life on the Dark Continent. Now he smiled down at her pale face crowned with the red-gold hair, not as intense a colour as in her girlhood, but beautiful and exciting to him. And her big eyes, they would never lose the leopard quality in their green goldenness.

"Well, darling, you're back and that's all that matters. Was the mission a success?"

"Yes, as much as you can trust a Kaffir's word. Lobengula agreed to do what we want."

"Good."

She lifted his wide-brimmed hat off and ran her fingers through his thick golden hair, loosening it from the damp scalp.

Then he unslung his gun and propped it next to the door.

"Brandy, darling—coffee?" she asked.

"A long brandy—I've been in the saddle for hours. And coffee too. But first I should have the boys pour water over me in the backyard and change into clean clothes. I'm not fit to sit with my beloved wife."

"Silly, don't you remember years ago in Lorenzo Marques how Mary said I love everything about Papa Paul. Even the smell of his perspiration makes me feel safe. Sit down and stretch out those long legs."

He settled into a chair and she hurried to the kitchen to order coffee, thinking of what a marvellous father Van Riebeck had been to her eight children that a fourteen-year-old like Mary should have said that she even loved the smell of his perspiration. Back in the living-room she got a brandy bottle and glass and brought them to the stoep.

"Thank you, Katje." He poured himself a big Cape brandy whilst she pulled up an oxskull stool bleached to whiteness, to sit beside him.

"So you succeeded with the Matabeles, as you always succeed."

"I'm not sure about that. Lobengula seemed to absorb our warning about Cecil Rhodes and the English but time will tell."

"It's extraordinary about Cecil Rhodes. In a letter from John he said that he'd met Rhodes in London and he offered to employ him out here when he comes down from Oxford. John's accepted and of course I'm delighted. I was beginning to think he'd never leave England."

Van Riebeck grunted. John, Katje's eldest child by her dead English husband, Captain Richard Eaton, had been a problem to Van Riebeck, for he had lacked the manliness of Boer boys. At fourteen he had fought well in a terrible Batlapin attack on this very house, then afterwards he had gone to pieces and since then he had lived in England with his paternal English grandmother and had been educated at Eton and Oxford as his dead father had wished. Typical of John, Van Riebeck thought, that an odd type Englishman like Rhodes would appeal to him.

"I'm surprised John wants to come back," he said. "I thought the luxurious life with Lady Eaton and the splendid shooting and hunting he got on the Duke of Rotherford's estate would have entirely absorbed him." He sipped his brandy. "So his father's cousin, your devoted admirer Lord Howard Aubrey de Rivers, 9th Duke of Rotherford, doesn't try to stop John from leaving England?"

Katie burst out laughing. "I see you give Howard his full title. It was he who introduced John to Rhodes and you know it was Nancy he admired—not me." She tried to lie convincingly.

"You never could lie well, thank God. The Duke liked Nancy when you were beyond his reach out in Africa and because being your daughter she reminded him of you, but, poor brute, it was *you—you—you*, whom he fell in love with. Well, and how was Nancy whilst I was away? Less moody, less tearful?"

Katie shook her head and frowned. "No —if anything she's worse. She's lying down with a headache and she's utterly determined to leave the Transvaal as soon as possible to go home to Abend Bloem. But I'm not going to burden you with it now; you've quite enough to fill your mind with at the moment."

His blue eyes gazed deeply into her worried ones as he leaned over and clasped her hand.

"Katje, my love—not all my thoughts are given to the welfare of the South African Republic. There is room in my mind to think of the family too. Not just the children I've sired but all of yours, too. Now tell me everything about them."

"Thank you darling. Well Madame Visele wrote about Mary. She says Mary's voice is more than fulfilling her early hopes. She advises us to try to send her to Milan to study with one of the great coaches there because she could well be a great operatic singer."

"That sounds a bit like a teacher's over enthusiasm."

"I don't know." Katie was a little indignant. "Mary's voice was beautiful a couple of years ago when we were in the Cape. I think we must consider what Madame Visele says. Thank God all the offspring are all right; Ken is at University, Eileen is an angel and Terence is beginning to make his way as a Doctor and Paul's a success running the ostrich farm. It's only Nancy who is a headache at the moment. Last night she burst into my room demanding hysterically to be sent back to the Cape. Poor Nancy!"

Katie had never seen her eldest daughter in such a terrible state before and she shuddered at what she believed was the unholy reason for her desperate unhappiness. Over the past few months, Katie had beseeched God to cure the beautiful girl of her terrible desires and had carefully kept her secret suspicions from Van Riebeck, but now as things worsened she was tempted to appeal to him for help.

He poured another brandy and sipped it. The news about Nancy was annoying. "It looks as if we'll have to find a trek going south and send Nancy back on it."

"Yes, I suppose so." But this would only lead Nancy into further temptation. She dare not let her remain at the Cape; she would have to sail for England. "I think she should go back to England." Now Katie brushed a flying insect aside and said as lightly as she could, "Was old Kruger pleased with your trip to Lobengula?"

"Oh yes. At the moment like all of us he is frantically worried about the financial state of the South African Republic. God knows we desperately need more colonists but of the right kind, not English; they just bring in rebellious ideas and before you know it they're appealing to England for protection."

"Yes, yes, it's a pity."

In an effort to interest people in Holland and Germany to emigrate to the Transvaal, Katie had written several articles from a European woman's viewpoint extolling life in the South African Republic, telling of the 6,000 acre farms, the crops that grew with magical speed, cattle that fattened as in fairy tales, servants almost begging to work for small rewards, the Boers' friendship and godliness. She described it as a Utopia for young men and women to help build a new world as the immigrants had and were building in America.

"Darling, I wonder if any of those articles I wrote for the German and Dutch newspapers were published and if they'll help to bring settlers in? I'm sure your translations into Dutch and German were excellent."

"I forgot to tell you." He suddenly sat upright, eyes alight with excitement. "The Volksraad have received over a hundred enquiries from people in Holland and Germany referring to your articles."

She clapped her hands in delighted satisfaction. "How splendid—oh, I'm glad if I've helped."

"You have and in addition there's been an official enquiry from Bismarck's Chancellory in connection with your articles."

"Bismarck! But that makes it all sound important."

"It certainly does. Kruger thinks, and I agree, that Bismarck's policy of isolation is doing a turnabout and the German people also want a colonial empire, but they can't have it in the South African Republic! If they settle here, they must swear allegiance to us. When I visited Germany with Kruger, we discussed all that with Bismarck. Being a north German, he speaks Platt-Deutsch which is a lot like our Taallow Dutch—so he and Kruger got along like brothers. Yes, Germans would be most welcome in the Transvaal as settlers."

"I'll write some more articles and we should also send them to Belgium newspapers too and this time I can say we have some schools. Whilst you were away I went into Lydenburg and arranged for the loan of the Church hall four days a week and I begged the Austrian doctor's wife to give lessons to the smaller children. I was writing letters to send to all the farms to tell them about the school when you came home."

"Katje, Katje, what a marvellous woman you are!"

"I want to do everything I can to help the South African Republic." Her voice broke on a sudden sob that surprised even herself and she finished softly, "I can never forget, Paul, that if you had not married me—an Irish woman instead of a Boer—that you had a very good chance of being President in Kruger's place."

He reached out and caught her hand. His hold was so tight she could have cried out in pain, then after a few seconds, he let go of her and muttered, "For God's sake don't ever fret about such things. We are so bloody lucky to be together—beside that nothing else matters. Now I'm going out to have the Kaffirs throw water over me. Then I'll come to our room." He unfolded his great height from the chair and stood up. "You'll be waiting for me?"

She nodded eagerly as she looked up at him like a tower rising above her. Her green-gold eyes seemed to merge into his eyes and her whole being felt it was floating up to become absorbed in his. Absurd! Ridiculous! She was forty-five, her daughter Nancy was so unhappy just down the corridor but Van Riebeck, this great blond giant of a man, filled her world.

"Do you wish to see your little sons after your shower? They're playing at the waterhole with Maarje."

"No, no, I'll see them later."

She understood him perfectly. "Then go quickly, my darling." She loved him now at this second, were it possible, more than she had ever loved him. "Is that what maturity means?" she asked herself feeling a little bemused by all of her emotions. Then she murmured, "I'll be in our room waiting for you. We've a good two hours before dinner."

"I'd like it to be two years," he

chuckled, then passed into the living-room, fitting his gun into the rack. Going through the house he reached the backyard where he called to some Kaffir boys lolling under the trees, to prepare the buckets of water.

In a small enclosure while he stripped, the Kaffirs climbed a tree and then commenced to pour buckets of water showering over him. Even they enjoyed the sight of the big boss's magnificent body.

3

"FORGIVE me, Papa Paul—I've tried to like the Transvaal as I know you've done your best to help me to like it." Nancy, almost a replica of her beautiful mother, looked up at Van Riebeck with great eyes streaming with tears. "But help me to go back to the Cape."

Van Riebeck's stern gaze examined her by the light of the oil lantern swinging on a cord from the stoep's ceiling just above her head.

Van Riebeck thought, "She is the incarnation of Katje at this age, hair, skin, eyes, lovely contours of the body, but she lacks Katje's guts, courage, stamina."

He spoke softly to be sure that Katje singing the youngest children to sleep in their room off the living-room should not overhear him. "Tell me, Nancy, *what* is eating into you like white ants that destroy furniture?"

In the evening gloom to Nancy he

looked like a demi-god, his bigness, his handsome blond security—so like the young Paul. The likeness tortured her and she blurted out, "Oh, Papa Paul, I can't tell you!"

"Rubbish! Of course you can! We've been good friends since you were a tiny girl, besides I'm your step-Papa. If you can't confide in me *who* can you tell your troubles to? Am I right in thinking that you've fallen in love with some young man in Capetown? A lawyer or a doctor?" He knew well that this was not the case.

"No! No!" She stamped her foot in the same imperious way that had been so common with Katje. "And I know you and Mama have flung every eligible young bachelor in Pretoria at my head and they've all been attentive, kind—also proposed marriage." Sobs suddenly burst from her. "But I want none of them!"

"Tell me," he put an arm about her shoulders, "who is the man whom you *do* want?" With deep sadness he already knew the answer.

He felt her shoulders stiffen under his arm. "I cannot tell."

With a quick decision he decided it was

timely to air the wound in her soul; covering infection created gangrene.

He murmured, "Then I'll tell you. It's Paul, your half-brother, you think you're in love with."

Her whole body sagged sideways against him, for it was relief beyond measure to be able to talk of this thing that was eating her soul away.

"Yes, yes; Papa Paul, you've guessed the truth. But how?"

"The day the Dutch finally beat the British at Majuba Hill and after his marvellous fighting Paul left at once for the Cape with Terence. You were half demented when you found he had gone. I easily guessed the truth."

"Dear God! I pray Mama never guesses. It would kill her to know I'm in love with my half-brother."

"I don't think she guessed. Certainly she's never spoken to me of it and ten months have passed since that day."

"Oh, Papa Paul, it's been such a terrible time for me. Life is nothing to me without Paul."

"Was that why you ran away from Abend Bloem to the diamond fields?"

31

"No—I wanted to get away from home to make a fortune of my own. I know it sounds silly because I hired a bodyguard to protect me from men, who offered me diamonds as easily as other men give flowers, but I thought I might earn a fortune in one of the gambling houses— dealing at Faro. Then Mama sent Paul to find me and that started it all."

"How far has this thing gone between you?" Incest was a serious business; he felt he must find out about Nancy and Paul.

In a low stumbling voice she said, "I'll tell you . . . but you swear you won't tell Mama . . . the shock would be too much for her."

"I swear I'll never tell anyone."

"All right—we were in Kimberley when a devil's wind storm swept in from the veld." Her mind flashed back to that night in the Faro Club when a sudden howling wind arose, and she told Van Riebeck how it had all happened.

"Well, Nancy." Van Riebeck's voice wrenched her from that wonderful night to the present. "You went to his room and I presume neither of you could withstand the temptation to make love. Paul should have been stronger."

"Don't blame him, Papa Paul, don't! We love each other! How could we have fought against it?"

"My poor Nancy. I remember you thought you were in love with that young officer I found you entangled with on the night of the shipwreck. Not long afterwards in London you eloped to marry Eric Preston and lived in Florence. After that there was your second cousin, the Duke of Rotherford, whom you thought you were in love with."

"But was I to blame because my husband liked to make love to boys? Rotherford came as a comfort to me, but I never made love with him."

She sobbed and blew her nose on the big silk handkerchief Van Riebeck pushed into her hands. "But still I burn with shame when I think about all of that. It was Mama Rotherford was in love with and came out to Africa to see—not *me*." She swiftly added protectively, "Although of course Mama never encouraged him ever, even while you were in St. George's

33

Hospital in London with your broken legs after the shipwreck."

"Bless you—I *know* that. I know my Katje." He chuckled with the comfort of complacency.

"Oh, Papa Paul, you and Mama are so lucky the way your love has worked out."

"Yes, yes, God at last smiled on us, but I can tell you, Nancy, that we wasted many good years in mad quarrels and partings—in unnecessary suffering."

"But at last you are *united*, whereas Paul and I can *never* be. It's cruel of God to have let us fall in love when there is no hope for us ever to belong together."

"Poor little girl, it's hard but you must face up to it. Why not go back to England and stay with your grandmother? Lady Eaton would be overjoyed to have you and you'll meet the most eligible bachelors in England. For God's sake make up your mind, Nancy, that you can never marry or breed with your half-brother. Incest is a terrible thing."

"Oh, Papa Paul, is that really true? Or is it only old wives' tales?" Her great green-gold eyes looked pleadingly at him.

"I'm speaking the truth. If you had a

child by Paul it would probably be crippled in some way or certainly weak in the head. Incest is ever a criminal offence. Centuries ago in England it was punishable by death and that applied to the female as well as the male."

Her head dropped forward on to her chest and her whole body sagged against him as she murmured, "What's to become of me? I just can't go on without him. Each day is a hell to live through and the longing for him instead of lessening only increases.

"Nevertheless you must completely give him up."

"But I did—I did. At the battle of Majuba Hill when I saw him climbing up amongst the Dutch, dodging and hiding from tree to tree so the English on top of the hill would not see and shoot him, I was so terrified that he'd be killed that I vowed to God if He spared Paul's life, I would never lie with him again, but now all I ask is to be allowed to *see* him, *talk* to him! This separation is cruel. Remember that for six months at Abend Bloem, when we returned from

35

Kimberley, we lay together in my room every night."

Nostalgia swept over Van Riebeck as he recalled how he used to ride from his own Cape homestead adjoining Abend Bloem, to lie with Katje in the great old house, *Magtig*—what lusting and loving those rooms had known. Against his sensible judgement he pitied Paul and Nancy. He said, "Has Paul written to you?"

"No—you see we quarrelled after the battle of Majuba when I told him I had sworn to God not to lie with him in thanksgiving for God having spared his life."

"But then why were you so hysterical when you discovered that he had ridden off without you?"

"Because at the last moment I couldn't bear the thought of parting from him and I ran to tell him that I'd defy God—break my vow and continue our love. But he had already gone."

"Well, well," Katie called out as she came from the house to the stoep. "There's going to be a full moon—how lovely." She wondered what Van Riebeck and Nancy had been so secretly talking about. Would to God the girl had confided in him.

Paul took his arm from Nancy's shoulders and turning around winked meaningfully at Katie, but Nancy remained with her back to her mother staring out into the darkness. She needed time to compose herself.

They were all quiet for a few moments as they listened to the far off roar of a lion then Van Riebeck said, "Nancy and I were discussing the possibility of her leaving Lydenburg."

Paul spoke casually trying to make light of the matter but Katie immediately sensed the air of tenseness and said, "Yes, we must discuss the idea—after dinner perhaps? Now, darling, Adrian and Franz are in bed and waiting for 'Papa's' goodnight kiss, so do go to them—they're ready for sleep."

When Van Riebeck had gone, Katie went and put her arm around Nancy's waist. She ached to be able to comfort her, but even whilst she guessed about Nancy's unholy love for Paul, the girl had never confided in her so she dare not voice her fears. All she said was "My darling one, whatever it is that troubles you, we will help you if we can. I think you should go back to England for a while—a complete change of scene is often helpful, and remember the Dutch saying, '*Alles sal regt kom*'—All will come right—and never stop praying."

4

IN the great four-poster bed, Katie lay stretched out along the length of Van Riebeck, her head on his chest, his arm around her. The oil lamps were out, the shutters open to let the moonlight stream in to the room.

Her eyes on the sky made pale by the brilliance of the huge moon drifting across the heavens, Katie said, "Before dinner, when you and Nancy were on the stoep, was she confiding in you?"

There was a moment's silence before he answered. "Yes, my love, 'confided' is exactly the word—so you know that I cannot tell you what she said."

"Ye-es—I understand and it all makes me desperately unhappy—she talks to you and not to me, which means she's ashamed to tell me things that have happened. God help us! Her reticence toward me confirms my fears." Katie shuddered at the unholy picture plaguing her mind. "I can't bear to think of it all. But how can we help her?"

"I've been turning that question over in my mind. It's a cruel joke of fate that Nancy has all your fire and impetuosity but somehow it's always stirred into a destructive form, whereas your energies have always been constructive. My advice is get her out of Africa as soon as possible and to Lady Eaton in England. The old girl will be delighted because John will soon be leaving to work for this bloody Rhodes in the Cape Colony, so Nancy can take his place."

"You're right, it's what I've been thinking. God help Nancy, what a troubled existence the poor girl has had since she grew into a young woman. Naturally, after her performance at Majuba when Paul left, I've guessed that she thinks she's in love with him—God help us. How do you think Paul feels about the horrible business?"

"He's a man; no need to worry about him. A young bull can lie with women all over the place. Nancy is the one who needs our help. I'd like to get her to join some safe trek going south as soon as possible.

Meanwhile you write to your sister Liz to book passage for Nancy on the first ship to England. After her arrival don't give her and Paul any time together in the Cape."

"You're right of course. I'll write to Liz in the morning."

"Good, we'll go into Pretoria tomorrow and make enquiries about a trek that she can join."

"Oh darling thank you."

"Now don't be so upset. Half-sisters and brothers thinking themselves in love has happened before today, you know. It will all blow over—they're young. Now let's get some sleep—I'm a bit fagged out after the last two weeks at the Volksraad and that meeting with Lobengula was a trial."

"Of course, my love, you sleep and God bless you." She leaned up to kiss him. Then she put her head back on his chest and lay still.

Within minutes he was asleep but she lay thinking that to send Nancy to England via the Cape was fine in theory but in actuality she knew once Nancy arrived at Abend Bloem and met Paul she would not leave for England. Deep within her Katie

41

knew that Nancy was unreliable. She still remembered the pain caused by Nancy in London when at fifteen she had eloped with Eric Preston to Florence. Then later there had been the agony of her disappearance from Abend Bloem after she discovered the Duke of Rotherford was not in love with her. A detective paid by Katie had found her at the Kimberley diamond mines and Paul had gone to bring her home.

Now Paul must be protected from the fascination of Nancy. But how? How was she, their mother, to rescue them from each other? A strong believer in prayer throughout her Roman Catholic upbringing, she held her rosary in her hand, playing the beads through her fingers as she silently repeated "Hail Marys" begging God for guidance.

Suddenly an answer came quite clearly to her. Paul and Nancy must not meet in the Cape! She would send Nancy down to Abend Bloem in the belief that she would find Paul there caring for the ostrich farm, but in reality Paul would be trekking North, for Katie would telegraph to him to come up at once, as gold had been discovered on the land ceded to him for fighting with the Afrikaner Korps eighteen months previously. In the vastness of the veld Nancy and Paul would unknowingly pass each other.

Infinitely relieved at what she believed to be an answer to her prayers, Katie had started to fall asleep when a bat flew in at the wide open window. Her first impulse was to awaken Van Riebeck, but she did not, and getting gently out of bed, she found her slipper and chased the ugly creature out.

She told herself despairingly that it was impossible to sleep with wide open windows in this horrible country for the veld claimed everything, even the interior of the homes. Bats, insects, snakes were frequent visitors. She closed the shutters quietly and returned to bed, where she lay along the length of Van Riebeck's big powerful back and in the far distance she heard a leopard cough. She shivered and sadly reminded herself that this was where her life must be spent.

She had no fears that wild animals would reach the house for at a good distance it was encircled by high fires which special Kaffirs tended throughout the night. The fires were there to protect the vast herds of cattle as well as the homestead.

It was the Kaffirs Katie dreaded. The devilish Matabele, the Zulus and other tribes even though they had pledged peace with the Dutch. Behind the house a part of her heart lay buried in the grave of her baby daughter Helen. Dead now more than six years, her body pierced through by a Batlapin assegai in this very room.

Perhaps Helen had been favoured by God by being preserved from the storms of life, such as poor Nancy seemed to be constantly confronting.

Nancy and Paul! What would she do when Paul arrived eager, excited, greedy to work the gold on his land? Well, she would think up something before he came. His trek up would take him almost three months. By then she would be ready with a profitable answer. She had actually heard rumours that gold had been discovered in the Witwatersrand district. She would explore the rumours and if Paul's land bore no gold she would somehow buy him some land that did. But she would say nothing of her plans to Van Riebeck. He disapproved of diamond and gold mining and might forbid her to telegraph Paul to come up.

Then wearied of her thoughts she placed her worries in God's hands, silently praying, "I've done my best, now it's over to You" and she fell asleep.

The following morning at breakfast, Van Riebeck told Nancy, "Your mother and I have decided to send you back to the Cape, but once there you must sail immediately for England."

She was ecstatic with the thought of being reunited with Paul. "Yes, yes, Father, I'll take the first ship sailing for England." She lied, for once she was back with Paul, nothing would make her leave him.

"We'll miss you terribly, darling," Katie told her, "but Lydenburg is not the place for you. It was wonderful how you and Terence and Paul came up to help Papa Paul in the Boers' fight against the English."

Nancy was almost hysterical with relief that she was to leave. "Oh, Papa Paul, we'll all come back again if you need us."

"Thanks, Nancy, but I think we should be at peace with the English as long as we can get this clause of the Queen's Sovereignty lifted from the Pretoria Convention and as long as this damned Cecil Rhodes doesn't press to get his hands on Matabeleland."

"But if John joins his staff," Nancy cried excitedly, "he could explain the Dutch viewpoint to Rhodes—perhaps even make a friend out of him for the Dutch."

"Perhaps—perhaps," Van Riebeck said. "Your brother John was a true dyed-in-the-wool English boy, even before he went to live in England. Now after all these years there—I think we're going to find that he'll see most of the South African problems from a thoroughly English viewpoint."

"Oh Lord," Katie sighed, "more difficulties. Is the family going to become a house divided against itself?"

"But, Mama, a mixed family is interesting. Terence, Paul, Kenneth, Mary and I are true South Africans—John is the Englishman. It was because our father was English that Kenneth felt he couldn't come up with Terence, Paul and me. He didn't want to fight against Englishmen."

"I wouldn't mind fighting the English!" Seven year old Franz, a small replica in looks of Van Riebeck, spoke up in between shovelling spoonfuls of porridge into his mouth. "I'm truly Dutch like Papa and so is Adrian but he's too young to know it." He nodded toward his golden-haired little brother.

They all laughed but Katie wondered in God's name what lay ahead. "Franz darling, we must pray that there won't be any more wars here. The Transvaal is bigger than all of France. There's plenty of land for millions of people to live here in peace."

"But *I* want to fight when I'm big like Papa and my brother Paul."

"You'll have plenty of chances, my man, to fight the unfriendly Kaffirs up here," Van Riebeck told him, "but now hurry and finish your porridge if you want to go into Pretoria with us."

"Me too, Papa?" Adrian asked.

"Of course you too." Van Riebeck leaned over and affectionately tousled his youngest son's thatch of golden hair, then standing up, he scraped back his chair. "Katje, excuse me, I must go and see Jantze about preparing the wagon and Obsete about the cattle and wheat whilst we're away. We may have to stay in Pretoria a week or more waiting for a suitable trek for Nancy to join."

"Oh Lord! I'm getting nervous of her going on a trek without us. She must take one of the maids. But which one? I can't spare Maarje. I need her for Adrian, but I'll talk to Joanna about which maid she should take."

"Mama, I don't need a maid," Nancy said, "if I'm going to join up with some nice family."

"Your mother is right, Nancy," Van Riebeck said. "You must have your own servant and I'm also going to send Jantze with you."

"Jantze! But don't you need him here?"

"We've got other good head boys including his sons, but you must have a man to help out in hunting for meat along the way and he's a fine shot. I'll give him two horses and he will ride beside the wagon you travel in. Anyone will be delighted to have the great Zulu on their trek."

"Papa Paul," Nancy cried, "I'm causing you and Mama a lot of trouble—I'm sorry."

"You're our girl, Nancy—anything we do for you cannot be trouble to us. We just want you to be happy."

Van Riebeck strode out of the dining-room and bursting into tears Nancy rushed to kneel beside Katie to sink her head on her lap where she wept convulsively.

Katie stroked her hair as she fought back her own tears. "Don't, darling. Everything will work out. I know your life up here has been very dull."

"Oh, Mama—I don't know how you can endure it—when I think of you dressed . . . in your beautiful ball gowns . . . going to wonderful parties in London . . . now—now, you're wasted up here!"

"Nonsense!" Katie tried to sound convincing. "Of course I miss the gaiety sometimes, but I've got Papa Paul and the wish of his life is to have the South African Republic grow into a fine country."

Nancy broke into fresh tears and Franz called out teasingly.

"Nancy's a cry baby—a cry baby."
Then Adrian joined in lisping. "Nancy's a cry baby."

Nancy looked up and dried her eyes. "All right, you two, wait until I find you crying again."

"Off you go, Nancy, and start packing," Katie said.

"I will, Mama," and with relief she ran to her room.

Sighing, Katie tinkled the brass bell and a coloured maid in a stiff white dress came in answer.

"Send Maarje to me, please, Josie."

"Yes, Missus," and the girl padded out on her bare feet.

"God help me to get through Nancy's departure." Katie silently prayed at the sudden realization that she was to be left with only two of the ten children she had borne. Then Maarje came in. Like the other maid, she was in stiff white but wore a white bandana on her head.

For several years the coloured girl had been the smallest children's nursemaid. She had travelled to England and Lorenzo Marques with Katie and she loved her mistress dearly. She was also reputed to have psychic powers.

"Missus, we go to Pretoria?" she asked.

"Yes, but how on earth did you know that?" Katie was amazed.

"By Missus' sad face—I know Miss Nancy is going away." She tapped at her heart with her long black finger as her smoky eyes glistened with tears. "I'm sorry for Missus. It will be lonely for Missus when Miss Nancy is gone, but later young Baas Paul will come, then many good things will happen for Missus."

"Maarje, you're extraordinary—how you know these things. Off you go and pack the children's clothes."

"Yes, Missus, and Philip, shall he come too?"

On the ship going to England a young English steward had fallen in love with Maarje and Katie had arranged their evening and given them their wedding breakfast at the house she had rented in London. Now she smiled.

"Of course Philip too. Have I ever parted you from your husband? You silly girl."

Maarje giggled shyly. "Missus is so

51

good. I'll go and tell Philip. He will be glad, he likes Pretoria." Maarje slipped away.

"Poor young fellow," Katie thought, "life up here was probably terribly dull for him, although Van Riebeck had turned him into a good shot and often took him hunting, when lions or leopard came too close to the herds to attack the cows."

"Well you two," Katie looked at the seven-year-old Franz and four-year-old Adrian, "hurry up and finish your breakfast."

They were true Van Riebecks with their father's marvellous blue eyes and corn-gold hair. How he loved them and what bitter gall that his eldest son Paul could never bear his name. Sad, for most Boers of Van Riebeck's age had sixteen to twenty children but he, loving her for all the years they had been apart, had never been able to marry until she was free. This too had been bad for him politically.

5

WHEN the children had finished breakfast, Katie sent them off with Maarje to play with the domestic servants' children in an enclosed playground made years ago when John and Kenneth, Mary and Eileen lived up here with her, before she had been obliged to leave them at the Cape under her sister Liz's care to be properly educated. In the playground were see-saws, swings and a tiny hut which housed all types of toys, mostly carved in wood by Van Riebeck. Tambouti trees and hartecoal trees lent the big playground shade.

In the large kitchen, where strings of onions, potatoes and biltong hung from hooks on the whitewashed rafters, and where the smell of coffee was always strong, Katie found the fat cook giving orders to vegetable maids to prepare pumpkins.

Lifting her long skirts as she climbed over several fat black babies crawling over the floor made of earth and dried ox blood and highly polished, Katie reached the cook near the great iron range.

"Good morning, Joanna."

"Good morning, Missus." The blue-black face broke into a wide smile showing teeth white as chalk. Joanna, like all the Kaffirs, adored both the Missus and the Baas, who unlike most Dutch masters seldom used the whip on any of his blacks.

"Missus like pumpkin stuffed with mince meat for lunch?" Joanna asked eagerly.

"It would be nice, Joanna, but we're going into Pretoria so use up the meat for frikadels and don't put too much onion in them because of the children, and also fry up some chicken and make mossboletjies, also a few without wine for Baas Adrian and Baas Franz—just put cinnamon in them. Oh, and I'll take the Hussapotheck too. Even though it's a short journey, someone might need some medicines. Will you see that the vinegar hasn't gone sour or the lavender water dried up?"

"*Ja, ja*, Missus. Leave it all to me. Joanna care for all."

"Good, and don't forget plenty of boiled

water, milk and coffee and a bottle of brandy for the Baas." Katie smiled at the black woman who was always so reliable. "Joanna, what a help you are to me. Tell me, how is your daughter? Did she have a good night?"

The dark face lost all its gaiety. "No, Missus, Janga is bad still." Joanna leaned her fat body across the wide wooden table that separated her from Katie so that the other servants polishing the great copper pots should not hear her as she whispered, "Missus, I think Janga smoke much dacca."

"No!" Katie was very upset. "She's so young, Joanna—only fourteen—who would have given her dacca?"

"That skelm son of Obsete, he wants to lie with her in the bushes, and she good Christian girl like Missus teach her—she say no—so he make her drunk on dacca and now she is half mad all night and talk like a fool."

"That's dreadful! I'll tell Baas Van Riebeck to punish Obsete's son. Which one is it?"

"Baja—he is seventeen, though for long he came to Missus' lessons about Christ he is no good Kaffir. He hates all whites. Better Baas send him back to the Amatonga tribe where Obsete come from."

"Don't worry, Joanna, we'll take care of Janga. Miss Nancy needs a maid to go with her to the Cape. I think she should take Janga with her."

"Ach yes, Missus—thank you, Missus; get Janga away from Baja, but please don't let Obsete be angry with me when Missus is gone."

"He won't be. Obsete is a good man. Don't worry, Joanna, I'll arrange everything."

Katie lifted the hem of her long full skirts, then leaning down she patted the heads of a couple of naked black doll-like babies and left the kitchen.

She was wondering vaguely if the very word "motherhood", apart from all its glory, comes hand in hand with heartache. Here she was grieving over Nancy and Paul and there was Joanna grieving over Janga smoking dacca. It was a horrible drug and taken in big enough doses could drive a person insane.

Shaking off her depression she went to

the bedroom to pack the clothes she and Van Riebeck would need in Pretoria.

Two doors down the corridor Nancy, almost feverish with joyous excitement, was throwing her clothes into her leather trunk. She felt half drunk with delight. Only the dreadful trek to be endured, then she would be in Paul's arms. She was too sure of his passion to worry whether he might have fallen in love with some girl in the Cape; besides her Aunt Liz's letters always said, "Paul doesn't seem to care for any girl in particular." No! No! She knew instinctively that she was as much a part of him as the blood that ran in his veins. If ever two human beings were made for each other she and Paul were that pair. As she packed she reviewed her plans.

In a vault of the Standard Bank in Cape-town she visualised her two big diamonds, given to her by gamblers hopeful of her favours in the Faro saloon in Kimberley. Nancy laughed to herself. She had rewarded the men with promising smiles —nothing more. The diamonds should easily bring £30,000!

With this fortune she and Paul would sail to America, a new, uninhibited land, that had won independence from England. There no one would ever know they were half-brother and sister, they would be free to marry. His passport was for Paul Kildare, hers was for Nancy Eaton. She had no passport in her divorced husband's name. They would buy a lovely home and land, settle down to a glorious life together amongst the Americans who were a freedom loving people.

She would keep her promise to her mother and Papa Paul and after her arrival in the Cape board the first ship leaving for England, only Paul would be a passenger with her. From England they would sail to America. Oh, thank God for those two diamonds. She wondered if she should write to Paul and tell him her plans. And send the letter via Durban, a shorter route than the one she must take; then she decided it would be wiser to put nothing into writing. "Aunt Liz is almost as shrewd as Mama," she warned herself. 'She might well look at the envelope and have a presentiment about a letter from me to Paul. Should she open it my plans would be ruined."

An hour later, Nancy heard her

mother's voice calling, "How are you getting on, Nancy?" Katie was in the living-room purposely not entering Nancy's room to spare herself the emotion of seeing Nancy packing.

Feeling a shadow of guilt because of her secret plans Nancy swiftly lifted the hem of her long full skirts over the lion skins and went to the living-room. Her heart thumped uncomfortably when she looked at her mother's slim, straight back as she stared out of a window. What a wonderful person she was. God had blessed her with such courage.

"I'm almost finished, Mama. Could I do anything to help you?"

"No thank you, darling. I've decided to write to Aunt Liz from Pretoria," Katie said turning around to face Nancy, "telling her to expect you. I'll post the letter to go via Durban so it will arrive well ahead of you. I wish you could trek to Durban and sail from there to the Cape but of course you can't possibly stay there alone awaiting a ship."

"Don't worry, I'll be grateful to be able to join a trek going the long route."

"Nancy—you've got to do something for me—will you?"

"Of course, Mama—what is it?"

"Joanna's daughter Janga is in trouble. She's only fourteen but fully developed with the usual beautiful body these Kaffir girls have until they've borne and fed their babies." Katie swiftly told Nancy the story, finishing up by saying, "Poor Joanna is sick with worry about Janga and I've got to help her. I want you to take her with you as a personal servant."

"But of course, Mama. I'll do anything you want." The question came to Nancy suddenly, as she thought of Obsete's son. Was sex the most violent passion in the world?

"Thank you, darling. If she stays here she might easily become a dacca addict. I'll talk to Papa about it as soon as he comes in. I'm all packed. . . ."

She broke off at the sound of heavy turning wheels. "That's the wagon coming up the garden path—I think."

They went on to the stoep with Nancy wondering if Janga was going to be a weeping love-sick burden to her. Anyhow she'd try to help the girl.

60

Outside the house the twenty-foot wagon with its great white canvas top was pulling to a standstill. Nostalgia caught at Katie, the same old wagon in which she and Sean had left the Cape almost twenty-eight years ago, and then it had been eighty years old. Wonderful old thing. She turned with resolute strength to face Nancy standing beside her.

"All right, we're ready to leave."

Then Van Riebeck rode up to her and dismounted and she said, "We're all ready, darling, but *please*, I want to take Joanna's daughter with us." She quickly outlined the reasons to him.

"Dacca!" He exploded. "Where the devil do the natives grow it?"

"Easy enough, darling, on a 6,000 acre farm. If Nancy takes Janga with her she can bring her round to normality with constant doses of coffee and rest, and, of course, Janga will get no more dacca. Later she can serve Nancy on the trek and once at Abend Bloem, Liz can always use her."

Van Riebeck gave a little shrug. "Whatever you want, Katje, but I warn you that you'll never change the blacks about lying together." He laughed teasingly. "You mustn't grow like Saint Paul who thought marriage and copulation was for the birds. Lead me to Joanna's hut and I'll pick up the girl and put her in the wagon." He nodded at the big bed that ran the breadth of the wagon behind the driver's box.

"You're the most marvellous man who ever breathed." Standing on tiptoe she flung her arms about his neck, kissing him on both cheeks.

"Hey—hey," he chuckled happily, "much more of that and I'll postpone our journey."

Laughing, Katie let go of him saying, "Follow me." She rushed back into the house to the kitchen and pulled the fat Joanna aside, then whispered to her, "The Baas will take Janga."

"*Aieu*, Missus," Joanna exclaimed with solemn relief. "This is an answer from Missus' God to my prayers."

She looked up with dark grateful eyes at the tall Van Riebeck who said, "Show me to your hut, Joanna."

The fat cook waddled out of the kitchen door and on to a clearing toward a group of huts on the edge of the outhouses and stables.

"I hope you won't miss Janga too much, Joanna," Katie murmured sympathetically as they neared the huts.

"I will miss her, Missus, even though I have seven others, but dacca is *so* bad. You remember Heraz—she was so mad on dacca, she hanged herself." Joanna glanced anxiously at Van Riebeck's face suddenly gone so severe looking.

He was remembering the beautiful Malay girl whom years ago he had found hanging from a rafter in a hut. When after discovering she and Paul were lying together he had sent Paul to Holland, Heraz had committed suicide.

Joanna waddled into her shadowy hut that reeked of human body odour and where Janga lay on a mattress on the earthen floor. Van Riebeck lifted the half-dead-looking girl up, together with her bedding and carried her off toward the front garden and the wagon.

Katie squeezed Joanna's fat shoulder murmuring, "Janga will get well, don't worry, Miss Nancy will watch over her." Then Katie hurried after Van Riebeck.

He settled the child on the bed in the wagon and told Nancy, "Unpack the food hamper and force her to drink some coffee."

Then he jumped off the wagon and found the head farm man, Obsete, waiting at the back of the wagon. He said severely to the big Kaffir, whom he had trusted with the farm for over twenty years, "Obsete, you know why we are taking the girl?"

"No, Baas." The man looked him honestly in the face. "She is sick?"

"From smoking dacca given to her by your son, Baja."

"Baas! I thrash him for this!" Obsete's face had gone hard and cruel looking. All sensible Kaffirs feared the effects of dacca.

"Yes, thrash some sense into him. You are my friend so I do not bring disgrace upon you by thrashing him myself, but I leave his punishment to you."

"This thing I, his father, will do well, Baas. He never smoke dacca again. I promise the Baas."

"Good, and make him show you where the dacca is growing and burn the devil weed out."

"*Aieu*, Baas—I will do it." Obsete's proud face showed the shame he suffered for he valued his great position of headman on Van Riebeck's farm.

By now the whole family was packed into the huge wagon. Jantze was riding one horse with a spare mount tied to his saddle. One Kaffir boy held Van Riebeck's horse waiting and another held his long gun which he now took and slung across his back, then he swung into the saddle and shouted to the wagon-driver, "*Voorwarts! Voorwarts*, Jong!"

The eighteen-foot-long whip snaked out and sounding like a gun shot cracked over the lead animals' heads, the oxen bent low dragging on the weight, until the team of sixteen beasts were all pulling and the great wheels started turning.

6

AN hour before sunset the Van Riebecks reached the outskirts of the twenty-two year old town of Pretoria.

The town was cradled in a bowl of low-lying, parched looking hills, and the air was dust-filled from the traffic of oxen and horses, yet Katie was pleased to be here for at least there was some activity. The street was lined with squat white buildings, willow and mimosa trees, and though a long cry from civilization, it was an improvement on the isolation of the farm. The Gothic type church boasting a spire, as usual in all Boer towns, dominated everything except the Volksraad's sturdy building and it warmed Katie's heart to see the Boers' beloved "Vierkleur" in colours of green, red, white and blue, hoisted about it instead of the Union Jack. It was justice that it should be so for the Dutch had trekked from the Cape, they had starved, fought, bled and died to create some civilization out of the land across the Vaal River, therefore before God—it was theirs.

In the main street many people called out greetings to Van Riebeck and Katie, who stood at the back of the wagon and waved to women pedestrians in their big sunbonnets and long voluminous cotton skirts.

"Well, here we are!" Katie exclaimed and turned to Nancy, who like herself wore a brayed goat's-skin mask and deep frilled Dutch bonnet to keep the sun's fierce rays from her face. Many years ago the golden-haired, fair-skinned Boer women had invented the masks as protection for their skins when they had first trekked from the Cape Colony.

"It's good to be here," Nancy said, relieved that the first small part of her journey was over. "Janga is much quieter —she's slept for the last couple of hours. Perhaps the dacca is wearing off."

"Please God it is. I hope she won't wake up craving for the rotten drug."

"Katje?" Van Riebeck leaned down over his horse as he rode beside the wagon. "We'll go straight to the Blesbok Inn and see if we can get accommodation. Can we manage with two rooms?"

"Yes, one for us and one for Nancy and the boys. Maarje and Philip with Janga can sleep in the wagon."

Katie knew Nancy would prefer a room to herself but they must economise. Both she and Van Riebeck had brought up most of their money from their ostrich farms in the Cape to help finance the Anglo-Boer war, then before that rinderpest had wiped out all their cattle which had cost a fortune to replace.

"Right," Van Riebeck told the driver, "Blesbok Inn, Jong."

Before the spreading white double-storied house of the Blesbok Inn, the courtyard was crowded with wagons and oxen but Van Riebeck guided his driver into a space, then he dismounted and went into the inn to obtain accommodation.

"I hope he'll get rooms," Katie said anxiously to Nancy for although she knew the beds were usually bug infested, it was still the best inn in Pretoria.

Soon Van Riebeck came out on to the stoep and waved his wide-brimmed hat in a signal for them to come in.

Inside the inn where the proprietor greeted them affably, Nancy whispered urgently to Katie, "Ask him if he knows about any treks going to the Cape."

Katie did, but he answered, "At the moment I don't, Missus Van Riebeck. Pretoria is overflowing with arrivals, come from all over the place. People trying to buy concessions, for shops, for hotels, for barbers—anything and everything. This rumour of gold has spread like a fire all over the country. But if I hear of a trek going south I'll let you know."

"Whilst you get settled in, Katje," Van Riebeck said, "I'll slip over to the Volksraad. When we passed there I saw there was a light in Kruger's office. I want to talk to him."

"You'll be back for dinner with us?"

"Yes, yes," and Van Riebeck ran down the stoep steps. He had thought up an idea and was longing to try it out on Kruger. He found him in his office with three other Volksraad members. He nodded to them all and slipped into a chair.

The long-bearded Kruger was speaking in his bull-like bellow.

"According to that Pretoria Convention

we have entire self-government with regard to our interior affairs, but we are forbidden to act against or with an outside Power, without permission of the Suzerainty of the English Queen."

He spat scornfully into a spittoon at his feet and Van Riebeck broke in saying, "It all means that for anything we want to do outside of the Republic we must wait for permission from the English. Actually we have no right to send our man to stay at Lobengula's court to keep that bloody Cecil Rhodes out, and stop him from getting that gold bearing land to the east."

"We shall send a man to Lobengula;" Commandant Joubert winked at the others, "as a friend, not 'Ambassador'. The English can't object to that."

The other members smiled and nodded and Kruger went on.

"Now the latest news is that England will make Swaziland independent." He struck his fist on the table. "Think of all the Dutch farmers living there under black rule. The whole of our Eastern districts should be given back to us! It is only just, that land was ours but as long as Queen Victoria retains her veto on all native legislation, we are powerless. *Ach, Magtig,* this British Resident in Pretoria has full powers and a seat on the Native Locations Commission, which holds land for the Kaffirs!"

"The English are mad! They should follow our law that does not permit Kaffirs to hold land," Joubert said. "But what could we do after the battle of Majuba? We were victorious, true—but we needed to agree to peace at once before the English reinforcements arrived."

"*Ja, ja,* Joubert, we all know that." Kruger nodded impatiently. "This business of equal civil rights to all is vordamnt! And worse is this tremendous debt England has hung around our necks like a yoke. In the name of God, how are we to pay it?"

"We proved at Majuba that we can outfight the English so why the devil do we allow them to saddle us with the conditions of the Pretoria Convention?" Breda—a great fighter and speaker— looked murderous enough to kill. "In the name of hell where will we find $748,162 for repayment of old debts to Britain and where will we find $1,272,000 to repay

Britain for civil expenses when she annexed us against our will?"

"When we signed the Pretoria Convention we lost our rights to appeal about the Sand River Convention which we morally hold to." Kruger spat again into the brass spittoon, it seemed impossible for him to carry on a debate for a few minutes without spitting.

With Van Riebeck's aristocratic background from Holland and the Cape Colony, his University education in Amsterdam, he was often revolted by Kruger's coarseness even whilst he valued his numerous qualities.

"I believe we must wait awhile," he said, "then appeal to the London Parliament to break the Pretoria Convention, but first we shall have to build up our finances."

"A port of our own is what we have *got* to have!" Smit, a heavily built man and a hero of Majuba, said. "It's a most important thing for us to be able to send our produce to the outside world, without the expense of travelling as far as Durban or the Cape and paying damned export and import taxes. *Magtig*, although we have a railway franchise from the Portuguese to build the railway to Delagoa Bay, we have used up the £90,000 that the Netherlands lent us and the machinery lies rusting in the bush."

"I've a wild idea but it might be workable." Van Riebeck pointed with the stem of his pipe at Kruger to emphasise his point. "What about Saint Lucia Bay for our port?"

"Man, are you voordamnt? It's in Zululand."

"Agreed, but the Zulus are now very friendly to us since they lost their war with England. I think we might be able to buy Saint Lucia Bay from them or barter it for service given them. I'll tell you my plan. The English were mad after the war to divide Zululand up under eleven kings, when Dinizulu is the rightful heir."

"Of course, Dinizulu is Cetewayo's eldest son." Kruger's heavily lidded eyes were shiny as he listened to Van Riebeck. "But what can we do about it, Paul?"

"Everything for Dinizulu—put him back on his throne! Offer to help him fight and beat the ten false rulers and regain the country as sole ruler."

"Yes! Yes! We could do it!" Joubert cried eagerly. "And in payment we get Saint Lucia Bay! It's splendid! But hell and damnation, to fight on Dinizulu's behalf, we must ask permission of the bloody English Queen."

"No, by God! We fight *first*, then ask permission afterwards," Kruger chuckled. "It's a fine plan, Van Riebeck, in any case two-thirds of the Zulus want Dinizulu for their King. We'll have an easy time restoring him to power. Do you all agree?"

"*Ja! Ja!*" the four men cried.

"Then let's get started on it at once!" Breda said. "Who will go to talk to Dinizulu about it?"

"You and Van Riebeck," Kruger said.

"It is agreed," the others called out.

"Right, men! When will you leave?" Kruger flung the question at Van Riebeck and Breda.

Van Riebeck hesitated a moment, thinking about his job of helping to get Nancy on a trek, then he said, "I've just arrived with my wife and some of the family. A daughter is waiting to join a trek to the Cape."

"Then she can go with a son of mine

74

and his wife who leave tomorrow for Paarl in the Cape," Breda said. "They have two wagons with their five children. There will be plenty of room for your daughter, Paul."

"Thank you, Abraham—that settles that worry. Will there be space for my daughter's little coloured maid?"

"*Ja, ja,* of course."

"My finest head boy will ride with the trek to help hunt for meat along the way —Jantze, the Zulu, you know him."

"A good man—he will be welcome. We are staying at the Blesbok Inn so after supper we shall arrange everything."

"Good, and when will you and I leave for Zululand?"

"Tomorrow evening," Breda said. "It can't be soon enough for me."

"Then that is settled," Kruger said swiftly. "When you two go to Zululand you must use all the wits God gave you to make Dinizulu agree to our scheme. Find out from him how many warriors he can muster, then we'll know how big a Commando we must rally."

"Above everything, keep your mission

secret," Joubert warned, "so that the voor-damnt English don't get scent of it."

"We must get Dinizulu to give us a document that says he cedes to us Saint Lucia Bay, when we have made him Supreme King of the Zulus," Van Riebeck told the others, then asked Kruger, "Whom have you chosen to go to live with that barbarian Lobengula, to keep him from granting land concessions to Rhodes?"

"Grobler," Kruger said. "We informed him this morning and he is willing to take on the rotten job. His wife and smaller children will follow him later."

"I'm relieved. Grobler is a good man and I've a feeling that Rhodes is going to give us plenty of trouble up here in the future. I think he's one of the worst Imperialists England has ever had out here. He wants the whole of South Africa from coast to coast for the English."

"Why need we fear him so much?" Kruger asked.

"Because I've heard he's power mad. Already he's bought up most of Kimberley's most lucrative diamond mines and formed the de Beer Syndicate. Now I don't want him to get his rotten hands on the gold of the North. He's an odd man who dislikes women. Even in his home only young men serve him. Such men I believe are against nature—they could be doubly dangerous."

"*Ja, ja,* he could be a bad enemy, but I have heard that he is a sick man," Smit said. "His chest is bad."

"Not too sick to have made himself a multi-millionaire out of diamonds in a few years," Van Riebeck retorted. "I put him down as one of our chief threats, I think you all should beware of him. Now, what about selling concessions to the greedy wolves who've come here really to hunt for gold? We must remember that gold could be our answer on how to pay our debts."

"Ach, no," Kruger spat into his spittoon, "Gold will bring sorrow and blood to our Republic. Let us leave it in the earth. You and Breda bring back from Dinizulu a document that gives us Saint Lucia Bay. With a port we will pay back the money we owe."

Van Riebeck stood up, nodded to the others, then flicked his hat from a peg and with a feeling of elation left his colleagues.

If his idea about Dinizulu succeeded and the South African Republic obtained a port, they could well leave the gold in the earth.

7

WOULD there never be an end to these dreadful partings? Katie wondered painfully as in their stuffy bedroom, Van Riebeck told her that he had found a safe place for Nancy on the Breda trek headed south tomorrow.

"Nancy will be delighted," Katie said, "and overjoyed that you've so swiftly found a trek for her to join."

"Yes, it was extraordinary luck." He thought with annoyance, "Nancy will be counting every minute until she is with Paul again."

Whilst Katie was thinking, 'If only Nancy *will* leave at once for England when she returns to the Cape, there will be no time for her love for Paul to grow. I must write to Liz to book Nancy's passage, also to Lady Eaton saying Nancy is coming.' "Now, darling," she smiled up at Van Riebeck, "I'm longing to know all about your talks with Kruger."

"After dinner I'll tell you."

Later, before dinner in the big dining-room of the Blesbok Inn, Van Riebeck introduced Nancy to Abraham Breda's family and at her obvious delight that she was to leave so soon with them, a sickening feeling invaded Katie.

Not only did Nancy not mind leaving her, but her joy at the idea that she was to be reunited with young Paul was so disgusting to Katie, that temporarily it turned her against Nancy. Only with a great effort could she hide her revulsion and join in the general chatter as they sat at a long table whilst barefoot Kaffir maids served heaped up dishes of rice and beef and tomato stew.

"Katje," she found Van Riebeck's voice was saying, "as our friends intend pulling their wagons out at three in the morning it is best that you and Nancy should say goodbye now. No need to disturb you in the middle of the night." He was convinced that a swift public goodbye would be less emotional for Katie and he hoped she would agree.

She sensed his thoughts and turned to look at Nancy's pale face. She found there no trace of sadness at the thought of parting and whilst Katie could have cried aloud with hurt, it decided her to accept the lifeline Van Riebeck had so understandingly thrown to her.

"That's a good idea, Paul," she said quietly, "and as it's almost ten, I think everyone must wish to go to bed and get a few hours rest." She stood up, shook hands all around the table wishing them God speed and then kissed Nancy on both cheeks.

"God bless you, Nancy. Enjoy your stay with your grandmother in England."

"I will, Mama—I promise you." Nancy lied without a trace of shame as her mind pictured her future in America with Paul.

They kissed and hugged, then Van Riebeck gently disentangled them and took Katie off. It surprised and rather gratified him that she was dry-eyed.

In their stuffy little room, he caught her by the shoulders and stared down into her pale, strained face, the beauty of which nothing could mar.

"Well, well, Katje my darling. You were splendid in your goodbye! No tears —I'm surprised."

"Are you, darling? Did you notice that

there were no tears from Nancy either?" Katie felt half dead inside. "She's her father's daughter. You know the English don't cry easily, but now *you*," she forced herself to say, "what has happened to you today? That's what I'm longing to know. You were gone with Kruger and Joubert and the others for ages, I haven't a notion of what's happening—please tell me."

"Get undressed and into bed. I can always explain things more easily to you when you're lying in my arms."

She shot him an understanding little smile and guessed that the news he was going to tell her would upset her. Saying nothing more she prepared for bed.

They lay in the big four-poster bed, slapping out at the bed bugs biting them whilst the grey mosquito net hung limply like a disgruntled ghost protecting them from mosquitoes. Then as he cradled her in his arms he said, "Darling, you know before we left the farm I told you my idea regarding Dinizulu, of trying to barter with him for Saint Lucia in Zululand, if we fought with him to gain his throne?"

"Yes, darling, I thought it was a brilliant idea. What did Kruger and the others think?"

"They are all for it and tomorrow, Breda and I leave for Zululand to parley with Dinizulu."

She swallowed her annoyance that he must again leave her so soon. "Oh Lord, you've hardly been home and you're off again."

"Forgive me, my darling."

"Yes, yes, I understand." She bit back her recrimination, 'The South African Republic must always come first' and said, "So you leave tomorrow?"

"Your voice sounds bitter, Katje my love."

"Do you wonder at it? I've turned into a recipient of goodbyes, but the main thing is I'm terrified of you fighting Zulus again. They're the worst of all the tribes."

"Don't worry, darling," he chuckled. "This time I'm not going to fight, I'm only going to discuss plans with Dinizulu."

"Thank God for that, because the battle of Majuba Hill seems like yesterday. Naturally I'm delighted at a chance for the South African Republic to gain its own port at last! Go to Dinizulu with my blessings, darling."

He fell asleep almost immediately, but she lay awake with her head on his shoulder listening to the grandfather clock striking the hours. Soon Nancy would be leaving. Katie was awake to hear the commotion in the big yard of the inn. Kaffir drivers were summoning the oxen by names, chains started clanking as the animals were secured into place on the dusselboom, she recognized sounds of stowing of water casks beneath the wagons, the noise of fowls as their crate was hung near the water casks, the muted voices of those who were about to travel. She easily visualized all that was happening for she had trekked so often.

By the sounds, she knew when the wagons—packed with provisions several days ago, were ready to leave. Then she heard the command: *"Voorwarts! Voorwarts!"*

There was the swishing sound of the driver's eighteen-foot-long-rhinoceros whip flicking out over the heads of the lead oxen, then as slowly they bent their heads low to their knees pulling with their great strength until the high wagon wheels started turning.

Nancy was almost gone! Too late for Katie to rush out for a last embrace. Who was it who had said, 'To say goodbye is to die a little?' Nancy had started on the first portion of her journey from corruption, for when she reached the Cape, Paul would be gone.

Deeply depressed Katie fell into heavy sleep, but awakened at 5 a.m. when a Kaffir maid brought Van Riebeck coffee and hot water for shaving.

Believing she was asleep, he moved about quietly, opening the shutters just a slit to give himself enough light to move about. He sipped the coffee, but it tasted like hot mud, so he left it. The coffee at Kruger's house would be good. He shaved, washed and dressed, then flicking his wide-brimmed hat from a wall peg, he tiptoed out, glad that Katie slept and Nancy's departure had gone off without any dramatic scenes.

Though her body ached and her soul was weary, Katie rose soon after Van Riebeck had gone. She threw the shutters wide open to admit the cool air and stared out into the early sunshine.

As soon as the telegraph office opened, Katie told herself that she must be there. She drank the coffee Van Riebeck had left, and, strong and bitter though it was, it helped revive her. Then she commenced to wash and dress, whilst from all around came sounds of the world of men awakening. It was six o'clock, the hour when the day's work commenced.

Later at the telegraph office, with a trembling hand, she filled out a form.

"Paul Kildare, Abend Bloem, Stellenbosch, Cape Colony.

"Gold discovered on your land concession but essential you be here to re-register your ownership come immediately stop Ask uncle Chris or cousin Stephan replace you on ostrich farm all love mother."

She handed the form across the narrow counter to the young clerk who glanced over the form with a surprised expression, then chuckling he said, "Gold, Missus?"

He spoke in a true colonial accent, English accented like Dutch. "Do you believe it? It's more than fifteen years that men have been digging around Pilgrim's Rest for gold, but never heard tell of a single one who's got rich out there. Now they're trying to find gold in Matabeleland I hear."

"Yes, it's probably a false rumour." She left unsaid that Paul's land was on the Witwatersrand; she did not want to help spread another rumour. "Yet it seems my duty to let my son know the rumours about his land."

"Ach yes—of course. My Missus would do the same. Now I'll just check the address." He stared in surprise when he saw it. "That's funny! I've only just received a telegram addressed to the same man—before you came in."

Katie's fingers gripped the edge of the wooden counter to give herself support. Nancy must have telegraphed Paul! But impossible, she left at 3 a.m.!

"How extraordinary! Perhaps my husband came in and sent a similar message, if so there's no need to send mine."

87

"No, a Kaffir from the inn brought it in with the money." He sorted through a few forms, picked one up, then smiled.

Katie ached to see the form he was reading and asked in an ingratiating voice. "Is it the same message?"

"No—no. This just says, 'Hurrah, leaving today longing to see you, all love.'"

Breathing as if she had been running Katie forced a laugh. "Oh yes, and I'll wager that it's signed Nancy."

"You're absolutely right—that's it. Your son's sweetheart I suppose?"

"Yes," Katie murmured, then as the clerk went on to say how he too was from the Cape where he had learned telegraphy she smiled politely, paid, then left.

Why in heaven's name did she not guess Nancy would telegraph to let Paul know she was coming? Would he wait for her, or come up? God, what a bitter problem it all was. Despair started to creep through her, for now she felt that instead of ending the revolting affair she might have given it an impetus by sending Nancy off. What now?

How could she trust Nancy to catch a

ship to England when she reached the Cape if Paul was waiting for her? Nancy was over age, her own mistress and with her wild character she would probably refuse to leave Abend Bloem even if Liz had booked her passage.

Katie walked slowly back to the Blesbok Inn trying to assure herself that her plan would work and Paul *would* come up in answer to her telegram, but supposing he did not? Supposing he waited for Nancy's arrival?

Back at the inn she started to write to her sister.

It was a difficult letter for she wanted to make it strong enough so that Liz would move heaven and earth to *make* Nancy leave for England, yet nothing could make Katie tell Liz, to whom she was so close, about her suspicion of the incestuous love between Nancy and Paul. It was too horrible to put into writing.

20th July, 1882

My darling Liz,

At the moment we are in Pretoria for a few days so I have not yet collected the weekly post from Lydenburg and therefore do not know your latest news. Mine is that Nancy left last night on a safe trek. As I have told you in almost all my letters, she had been miserable up here and at last implored Paul to let her leave. We think the wisest thing is for her to return to England and I shall write to Lady Eaton whom I'm sure will be delighted to have her. Please, darling, do all you can to make her sail for England. I feel something horrible will happen if she stays at Abend Bloem, I don't know why—but I really do.

It's splendid news about Mary's wonderful voice and I shall write to Madame Visele and tell her that I hope to arrange to send Mary to Italy. Someday we may sit in a great opera house and listen to her singing.

Oh, Liz darling, I feel so homesick for you and all the family. Now I am alone with Paul and my two little Van Riebecks and he works, lives, eats, breathes for his beloved South African Republic. There is trouble threatening with the Kaffir tribes near Lydenburg, but I don't think it's serious.

Forgive me for writing all about us,

whilst actually I am longing for news of all of you. Are your Stephan and Jan as keen on farming as Paul? I do hope so and that later they can run the ostrich farms and our vineyards when the bushes start to yield grapes.

Well, darling, no more now as I wish to catch the mailcart that is leaving for Durban.

God bless you all,
All my love,
Katie.

P.S. Paul has undoubtedly shown you the telegram I sent him. I eagerly await his reply telling me when he can come. There is so much talk of gold in the Witwatersrand that I don't want him to lose a chance of making a fortune, so, darling, *do* give him a push to come. Thank God the Cape-Basuto war has been settled and none of our boys were wounded, but I wonder if there will ever be peace of unity in South Africa.

All love K.

8

KATIE had been back at the farm for three days and she had already driven into Lydenburg to pick up her letters, but she decided to go again for she was impatient to receive a telegram from young Paul. She instructed Hendrik, Jantze's son, to accompany the wagon, and with his gun on his knees he sat beside the driver. Inside the wagon were Franz, Adrian, Maarje and Philip. Both Philip and Katie had loaded guns, for rumours had grown that the Mapoochi tribe were being troublesome in stealing cattle and they had even murdered some English miners in nearby Pilgrim's Rest.

On the big bed that ran the width of the wagon the children slept. Katie sat propped up against cushions reading, for Liz kept her well supplied with books from the Cape. Dickens was a favourite of hers and now she was reading *Pickwick Papers* aloud to Philip who, being poorly educated in England, read with difficulty.

Katie had and was improving his education but had given up trying to educate Maarje, who after several years of lessons could still only just spell her name, but the coloured girl enjoyed listening to Katie, for she had been to London with her as nursemaid and thought she recognised some of the scenes in the book.

They were all laughing at a particular passage when suddenly Katie felt alien eyes on her, and she looked up—at the back of the wagon were men's black faces, their red-ringed bloodshot eyes staring into the wagon. The naked men, spears poised, started to climb aboard.

"What do you want?" Faint with terror Katie grabbed the gun by her side and cried out, "Hendrik! Hendrik!"

Before he could swing around on the driver's seat, an attacker's spear flew into the driver's shoulder; he collapsed, and the reins of the oxen went loose.

Philip with surprising swiftness shot straight into a savage face that splattered everywhere as the body fell backwards off the wagon.

"Guns! You give guns or we kill!"

The leader shouted into Katie's face, his

spear raised to strike. She pulled the trigger of her gun and screaming in agony the Kaffir collapsed sideways over Maarje. Then Hendrik jumped down from the driver's seat into the wagon. Clutching his gun barrel he swung it like a club first at one savage with raised spear, then at the other. Their heads were shattered and they collapsed.

The four Kaffirs were dead and Katie cried, "Quick, Philip, Maarje, throw their bodies out! Hendrik, take charge of the oxen! They'll end up in the bush and over-turn the wagon."

Maarje and Philip were rolling the corpses out of the wagon, whilst Franz and Adrian, awakened by the shots, were screaming at the macabre sight of dead men, blood and scattered flesh.

"Everything's all right," Katie tried to assure the children as she helped the wounded driver off the seat and into the wagon and started to care for his wound.

"Load our guns, Philip, for God's sake and Maarje bolt the back of the wagon. There might be more of the devils coming. Who are they, Hendrik?" she called up to

Hendrik driving the oxen. "Will more attack us, do you think?"

"No—no, Missus, I think those are from the Mapoochi tribe; they were a few young ones hunting for guns. Now I drive the oxen fast. We are not far from Lydenburg." He lashed out with the long whip and the beasts increased their speed.

Philip helped Katie disinfect the driver's wound with turpentine from the hussapotheck, then they bound it up, whilst Maarje washed away the blood splashes and picked up pieces of flesh and flung them out of the wagon.

"We all need a big drink of brandy," Katie said, her voice quivering. "The driver first—thank God his wound is not deep."

They drank brandy that Maarje poured into tin mugs. Katie was shaking from head to foot and she could not stop it. The killings had been horrible. She had killed many men in battles, but none had terrified her as these men had, coming upon her with such surprise. She wiped blood from her face and hair, but her dress was too blood-soaked to do anything about.

"Mama! Mama! Are you bleeding?"

Franz cried in horror, as his little hands wiped blood off her cheeks.

"No, no, darling. There's nothing wrong with me. Maarje, give me a cloth."

But at that moment the terrified girl became hysterical and started to laugh loudly. Philip looked in amazement at Katie and suddenly she could not help laughing too, then Philip joined in. They were all semi-hysterical from shock but it minimized the terrible affair for the children.

Ten minutes later the first squat white buildings of Lydenburg came into their relieved view and the oxen entered the wide, deeply rutted main road flanked by white-washed buildings with the usual wooden church and canals running along the sides of the street. In the dirty, sluggish water, fruit peelings and filth drifted slowly along. But it was a blessed sight for those in Katie's wagon.

The Dutch flag, their beloved Vierkleur, hung limply from a pole of the Field Cornet's building where the oxen slowly came to a halt, Katie gathered her skirts around her hoping to hide the bloodstains, then went down the step and darted into the Police Cornet's office.

The big man, Rix Huton, looked up in surprise at seeing her and called out, "Ach, Vrou Van Riebeck, it is good to see you."

"Oh, Mr. Huton—we were attacked by Kaffirs!"

Swiftly she told him what had occurred ending with the warning, "It isn't safe for a wagon to make the journey alone. There may be more Kaffir gun thieves in the bush."

"*Ja, ja,* I send you back with an escort of the Afrikaner Korps and now I must post a warning at both ends of the road to stop wagons from leaving. *Magtig,* the Kaffirs are out of hand since they saw white men fighting each other, though since our victory at Majuba they fear us more than the English, but trouble is coming up like a bad storm with the Mapoochi. We shall have to fight them to show them who is Baas."

Then he rushed out and Katie made her way to the Telegraph Office next door. A telegram awaited her and with trembling hands she tore it open and read.

"Impossible leave stop You please try re-register Land. Love Paul."

Disappointment made her feel more faint than the Kaffir attack. She sank tremblingly on to a nearby stool.

She had lost! Nancy had won! The thing that she had so feared had happened. Paul was waiting for Nancy. What now? What now?

She sat on with her mind whirling. She just had to make Paul come here! He and Nancy must not meet! The incestuous affair must be broken!

Suddenly she knew what she must do. She stood up and asked the clerk behind the counter for a telegraph form, then with almost a firm hand she wrote out a telegram to Paul.

"Regret changed plans not coming to Cape please come up here All Love Nancy."

Katie paid for the telegram and left the office telling herself that this ruse would surely bring Paul up here. Nancy could not telegraph him from the middle of the veld where she now was, so he would take this telegram as final.

She went back to the wagon to give Maarje money to go with the boys to buy toys at the old German's toy shop.

"I'm going to the Rooibok Hotel, Maarje, to try to book rooms for us so come back there. I don't think it's safe for us to return to the farm tonight."

"*Ach ja*, Missus—better we stay in Lydenburg unless we have many Afrikaner Korps to ride with our wagon and. . . ."

She broke off at the sound of shouting coming from the far end of the road leading from the bush. Philip and Katie rushed forward with a crowd of people to see what was happening.

Down the wide road raced a team of frightened mules pulling a covered wagon that was rocking from side to side on its big wheels. The mules were driverless and from all over men rushed forward to grasp at the beasts to pull them up to a halt.

People crowded around and peered inside the wagon, then came horrified shouts.

"*Magtig!* It's the La Rue family!

Mother! Children! All murdered by assegais! The bloody Mapoochi have risen!"

9

THE entrance, lounge and bar of the shabby Rooibok Hotel were crowded to the walls with fat Dutch women, girls and children of all ages. The men and boys of fighting age were riding out in every direction to summon the farmers to join the Commando and to help bring their families into Lydenburg. The fastest riders had been despatched to Pretoria to acquaint Paul Kruger with the bad news that Mampuru, Chief of the Mapoochi, had, in his own way, declared war.

Katie and her little group were squeezed into a corner of the hotel's lounge, hemmed in by women from neighbouring farms. Though Katie met these women seldom—usually for betrothal parties, weddings, christenings or when they accompanied their men in the great wagons at time of battle—they were all good friends.

Now Josie Oliphant said, "Mampuru is

a very skelm Kaffir. He murdered Secocoeni—the true chief of the tribe—and for months he's been stealing white men's cattle and murdering miners at Pilgrim's Rest, and that's in the South African Republic. Our men must punish him."

"*Ja, ja,* we should have finished him off months ago." Stella Hofmeyer answered, then she shrugged. "But most of the miners are English and of the worst kind."

"But they are *white* men! We should have given them more protection." Josie argued as she mopped at her round perspiry face.

"Well at least the miners can help fight in the coming war against Mampuru and his Mapoochi." Katie started shuddering again at her terrible experience in the wagon.

"This verdamnt Pretoria Convention ties our hands and the Royal Native Vocations Commissions just don't know what it's doing, the way it pardons Kaffirs," Stella exclaimed. "How can the English know what *we* know about Kaffirs? They sit in London making mad laws for people they know nothing about." She sniffed with disgust. "It's made it hard for our own government to keep order with the Kaffirs, for they know how the white men quarrel amongst themselves."

"*Ja, ja,*" Josie's big blond daughter opened up her bodice to give her screaming infant the breast. "My husband has been saying for months we must fight Mampuru and the Mapoochi and show all the other tribes that the South African Republic will stand no nonsense from them."

"Do you think there is trouble along the Cape route with the Kaffir tribes?" Katie anxiously asked her friends, her mind on Nancy.

"Ach no, Katje. The main trouble is up here. The Kaffir devils think the Boers are tired and weak after our war with the English." Josie smiled triumphantly. "Fools! They should have seen our men's victory at Majuba."

Katie thought despairingly that the very word "Majuba" would go down for centuries in the Boers' history, but God knows it would not be enough for the years to come, to ensure their freedom.

"Yes, yes. The Boers were magnificent," she murmured. "I was so glad that my son Paul was in the battle—but now —I do wish my husband were here."

"Don't worry, Katje. Van Riebeck will come in time, you will see." Stella laughed easily as if she had no cares. "There would be no war without him, but I think we should start at once to prepare for the battle. Most of us only have enough supplies in our wagons for a day or two. We should order our Kaffir servants now to kill and dry meat."

"You're right!" Katie cried. "We must buy up whatever food there is in Lydenburg and supply ourselves. I've got no clothes for the children or myself; I must buy some cloth and cotton. The wagons coming in from the farms will have supplied themselves." She turned to Maarje. "Stay here with the children. I'll get Philip off the wagon to help me shop for supplies."

She started to elbow a way out of the crowded lounge but she made slow progress for almost like a miracle the thought had flashed to all of the women. 'Take action and buy supplies so that the wagons will be in readiness when the Commando had gathered to ride out against Mampuru.'

Preparations to withstand a possible surprise attack from the Mapoochi tribe had already been swiftly taken by the Afrikaner Korps. The Field Cornet had planned that the women and children would occupy the hotel, post office and all the sturdy buildings from which the women, all good shots, could fire at the Kaffirs. The church, being built of wood, was considered unsafe, for the Kaffirs could fire it with burning shrub tied to well flung assegais. The great covered wagons were spread out, tied to each other in a type of square laager, and thorn bushes were stuffed between the wheel spokes. The oxen, horses, mules and cattle were milling about in groups inside the protective laager.

Katie decided not to look for Philip but to start her purchases. She moved down the street to stalls which bravely stood on display. Swiftly she and all the women made the purchases they needed and soon the stalls and small shops were sold out of sugar, flour, coffee, dried beans and anything else that could be used during the forthcoming battle. Bales of calico and coloured cottons were bought to make clothes, for everyone now in Lydenburg had come prepared to be absent from home for a few hours, not possibly a few months.

Under the Boer women's instructions Kaffir servants were slaughtering cattle at a square usually reserved for cattle auctions and weighing elephant tusks. At a spot close by fires had been built for other servants to roast the newly killed flesh, for there was not time to dry meat in the sun to make biltong of it. But thin strips were hung out on the sides of every wagon to dry into biltong for it was one of the best foods a fighting man could carry in his saddle bag.

Where was Van Riebeck? Katie started to wonder frantically. Still in Zululand, or by now had he returned to Pretoria where the news of Mampuru's uprising would reach him? When would he arrive in Lydenburg?

Before Paul Kruger's small white-washed house in Pretoria's main street, just after sundown, Van Riebeck and Breda cantered up. They each had a lead horse as well as the one they rode.

Hot, dusty, with shirts dark with sweat, they dismounted. Coloured boys came up to tether their horses to the wooden posts and the two big men tramped up the three steps to the stoep where Paul Kruger sat in his armchair, one mottle-skinned hand resting on his big worn bible on the table beside him, the other combing through his long grey beard. He rose hastily to greet the men and shake their hands.

"You're back so soon. Good men! What news?"

"Fine!" Breda exclaimed. "Dinizulu is jumping somersaults with joy at the promise that we will fight the other rulers and restore Zululand to him and his throne."

"And here is his deed of sale to the South African Republic of Saint Lucia Bay."

Van Riebeck triumphantly pulled from his pocket a light leather wrapping, undid it and then unfolding a paper, handed it to Kruger. Looking over the President's shoulder Van Riebeck pointed to the "X" and then "Dinizulu" written as if by a child.

"I had to hold his hand to help him write his name."

"Once more God has taken care of His chosen people." Kruger's words were devoutly spoken as his heavily lidded brown eyes studied the document granting Saint Lucia Bay to the South African Republic, in return for them establishing him on his rightful throne.

"You men have done well," Kruger smiled.

"Thank you, President." Breda unslung his gun from his back, stood it in a corner and sank down on to a wooden armchair. "We have been fifty hours in the saddle."

Van Riebeck unslung his gun from his back, propped it up against a wall and hung his wide-brimmed hat on a peg, then he sat down and felt in his trouser pockets for his pipe and tobacco, whilst a Kaffir houseboy brought out coffee and brandy.

"We came as fast as we could to give you the good news," he said.

Both Breda and Van Riebeck were stiff and aching all over from the long ride.

"We just gave the horses time to eat and to roll," Breda chuckled, "then we were off again to share the good news with you."

"Good, good, that is the way we Boers move with good news as well as bad." Kruger was holding the treasured document between his sausage-like fingers. "How big a Commando does Dinizulu want from us? And when?"

"As soon as we can send it." Breda happily sipped his coffee, this simple way of making plans on Kruger's stoep pleased the Boers. "He will raise an army of 15,000 impis, and after consultation with him we believe a Commando of 500 crack sharpshooters will be enough to beat the other 50,000 Zulus."

"We have them all ready and eager to leave. Joubert has hand-picked our best men. Give praise to Almighty God that we are to have a port at last!" Kruger snapped his big, bulging fingers to a nearby Kaffir servant. "Go quickly, Jong, to Baas General Joubert and ask him to come here at once."

When the Kaffir had left, Kruger turned back to Van Riebeck and Breda. "Joubert wants to lead the Zulu campaign himself so we know we shall have. . . ."

Kruger broke off as two horsemen came galloping up the dusty street scattering the pedestrians to the sides. They dragged their horses to a halt before Kruger's stoep and jumped to the earth. They were hardly more than boys Van Riebeck noticed as they rushed up the steps.

"Bad news this time," Van Riebeck muttered.

"Mr. President, the Lydenburg district is threatened with attack from the Mapoochi!" one of the young messengers cried.

Van Riebeck and Breda both sprang to their feet, then reaching for their guns they slung them across their backs as the messengers went on breathlessly, "A family in a wagon, the La Rues, were murdered just outside the town."

"The Field Cornet has summoned the local Commando?" Kruger asked.

"Yes, sir, immediately. We were sent to ride non-stop to inform you of what was happening and to tell you that we do not think we shall need help. The Field Cornet believes we can settle with the tribes with our local Commando!"

"We must leave at once!" Van Riebeck swiftly told Kruger. "Breda's family and mine could be in danger." He reached down, poured two big brandies, gave one to Breda and tossed one off himself. "So we're off." He shook Kruger's out-stretched hand.

"God ride with you, Van Riebeck." Kruger's deep voice was like a blessing. "It is not good that we have the Dinizulu business coming up at the same time as the Mapoochi trouble, but with the Lord's help we shall be victorious."

Van Riebeck and Breda dashed down to the horses which the Kaffirs were swiftly saddling up.

"Where is the Commando meeting?" Breda called to the dust-covered mess-engers.

"In the town of Lydenburg. Mynheers, don't worry, I saw both your wives .there so they are not in danger on your farms."

"Thank you! Thank you!" Van Riebeck and Breda cried out as they swung up into their saddles.

"Alles sal regt kom," Kruger called out to them as they nodded and turned their horses. 'Yes, yes, all will come right someday,' Van Riebeck thought, then he and Breda were digging their heels into the animals' flanks and they broke into a gallop.

Mrs. Kruger, her fat body covered by a stiff black taffeta dress came out of the house on to the stoep. From her front parlour window where she had been sitting knitting she had heard all that had occurred and was thinking of one of her sixteen children who was farming in the Lydenburg district.

"Van Riebeck and Breda have been in the saddle for fifty hours, yet they're off again," Mrs. Kruger told the messengers.

"Ja, ja," Kruger said. "They are true Boer leaders."

"Rest and drink coffee," Mrs. Kruger invited the young men but they refused. Having delivered their news to Kruger, they were anxious to be off.

"We must return at once to Lydenburg! All our men are needed there."

"Good. Good." Kruger slapped one young man on the back and handed the other one the brandy bottle. "Drink as you ride. *Voorwarts*, my boys! To Lydenburg! Shoot straight! Remember Majuba!"

10

IN the Cape on the Abend Bloem estate, young Paul was working in one of the brick incubator sheds on the ostrich-feather farm when his young sister, Eileen, opened the door a crack and squeezed her way inside as she beat off and shut the door on the baby ostriches trying to follow her in.

"I came to give you this telegram that's just arrived for you." She held the orange-coloured envelope up to him.

Feeling apprehensive he took it and opened it, hoping nothing was wrong with his mother or the family in the Transvaal. Then he read Katie's telegram and whooped with delight.

"It's from mother! They've discovered *gold* on my land up there and I've got to go there!" He grabbed Eileen's hand. "Come on! I must see Aunt Liz and Uncle Chris at once."

He pulled the astonished girl out of the brick incubator shed.

"Gold! Oh, Paul, will you be a million-aire?" she cried wildly.

Outside they were immediately sur-rounded by flocks of ostriches, but Paul shoved them off and ran with Eileen to where she had tethered her pony next to his horse under some tall gum trees.

"A millionaire! Not so easily as you think. Come, I'll ride you back to the house and send a stable boy for your pony."

He lifted her on to his stallion's back, then swung into the saddle with his whole being singing.

"Nancy! Nancy! Nancy! I'll soon see her again! My God—to hold her in my arms again—to forget all these cows I've been lying with when I was agonizing only for her. But her bloody vow never again to lie with me? What about that? Once I am with her I'll make her break it."

He galloped away from the dusty land, where in the distance flocks of ostriches were strutting about in their ugly fashion, then Paul slowed his horse down as they started to reach the cultivated grounds of the estate. Now the animal daintily picked a footing between huge clumps of gladioli

115

and irises, and camphor trees with their trunks embraced by honeysuckle and yellow bramble roses that also showered over bushes heavy with blue mayflowers.

Paul rode up to the stables and called, "Sannie! Sannie—are you there?"

A tall, slim, beautifully built young man, his shiny brown skin helping to make him look like a bronze statue, came forward from the back of the loose boxes.

"*Ja*, Master Paul." His white teeth flashed, lightening his handsome face.

"Hello, Sannie." Paul and Eileen greeted him warmly for he and his family were favourites with the whole of Katie's family. As children they had played together.

"I left Miss Eileen's pony near the incubator sheds," Paul said, "Will you send a boy for him soon—it's too hot out there for him."

"*Ja—Ja*, at once, Master Paul."

"Thanks, Sannie—I've just heard from my mother that they've found gold on my land in the Transvaal and I'm going up there at once!" Paul excitedly said. "Like to come with me perhaps?"

Sannie chuckled. "Oh yes, I like to

come, *ja*—but life here is good, too. Here I was born." He spread his arms out to take in the huts of the hundred coloured and black people employed on the estate.

"Don't you go too, Sannie!" Eileen cried. "If you do—who will take me fishing?"

"That's true." Paul laughed and whirled his horse around making for the back stoep.

"I love Sannie," Eileen said, "and really he's very well educated, thanks to Mama. You can't imagine what care she gave him when I was too small to join in the lessons with Mary and Ken and the servants' children of that age. She often said Sannie was the brightest of all the blacks."

"What a chatterbox you are."

"All the housemaids are in love with Sannie," Eileen laughed as Paul reined in.

He jumped down and lifted her to the ground. "You're a terrible little gossip—that's what you are—leave Sannie's business alone—he's a man now and he knows what he's about."

He sprang up the wide steps and strode into the back hall with Eileen running at his heels. "I'm not really a gossip, Paul, but none of the housemaids is good enough for Sannie and that's what bothers me. The other day he was reading a play of Shakespeare's that Aunt Liz loaned him. Imagine that."

Paul now ignored her and bellowed out. "Aunt Liz! Aunt Liz—where are you?"

"I'm in the yellow room, Paul," came his aunt's answer in a voice like his mother's, but with a slight Irish brogue.

Paul strode into the small drawing-room and Liz looked up from her sewing. Her thick dark hair was swept up from her high, pale forehead, emphasizing her wide-apart grey eyes. She was blessed with a serenity that reached out even to strangers.

"Paul, darling! What's the excitement?"

"Gold! I've had a telegram from mother. They've found gold on my land and I've got to go up to the Transvaal and re-register my claim."

"Oh, Paul! This is most exciting!"

"But do you think that Uncle Chris could relieve me or Stephan or Jan so I can get away?"

"Of course! Of course—the House of Representatives is in Recess. I'm sure

Uncle Chris will replace you. Eileen, ring the bell for tea, will you?"

Paul was pacing the room speaking excitedly. "Splendid! Wonderful, if Uncle Chris will replace me. Just think of it, Aunt Liz, I may make all my cousins and all my brothers and sisters *really* rich!" 'Nancy—oh, Nancy! I'll get you back again.' The words sang silently in his head. Then again he spoke out loud. "I'll travel up in the fastest way on the first ship from Capetown to Durban, then I'll join a trek going to the Transvaal. It would be too dangerous to attempt to ride the 400 miles alone on horses."

A coloured maid came in answer to Eileen's ring and she also held out an orange-coloured telegram to Liz, saying.

"Missus, I find this on the front hall floor. I think maybe someone drop it."

Liz took and read it with surprise, then handed it to Paul, saying.

"*Another* telegram for you."

He tore it open and read.

"Hurrah leaving today longing to see you all love Nancy."

Paul's entire six foot four frame started to shake. "All love—longing to see you." Those words could only mean she had relinquished her vow not to lie with him. In the name of God what could he do? Leave for the South African Republic just as she was returning? Impossible!

He felt his aunt and Eileen's curious eyes on him. Of course people always wanted to know what a telegram said. What could he tell them? What?

"Paul, you look shocked," Liz said gently. "Is it bad news?"

She gave him a lifeline of an idea and he grabbed at it. "Yes, Aunt Liz, a friend in Capetown is very ill. I'll go in tomorrow." He tucked the telegram into his trouser pocket and sank into a deep chintz-covered chair.

"I'm sorry, Paul. I hope it won't turn out to be serious."

Liz did not believe it could be a girl, for Paul never brought girls home. He went to all the balls around the countryside, danced and flirted at the parties she organised at Abend Bloem when girls almost boldly flung themselves at him but never did he seem close to any particular girl.

She tried to get his mind off his friend's sickness and said, "Why not ride over to the Van Riebeck place, you know your Uncle likes to work over there on his speech for the House of Representatives. Discuss your trip north with him—or do you want tea first?"

"No, no. I'll ride over and talk to him now." Paul gladly stood up. It would be a help to be alone—to think. Think of what he was to do.

A few minutes later he was riding slowly over the lush green land that joined Abend Bloem with the Van Riebeck homestead.

As he rode slowly Paul decided that he did not wish to see his uncle yet. He must first make his own decision. Either to wait here for Nancy or go to re-register his land in the North. His longing for his half-sister had been an ever present ache ever since that day in the Transvaal when the Boers had been victorious at Majuba. The last day he had seen her when she had sworn to God if he were unhurt in the battle she would never lie with him again.

He had left the Transvaal feeling like a madman, and once back in the Cape he had taken women wildly so that the

German Madam in Capetown who ran the best brothel complimented him.

"Never have I, or my young ladies, known a man with such strength as you have."

But none of the beautiful women had helped. It was Nancy—always Nancy whom he sickened for. Her white face framed by her red-gold hair, her tiger-green-gold eyes staring up at him. He was cursed, just as his mother and father had been cursed by their wild love for each other.

In all the time they had been separated, he had received no word from Nancy and in his mad jealousy he felt she had fallen in love with someone in the Transvaal, but today had come the telegram with "All love". It meant that she had relinquished her vow to God and was ready to lie with him again. To hell with the gold! He would wait here for Nancy! Later, together they could go to find the gold.

Elated with what the future promised, Paul swung his horse's head around and started to gallop to Stellenbosch and the Telegraph Office. There he telegraphed to his mother to say "Impossible leave the ostrich farm".

Later when he returned to Abend Bloem, running his fingers through his thatch of moist golden hair, he lightly told Liz what he had done.

Amazed, she stared into his blue, laughing eyes, wondering why he seemed so happy with his decision. "But it's extraordinary that you didn't even go to discuss the whole thing with Uncle Chris! I'm sure he would have taken over here for you."

"No, Aunt Liz, I don't have the right to ask him to and I am sure Mother will manage to re-register the land for me. You know how wonderful she is about arranging these things."

Liz nodded a smiling assent. "Indeed I do, nothing has ever been impossible for her to achieve." She imagined how disappointed Katie would be not to have her marvellous son with her, for Paul—her love child—Liz sensed was Katie's most dearly beloved offspring.

Smiling down at his aunt's upturned face, Paul suddenly thought it was strange that his mother had not telegraphed to her to tell of Nancy's departure. Perhaps she had already written of it and the letter would come later. He regretted that he could not joyously announce. "My beautiful, glorious Nancy is returning soon."

11

TWO days later at noon, the Cape-town newspapers, as usual, arrived by train at Stellenbosch railway station where Sannie picked them up. Before putting the papers into his saddle bag, the black boy, educated by Katie and Liz, read the headlines and was worried by them. He swiftly stuffed the papers into his saddle bag and rode at a swift trot through the town, then galloped through tree-lined country roads to deliver the papers quickly to Abend Bloem.

In the grey painted dining-room, with pale yellow curtains and beautifully polished mahogany table and chairs, lunch was being served. Tall, big-framed Christopher Van der Byl sat at one end of the table and his wife, Liz, at the other with Paul on her right. Her own sons and daughters and all of Katie's young children who lived at Abend Bloem were also there.

Mary, with waist-length golden hair, was seated on Van der Byl's right. Her eyes and fair skin were not beautiful in the way of her sister Nancy, yet a certain fragility made men feel protective towards her.

"Uncle Chris, do you think there is a slight chance that Mama will send me to Italy to perfect my voice?" Mary eagerly asked the big blond sun-tanned man.

"*Ja*, of course, Mary, why not? It's your turn to go to Europe. Nancy and John have been and Paul went to study law in Amsterdam. Now it's your turn. Kenneth, of course, must stay in the Cape until he's finished at the University."

At that moment four young coloured maids came in. They were wearing stiff white shapeless dresses and as they moved about their bare feet slapped gently over the dark tiled floor. Each carried a huge blue-and-white Batavian dish, piled with rice and topped by minced fish fashioned into balls the size of tennis balls— kedgeree was a favourite dish with the family.

When everyone was served, they all stood up and turned toward Van der Byl who solemnly intoned, "Dear God, for what we are about to receive make us truly thankful."

Everyone murmured "Amen", made the sign of the cross, all but Van der Byl who was not a Catholic, then sat down and started to dig their forks into their rice and fish as the maids returned to hand around flat silver dishes heaped with moss-boletjies, the spongy buns filled with half-fermented grape juice.

The dining-room was filled with laughter and chatter for unlike most parents, Liz and Christopher allowed their young to enjoy each other's society at meal times.

A few minutes later a maid came in with a silver tray holding the folded newspaper and giving it to Van der Byl said, "Baas, Sannie send me. He say Baas like see paper at once! Important, he say."

Chris took the paper, opened it and read the headline.

"South African Republic attacked by Mapoochi tribe."

"What's so important about the news?"

Paul asked and his uncle re-read the head-line aloud.

Everyone stopped eating to listen as he went on to read the text.

"Once more the white man is under pressure from the black man. From Pretoria we hear that a large force of Chief Mampuru's warriors have gathered in the mountains behind Lydenburg with countless caves to hide in. They are well supplied with guns and ammunition from German traders from the Zambesi and from workers returned from the diamond mines.

'The local Commando has gathered under the leadership of Commandants Paul Van Riebeck and Abraham Breda. Their wives and wagons are backing them up, for a Boer's wagon is his second home, also the women will act as nurses. In addition it is considered dangerous for women and children to be left on isolated farms.

'Let us hope that the Boers will swiftly win the war and it will not drag out like the wars on our own borders, and the Basuto wars with the Dutch of the Orange Free State, otherwise the white man's prestige will severely diminish."

"Oh, my poor Katie!" Liz burst out, "God help her. Yet another battle to be fought. Will she never be allowed to live in peace?"

"This new trouble doesn't sound so bad to me, Aunt Liz," Paul assured her. "I know that countryside and those Kaffirs. I fought with the Afrikaner Korps against Secoceni, the chief whom Mampuru murdered and replaced. I think the Boers will make short work of them." But secretly he was worried about his mother and two little brothers and thanked God Nancy had already left the Lydenburg district and was on her way down.

"Oh, poor Mama," Mary broke into sobs. "I'll never forget the awful attack of those brutes—the Batlapin on Papa Paul's farm."

She shuddered and hid her face in her hands, as the terrible memories of that night flooded through her.

Then she suddenly felt her Uncle Christopher's arm around her shoulders as he said quietly, "Don't be upset—don't think of the Batlapin attack. Then the Boers were taken unawares. It's different now. At Lydenburg they'll be ready with a big Commando; it won't be the same thing at all. Your mother and Nancy won't be exposed to danger. Don't worry, my dear Mary."

Mary pulled her shielding hands from her face and swallowed her sobs.

"No, Uncle Chris—I'm sure it won't be as bad as *that* time, only I do wish the family could all live together down here."

"Ah, Mary darling, I'm afraid that's a vain prayer." Liz spoke in a sad, philosophical way. "Your Papa Paul's life's work is to help the South African Republic grow into a fine healthy country.

"But see, darling—as nearly all the young at the table are of mixed British and Dutch stock, they must not be prejudiced against the Dutch or British. They must be real South Africans—neither English nor Dutch."

"Yes, Aunt Liz, that's how we feel," Mary assured her. And of course John's ship will soon be in, won't it, Aunt Liz?"

"In three days," Liz said, "I wonder

how he'll like the Cape after all his years in England?"

"I hope he's not going to be too damned English." Paul caught his aunt's arm. "Sorry for swearing, Aunt Liz."

"Don't be, Paul." She smiled acquittingly into his bronzed face. Only one other man was so like a Michelangelo statue and that was Van Riebeck. She had always understood her darling Katie's utter madness over him. Thank God they had found happiness at last.

"I bet John will be a prig," Eileen said, peeling the soft yellow skin off a guava, then digging her fork into the pink fruit. "You remember, Mary, he was always so bossy."

"He can't boss us now," Mary consoled her. "We're too old and in any case I hope he's grown out of his bossiness. He must be very clever if Cecil Rhodes has engaged him, don't you think so, Uncle Chris?"

"I should think John is very clever." Van der Byl had never really liked John and was apprehensive of the effect he would stir up amongst his brothers, sisters and cousins. Chris turned to his own son, Stephan, and asked, "How do you think you'll like working with Paul on the ostrich farm?"

The young man, so like his mother with her dark hair and soft Irish looking eyes, hesitated a moment then said, "I think I'll like it well enough, Father, but I'd like to have more time before I make a final decision. You see, I'm still interested in the idea of entering the Church."

This was a deep grief to Christopher who had loved Liz so much that before marrying her he had willingly signed the Catholic Church's stipulation that children of a mixed marriage must be Catholics. He hated the idea of Stephan being a priest. Still he knew that Liz prayed for it so he kept his thoughts to himself, and said, "Well, time will tell, Stephan." He nodded toward the newspaper on a side table. "Too bad about this Lydenburg business. I wish your Aunt Katje with Nancy and the little lads were down here."

Hearing him, Paul ached to shout out to all of them. "Nancy *is* on her way down here!" But until Aunt Liz had the news from his mother he must keep his happiness to himself.

12

THAT evening a coloured messenger from the Stellenbosch Post Office rode up to Abend Bloem to deliver Katie's telegram to Paul.

"Regret changed plans not coming Cape please come here all love Nancy."

"God in Heaven!" Paul swore to himself as he crumpled the telegram and stuck it deep into his trouser pocket. He was sitting alone smoking on the front stoep so there was no need to explain to anyone about the telegram. He knocked the bowl of his pipe out on the heel of his soft leather veldenhoen.

He would go the quickest way. Leave on the first ship sailing to Durban and trek up from there. But what explanations to give Aunt Liz and Uncle Chris for his sudden change of plans? Easy enough— the war with the Mapoochi—he felt his gun should be there to help his father protect the family. Also he could re-register his land on the Witwatersrand.

At dinner, he announced his decision, which the whole family applauded, and Van der Byl and Stephan promised to take over the responsibility of the ostrich farm.

"If it's all right, Uncle Chris, I think I'll ride into Capetown tonight," Paul said excitedly, eager to make even so small a start. "I'll doss down at Terence's place and in the morning find out when a ship leaves for Durban. I'll telegraph Mother from town to say I'm coming."

"That's best." Van der Byl agreed but Liz said, "Don't ride in, Paul—have Sannie take you in a carriage and. . . ."

"Oh yes, do! Do! And we can ride in with you," Eileen pleaded. "I just love to see the electric lights at the railway station; they're like magic."

"Yes, it's such a lovely evening," Mary said, "and we can all see Terence. I miss him, he hasn't been home for weeks."

"Because he's on duty in the hospital," Liz said.

"All right then," Paul agreed. "Who's coming into town with me?"

"But the girls can't come home alone."

Liz shot a glance of enquiry at her husband who gave a negative shake of his head.

"But, Aunt Liz, it's all right if Sannie drives, isn't it?" Mary said gently. "After all, he drives me to town to my singing lessons and we go fishing and swimming with him. He's like one of the family."

"Of course he is, but a maid always goes with you to your lessons."

"I'll chaperon the girls, Mother," Stephan said with a quiet laugh. "I also would like to see Terry."

Liz savoured the fine rapport that had grown between her eldest son and Katie's eldest son, Terence. "Good, Stephan, that solves the problem." She turned to Paul. "But you'd better pack."

"Right—I'll start if you'll excuse me." He stood up.

"I'll help you," Eileen cried excitedly.

"No! No, thank you," Paul laughed, "but perhaps Stephan will lend me a hand."

Half an hour later, the big carriage stood at the steps of the front stoep, and Paul's guns, ammunition and two portmanteaux were loaded into the back. There was also a small package of special delicacies swiftly packed by Liz for Katie.

Sannie, wearing spotless white jacket and trousers, was seated on the driver's seat with one of his young brothers, also in white, beside him.

Paul shook his uncle's hand, kissed his aunt and the rest of the family and climbed into the carriage to sit beside Mary with Stephan and Eileen opposite him. The night was so warm the carriage hood was down and as Sannie called to the horses with a clicking sound and turned them around to face the long avenue of great oaks, Paul looked back affectionately at the group on the stoep waving to him and calling out, "A safe journey." "God bless you." "Give the family our love."

Shame lightly brushed his soul. How they would suffer should they ever discover his love affair with Nancy. He was the second oldest of his brothers, sisters and cousins and he knew well that all regarded him with a type of hero worship. Why? Because he stood 6 feet 4 inches and had wide shoulders, and because he looked like his father? Because he was a fine shot, could force an ox's head to the ground, by its horns, break in devil horses that could never throw him? Because he ran the ostrich farm profitably? Madness! He did not deserve all the respect. Inside this great frame of his was a coward, a man rushing to embrace his half-sister. A man weak and corrupt for what could be his future with her? Only God knew, then with a mental shrug he thought, "To Hell with it. I didn't make myself and I fought against loving Nancy for several years—long before we touched each other."

Three days later he sailed on the *Millicent* for Durban.

Up in Lydenburg that was crowded with men of the Commando and their families still coming in from the outlying districts, Katie made her way to the Telegraph Office. God willing Paul had telegraphed to her. Van Riebeck had joined her and had just decided to pull out with most of the Commando and wagons that evening, so this was her last chance to receive a telegram.

She gave her name to the clerk who

handed her a telegram, and with relief she read.

"Changed my mind sailing on the *Millicent* next week to Durban love Paul."

He was coming! Praise God! She had succeeded in preventing a meeting between him and Nancy. But merciful God, how besotted he must be with Nancy to have so swiftly decided to come up after having received the telegram she had sent in Nancy's name. But enough—he was coming!

Outside the Telegraph Office, Katie tore the message into shreds and scattered them into a canal of stagnant water. She then walked slowly back to her wagon. As Paul was coming via Durban she thought, he might arrive in less than two months, and by then Nancy would be nearing the Cape.

He could never discover that it was Katie who had sent the telegram in Nancy's name and as for gold at the Witwatersrand, on his land, she felt in her very bones that all the odd rumours about it would materialize into reality. But should there be no gold and Paul be furious with her for bringing him up on a fool's errand, then she and Van Riebeck must face their son with the truth. Tell him they knew of his incestuous love. Somehow Van Riebeck must make him end it and God grant that Nancy, reaching Capetown and finding Paul gone, would sail for England.

"Well, I've done my best," Katie wearily told herself, "No one can do more than that." Then she put the matter aside in her mind and started hurrying to the wagon to check on the last minute affairs before the wagons pulled out of Lydenburg to start for the Mapoochi country.

On the great spreading plain at the base of high, thickly wooded mountains that rose up with their peaks to pierce the dome of the sky scorched to whiteness by a devil-sun, the wagons of the Commando were halted near a small river.

After two months of fighting, the Boers had still not conquered Mampuru and his tribe. They had now taken to avoiding open fighting and were hiding in the caves of the mountains from where they come down in the darkness as silently as shadows, to kill the look-outs and steal the cattle and worst of all to hurl assegais with flaring grass tied to them, to start fires on the wagons' canvas hoods.

But the Boers were not easy victims for they kept great fires burning all night around the laager and vigilant sentries were always on duty; yet sometimes Kaffir assegais, thrown from the darkness, managed to pierce a man's back.

In her wagon, lying in the great bed that stretched across the wagon's width, Katie could not sleep, so she quietly left the bed where Van Riebeck, wearing trousers and shirt, his gun and veldshoen on the floor beside him ready for a possible attack, was sleeping soundly. Katie, in her voluminous cotton nightdress, went to stand at the back of the wagon to stare out at the night.

It was a scene that fascinated, yet repelled her. A huge moon spread its silvery-golden rays across the purple sky making the silhouette of the mountains seem even greater and starker than in daylight. In those wooded mountains were thousands of warriors of the Mapoochi tribe, longing for the command to come from Mampuru to satisfy their blood lust and spring down to attack the white devils. Might the command not come tonight?

Katie shivered though the night air was warm. Her eyes travelled over the huge laager for there were a thousand fighting men gathered there with their wagons, families, servants, horses, trek oxen and cattle for eating. The great fires lit up a huge perimeter, for the Boers always followed the precaution of going into laager to protect themselves against surprise attack.

The wind changed direction carrying with it the stench from mounds of human and animal excrement piled high outside the laager where each day Kaffir servants dumped their masters' full pails from the previous night, adding to the height of the dungheaps. Katie held a fold of her nightgown to her nose until the breeze blew the stench in another direction.

God, oh God! She was so bitterly weary of this crude life. The savage conditions, the hardships, the flies, the mosquitoes. The total lack of privacy in this type of living, where the wagons remained stationary, was hard to endure. When trekking conditions were not as bad for during the times of travel she could sit in her wagon and read but now everyone seemed to be a part of everyone else's life.

Worst of all, were the times each day when the men rode off to the mountain's base, left their horses and climbed up through the wooded areas to try to smoke out and fight the Mapoochi. Then she trembled as she listened to the firing, always beseeching God to let Van Riebeck return, unhurt.

"When will it end, darling?" she had asked Van Riebeck that very evening before he had gone to rest.

"When we've wiped the Mapoochi out or we're sure that we've frightened them sufficiently so that they desert this part of the country, get right out of the South African Republic, and *when* we catch Mampuru himself and string him up."

"It's too awful that this fighting and killing must continue when the South African Republic is the size of France. In God's name there's land enough for all the blacks and whites."

"Yes, when you put it like that it sounds

sensible, but the blacks don't want the white man here at any price, and that's the crux of the matter. Until all the tribes accept that we're here to stay, that they can't drive us off, I'm afraid the killing will continue. But at least after all the years of terrible slaughter with the Zulus, we are now at peace with them. Better still, we are now Dinizulu's ally," Van Riebeck chuckled. "Pray God that the war between the Zulus will soon be over and the South African Republic will win its own harbour. Saint Lucia Bay—an outlet to the sea! By God, how badly we need it." He tamped tobacco into the bowl of his pipe. "Well, we can't wait around here much longer for the Mapoochi to come out and fight. We'll have to use dynamite and blockade them in their caves."

"God—how horrible! That means closing them up in the caverns, burying them alive!"

"War isn't humane, Katje, and we've got to beat the bastards. We can't afford a failure up here in the South African Republic like they've had in the Cape with the Basutos. It's cost them millions of pounds and the Basutos have really won

143

the day. They've *not* turned in their guns and the government has to 'allow' them to keep them."

"That's what I'm so afraid of. The Mapoochi have guns too—every time you go out and fight in the mountains, I listen to the firing and I'm terrified."

"Don't be. The Kaffirs are bloody awful shots," he laughed with satisfaction. "They all aim their sights too high. Well, I'm for bed."

He had kissed her, then lay down in his clothes, his gun beside him and immediately fell asleep.

Heavy with a deep depression more profound than usual and which she could not shake off, Katie now stayed at the back of the wagon. She glanced at the next wagon lashed wheel to wheel with hers. Franz and Adrian slept in there with Maarje and Philip. All seemed well with them. Then her mind roved to Paul trekking up here. Soon he would be arriving. Would he come out here to the camp? Soon too, Nancy would be arriving at the Cape.

What a sorrow it all was. How deeply one must pay for the gift of love. To remain with Van Riebeck she had sacrificed the possibility of being with all of her children. Out of ten she now only had little Franz and Adrian with her, and only her beloved sister Liz's letters kept her a little in touch with all of her other children.

"God—dear God!" she silently prayed, "Help me to bear this existence. I love Van Riebeck deeply—help me to be satisfied with him in this semi-wilderness. You granted my years of prayer to be his wife, now let me be a good one and satisfied with my lot."

"Katje, darling. . . ." His beloved voice in low teasing tones reached her. "Just why are you playing the part of sentinel? There are many good men on watch—I assure you."

She turned back into the shadowy wagon. "You're awake, my love. Why? I didn't make a sound to disturb you."

"Ach, no, you didn't but there are two parts of me—one asleep—one awake—so I missed you when my left arm was empty. Come, don't leave me."

"Never, never." Her bare feet swept over the silver fox covering on the wagon floor then she sank on to the bed beside him.

He gathered her into his ironlike arms, pressing her against the length of him as he murmured.

"Katje! Katje! Even though we've been married almost nine years, I still can't believe you're mine at last."

"My love—I know, I so often feel the same."

Then his hand, calloused by his gun, found her breast as he kissed her and her mind was swiftly emptied of everything but the joy of his love-making.

13

IT was the hour before dawn when all the earth seemed still. Suddenly three shots split the quiet, dogs started furiously barking, then came warning blasts on the sentries' horns.

"The Mapoochi are coming!"

Van Riebeck muttered as he jumped up, slipped his feet into veldshoen, grabbed his hat, his gun and bandolier, and strode from the wagon. He jumped on to his already saddled horse as a Kaffir boy untethered it from the wagon and galloped off to the speaker's box on a small dais in the centre of the laager as from all the wagons men poured out and on to their horses.

"They're coming! They're coming! Prepare!" came the warning shouts.

Hundreds of mounted men were riding up to Van Riebeck and Breda who had joined him on the small dais.

"We'll fight outside the laager and drive

147

them back!" Van Riebeck shouted to the men.

"If we can't drive them back," Breda called out, "three blasts on my horn means ride for the laager. Understood?"

"*Ja, Ja*," came from almost a thousand throats.

"*Voorwarts!*" Van Riebeck cried. "And may the Lord ride with us! *Voorwarts!*"

Two wagons were being pulled back to form an exit for the fighting men who now cantered out of the laager to meet a black mass of thousands of naked black men, oiled bodies shining in the rising sunlight as they rushed from the mountain's base toward the laager.

The Mapoochi came with spears held high poised to throw, some waved their guns triumphantly. They seemed a never-ending black wave of death, rolling quickly toward the whites as they screeched.

"*Bulala! Bulala!* Kill! Kill!"

By now the mounted Boers had spread out in a line, and waiting for the Kaffirs to get closer, suddenly commenced to fire into the advancing black mass of Mapoochi warriors who started falling in heaps.

On the wagons, the women and children stared out as fighting began, and when the childrens' wails added to the guns barking, the cattle lowing, the murderous cries of the Mapoochi, it was like Bedlam.

Katie went swiftly into the wagon to Franz and Adrian who were yelling in fear.

"Don't be afraid, children," she comforted them. "You've heard guns firing often."

"But mama, the Kaffirs sound so close this time." Franz whimpered and Adrian clung to her sobbing, "I'm afraid, Mama." She cuddled him and kissed him. Maarje muttered, "*Ja, ja,* Missus, they are just outside it seems—nearer than before."

"Don't worry, the Dutch will drive them off. Each time a gun fires it means a Kaffir is killed. Help me dress the children, Maarje."

When the boys and Maarje were dressed, they went to Katie's wagon where she rapidly got out of her voluminous nightgown and pulled on her clothes. As always she stuck her long knife into her waistband, then bundled her hair into a knot on her neck and she never ceased silently praying, "Take care of Van Riebeck, I implore You."

The sounds of the guns barking and the Kaffirs screaming was non-stop. From nearby trees birds rose chattering to the sky. The dogs barked incessantly, the cattle lowed in fear. But the Boer women left their wagons and calmly helped the Kaffir maids to prepare breakfast at the same time scolding servants and children.

"Ach, you are fools—there is nothing to fear. Our men will kill and drive the devils off—don't worry."

For a few minutes Katie stood on her wagon staring out at the battle. Through the air filled with dust and gun smoke, she saw that already there was a terrible carnage of the Mapoochi. Desperate to kill the hated white men, they flung themselves forward within reach of the gunfire and even before their spears could leave their hands they were dead men. The Boers fired from their horses trained to stand still. Piles of dead blacks lay before them and yet the Mapoochis came on, jumping over their dead. It was as if Mampuru had ordered the warriors to make this their day of victory or die where they fought.

The Kaffirs' courage amazed Katie; they seemed to care nothing for death. The fight was near enough for her to see that those with guns used them awkwardly. Whilst the Boers, crack shots that they were, never missed their target. But thousands more of the Mapoochis were pouring out from the trees at the mountain base and rushing forward to replace their dead.

Could the thousand Boers fight out there without being mastered by the force of numbers of the Kaffirs who were rumoured to be thirty thousand strong? Some of the blacks must surely manage to get close enough for their throwing spears to kill. Oh, why didn't the Boers come back to the comparative safety of the laager?

Now the terrible black wave was advancing so fast it was forcing the Boers back, and they were losing ground. Then above the bedlam of sounds, Katie heard the horn blast three times and cries floated out.

"To the laager! Back to the laager!"

Whirling their horses, the Boers came

charging back in clouds of dust and around the cooking fires women cried to each other in relief, "Thank God! They're coming back! Praise the Lord!"

Galloping through the space made by the two wagons being pulled back, the Boers were looking backwards firing from their horses which they controlled with their thighs. When the last man was in the laager, the wagons were dragged into place and the circle tightly shut. The men jumped from their horses and mounted anyone's wagon where they continued to fire into the black masses coming close to the laager, whilst the women loaded for them.

Two men whom Katie slightly knew, Conrad and Falks, jumped up on her wagon, crying, "Get back, Missus! Get back inside the wagon!"

"I'll load for you," she cried and went to grab her own gun and a spare of Van Riebeck's which was already loaded. She pushed the spare gun into Conrad's hands and grabbed his gun to reload.

"Get me the bowl of bullets, Maarje! Quickly! Quickly!" Katie ordered the frightened coloured girl who with the children was crouched into a corner of the big bed. "Hurry! Remember Philip is also fighting in this battle."

This brought action into Maarje's numbed limbs and she jumped to obey.

Now the Mapoochis were all around the laager, but just out of distance of the guns, as if they were conferring, they slowed down.

"Another tribe must have joined the bastards," Falks cried as he stood with gun raised. "They seem double their number."

Then suddenly the warriors rushed forward with their terrible assegais poised, and screaming, *"Bulala! Bulala!* Kill—Kill!"* Guns barked from every wagon and in terror, Katie loaded and reloaded guns for Falks and Conrad as they fired into the black hordes of shiny naked bodies wet with sweat, head feathers tossing. The long animal hide shields held to protect the Mapoochis were useless against bullets. Now their assegais were coming dangerously close; some had burning grass tied to them.

But the Boer guns were barking, barking, their fire shattering into black men's faces or stomachs. It was too horrible and the savages were coming closer. Katie could see their bloodshot eyes as like a machine she loaded a gun, gave it to Falks or Conrad, took an empty gun and loaded it—on and on she went.

Now smoke from the guns mixed with dust raised by thousands of warriors' feet was obscuring the view. Impossible to see if more blacks were still coming behind those so near the wagons. Yes, yes, more were rushing up.

Would the black horde never stop coming? Dead bodies were piled up so near the wagons that warriors could hide behind them and creep up to reach the wagons. There—a Kaffir had got through the range of fire and was making for a wagon, but someone spotted him and a gun blew his head off.

At that moment a horn started blasting. "It's the Mapoochi signal for retreat," Conrad cried, but went on shooting.

The mass of warriors hesitated for a second then turned and started to flee from the barking guns that the Boers kept shooting until the enemy was out of gun range.

"Oh, thank God—thank God!" Katie cried and sank down to her knees, then almost fell over sideways to sit on the silver fox covering the wagon boards.

"*Ja, ja!* We've given the bastards a good beating." Falks stared triumphantly out at the plain as with the back of his arm he wiped sweat from his face.

Through the smoke and dust people were peering from every wagon at the earth dark with black bodies.

"We've killed them by the thousands, the bastards," Conrad roared in triumph. "Now let's see what's happened on our own wagon. Goodbye, Missus," they cried to Katie, jumped off the wagon, found their horses nearby and went off.

Seconds later Van Riebeck galloped up, dismounted and sprang into the wagon. Seeing Katie on the floor he cried, "My God! Are you hurt, Katje?"

"No! No—resting. And you?" Her eyes flashed over him. "You're all right—praise the Lord."

He nodded. His shirt and moleskin trousers were clinging to him with sweat, his golden hair was wet and clamped to his head as he went to his two small sons and caught them in his arms.

"And Philip is all right too, Maarje; he'll be here any minute."

"Papa! Papa! Is the awful fighting over at last?" Franz's arms had a stranglehold on Van Riebeck's neck.

"No, my son. We've beaten the Kaffir attack but now we're going to follow them into the mountains and dynamite their caverns to finish them off—but you must get used to battle, Franz, for someday you, too, must fight."

"Must you go right away?" Katie murmured. "What about all that out there?" She waved an arm toward the mounds of dead so near the wagons.

"We'll care for everything first, don't worry. Make coffee, Maarje. I'll be back, but first I must address the men and see if we have any casualties."

The roll call was swiftly taken. Three Boers had been killed and fifteen wounded. Then Van Riebeck and Breda sent two parties of young men out to finish off the Mapoochi wounded and to count the casualties. Later they would clear the dead away, but now they must follow up with their victory and break up the Mapoochi tribe for all time.

Soon it was known that eleven hundred men lay dead around the wagons alone. There was not time yet to count the number killed in open fighting, but it was reckoned to be at least four times that amount.

Half an hour later, having swiftly eaten and restocked with ammunition, and carrying a large quantity of dynamite, the horses having been well watered, the Commando numbering 950 men rode out toward the mountains. Forty men were left behind to guard the laager lest there be stray warriors hiding in the bush who might attack the wagons when the main force had gone.

Watching the Commando ride out, guns across their backs, wide-brimmed hats pulled over their eyes, Katie marvelled at the courage and strength of these men. They had been fighting almost non-stop for four hours yet they sat their horses as if they knew no fatigue. As for fear it was something she had never seen in these extraordinary tenacious people.

She felt too weary to move, to sip the

coffee Maarje had brought her, but she told herself to drop the canvas flap at the back of the wagon, to hide from the children the appalling carnage—also to keep out the sickly-sweet stench of blood and death.

"Maarje, we'll stay in the wagon but the children must be fed. Would you go down and cook some pancakes for them and bring them up? We've enough water up here."

"Yes, Missus." Maarje reluctantly started for the back of the wagon. She too did not want to see the mounds of dead, but then she was encouraged by the sounds of Dutch women's voices on the ground; they were bossing servants up to build cooking fires and commence the childrens' mid-day meal.

"We must start the stews and babootie; we must eat and when the men return from the mountains they will be hungry and want a well cooked dinner," Katie heard a woman call out and marvelled at the Dutch stoicism. How could they eat with piles of dead men so close, with the smell of blood so strong on the air, rising above the smell of smoke of the cooking fires?

For a nasty moment Katie's head felt almost empty and she swayed on her feet. Was she going to faint? The blood seemed to be draining from her heart. Then the moment passed and holding on to the side of the wagon she groped her way to the bed and sank on to it.

Adrian immediately snuggled up to her, and on the other side Franz smoothed the hair off her forehead saying, "Poor Mama —you are tired from loading all the guns; you must rest till Papa gets back. I can hear the sound of the horses growing fainter. They must be near the mountains."

Over the sounds of the intermittent barking of the nervous dogs, she heard the distant clap clap of horses' hooves. In her imagination she could see Van Riebeck giving the Boers orders to climb up to find the Mapoochis—then they would lay the dynamite and explode it so that the earth would fall into the caverns and blockade them, and thousands of Kaffirs would be buried alive. Cruel! Cruel! She could not tolerate the thought, it was too unbearable.

Also the dynamite would surely bring parts of the mountain sliding down on the outside of the caverns—would some of the Boers be trapped?

Her head thumped with a drum beat and despite the heat she felt shivery.

"Dear God—don't let me be ill, don't let me be." Then her teeth started to chatter as if with cold. "Malaria! It's catching hold of me! I mustn't be ill at such a time. I mustn't be a burden to Van Riebeck, I, who am never ill." Then again came the slipping away feeling and from far off she heard Adrian's baby voice calling her, "Mama—Mama—answer me." But she was too tired to answer and then Franz was calling, "Maarje, Maarje! Come quickly, Mama is sick!"

Then she completely lost consciousness.

Maarje rushed on to the wagon and seeing how Katie's body was shaking with her teeth chattering, she dashed out to call the nearest Dutch woman from a neighbouring wagon.

"Come quickly, Vrow Van de Merwe—my Missus is very sick."

"What is it, Maarje?" Gerta Van der

Merwe looked up from her cooking fire where she was frying fritters.

"I don't know, but she shivers and shakes and can't speak."

"Ach, she has malaria I suppose. Don't worry. I'll give her some arsenic and soon she'll be well. I'll get my hussapotheck and bring it to your wagon. If the children are with her get them into their wagon."

She handed the frying pan with golden fritters to a servant, then heaving herself off a folding canvas chair she waddled to her wagon for her medicine box.

Almost all day Gerta stayed with Katie, who, although her body felt on fire to the touch, shivered with cold so that her teeth were chattering. Though well accustomed to malaria, Gerta was upset that her friend had such a heavy attack for she was out of her mind and the dose of arsenic Gerta gave her did not bring on the usual sweating that would reduce the fever in the brain.

Katie seemed quite unaware of the sounds of the dynamite blasting all around the mountain's base, of the Boers riding down and shooting the Kaffirs who came running madly from their hiding places.

She just kept muttering about strange things Gerta knew nothing of—a house in the Cape, the sea, which Gerta had never laid eyes on.

"Perhaps Katje is better off like this for now," Gerta thought as she worried about her husband and two sons who were on the mountain. For a few minutes she went to stand at the back of the wagon, but the sight of flocks of vultures gorging on the bodies of the Kaffir dead sickened her and she went back to bathe Katie's face and arms with water sweetened by lavender from her hussapotheck. As Katie's shivering increased she sent Maarje for more blankets from her own wagon and piled them on to Katie, but still she did not sweat.

Evening and at last the blasting was finished, then the gun shots grew intermittent, then at last stopped.

"Thank the Lord," Gerta prayed, "the men will soon be coming back—they have fought all day and without eating." But another hour passed before they came galloping back crying triumphantly, "It's all over! All over!"

They cantered into the laager and told

the women and children gathering around them, "We caught Mampuru and strung him up to a tree branch." "What's left of the tribe and it's not much, has fled over the mountains to the north." "They won't trouble us again."

Covered in dust from climbing the mountain on his stomach, face and arms scratched from brambles, Van Riebeck reined in at his wagon, surprised that Katie was not waiting for him. Then he went inside and saw her in bed with Gerta seated on a stool beside her.

"Malaria," Gerta said, "and don't look so worried, she'll be better tomorrow. Are my husband and sons unhurt?"

"Yes, we had no deaths, thank the Lord."

Bending over Katie he felt heartsick at the way her lovely face had fallen in during the hours he had been away. He tossed his hat on to a peg and unslung his gun.

"When did it start, Gerta?"

"Just after the Commando rode out. If only she would sweat it would be better, but you go and wash and eat at my wagon. Tell my family I'll come soon."

"No, Gerta, you go and see them. I'll

take care of Katje. Ask the Predikant to start the prayers of thanks, will you, but I'll stay here."

"All right, Paul." Gerta slowly manoeuvred her big body to a standing position. "But when will we leave here? Those bodies out there are stinking from the day's sun blazing on them. The assvogels are so heavy with eating they can't rise on their wings."

"We'll pull out for Lydenburg at dawn. The men are too tired to travel tonight."

"Ach, Paul! That is verdamnt! *Our* men —too tired!" Gerta blazed at Van Riebeck. "We should inspan at once and pull out straight away, or we'll have sickness from those corpses. The air is full of filthy flies that have been on them. I don't like it. I've never seen malaria like this attack of Katje's." Gerta was annoyed with Van Riebeck who in his man's way had forgotten the hellish day the women had endured. "Who knows what sickness Katje really has, so for God's sake, Paul, let's move out!"

He hesitated a second, listening to Katie's unintelligible numblings. "All right, Gerta, I'll go and give the order to inspan at once. The Predikant can conduct thanksgiving prayers later, and the men can eat when we are a safe distance from this filthy graveyard."

"Good man, Paul. That is right. I'll stay with Katje to keep the flies off her face whilst you hurry to get us trekking."

He rushed away, telling himself that he would not settle anywhere that night but leave the Commando and go on until he reached Lydenburg, where there was an old Austrian doctor who could care for Katje.

An hour later, the oxen were all inspanned, cooking utensils and folding furniture were packed, the chickens back in their crates beneath the wagons, the cattle rounded up and the wagons moved forward. As Paul watched beside Katie, he wrote his despatches to Kruger, then gave them to two young men especially riding beside his wagon for the despatches. They would gallop ahead with them to Lydenburg where fresh riders would take them and gallop on to hand them to Kruger in Pretoria.

But the victory over the Mapoochi tribe had lost much of its glory for Van Riebeck now that Katie was so ill.

166

14

NEWS of the Boer victory over the Mapoochis had, of course, reached Lydenburg by the two despatch riders to Pretoria before the arrival of the Van Riebeck's wagons. As they pulled up and Van Riebeck jumped off his wagon, cheering broke out and people rushed up to congratulate him, to shake his hand, but he swiftly shook them off explaining "I've got to get Doctor Mayer for my wife at once. She is sick with malaria or something."

"I'll run and get him, Commandant," an eager young boy offered and went charging down the street and whilst Van Riebeck told the people around him of the Boer victory, he saw the old doctor, with the boy carrying his black, bulging bag, hurrying toward the wagon.

Katie was still delirious, but now sweating so much that Van Riebeck needed clean sheets and decided to borrow them and blankets from some of his friends in town.

The silver-haired Doctor Mayer examined Katie and took her pulse. "Ach, yes, it's malaria and a nasty case of it. I'll give her a good dose of arsenic. Poor, lovely lady, I fear she has suffered through too much. She is so fragile, not like these great strong women of your race, Commandant Van Riebeck. I think it is hard for her up here."

His remark came as an annoying surprise to Van Riebeck, who had considered Katje to be indomitable. He said quietly for the doctor's tone had sounded reproachful and he resented it.

"Shall I get a room for my wife at the Rooinek Hotel or take her straight back to the farm, Doctor?" he asked.

"Take her to her home. The hotel will soon be crowded and noisy with victory celebrations. On your farm she has all her belongings and is surrounded by her own servants. I will visit her tomorrow."

"She'll be all right, won't she, Doctor?" Van Riebeck asked gruffly, trying to disguise the emotion in his voice. If she died? But he dare not even think about that.

"Yes, yes, man, she'll recover from the malaria, but, good God, take care of her! Don't put her through such awful experiences again. Not only was she attacked by Kaffirs on her journey into Lydenburg, she then went through the battles you've just fought." He shook his head sorrowfully and his deep brown eyes looked compassionate. "All the horrors she has forced herself to endure have built up inside her and have weakened her constitution so that the malaria has taken a strong hold of her. A delicate lady like your wife is not meant for this rough hard life, Commandant."

Damn the doctor to hell, but he was right. "I should have sent her down to the Cape after the war with the English," Van Riebeck said.

"That would have been a good idea. Now I'll go and you get off to your home. Give her this tablet tonight." He handed Van Riebeck a round pink pill. "The more she sweats the better and try to make her drink as much water as possible. Boiled water, of course."

He glanced with admiring eyes—whose commiseration showed—at Katie's pale, sunken face, shook his head and hurried off the wagon.

He left Van Riebeck with a feeling of heavy guilt as if having been trusted with a rare jewel he had dropped it in the mud. Not waiting to borrow fresh bedding, he gave the driver orders to head for the farm, adding, "And make these damned oxen move."

Hours later the two wagons pulled up before the squat white homestead and servants came running out to greet their Baas and Missus.

"All is well here, Baas," Obsete the head man smilingly assured Van Riebeck. "No Mapoochis raid the farm."

"Good, good, Obsete." Then Van Riebeck turned to the cook-housekeeper. "Joanna, quickly go turn down your Missus' bed; she is ill."

Joanna with a worried face hurried away whilst with immense tenderness Van Riebeck carried Katie into the house and laid her in the big four-poster bed and covered her up with many blankets.

170

"What is it, Baas?" Joanna asked. "What is wrong with Missus?"

"A heavy dose of malaria, she must be sponged and changed into a clean nightgown. Hurry and get warm water."

He went to a chest of drawers where he knew Katje kept her underclothes and pulled out a nightgown. Then when Joanna returned, together they sponged her whilst she murmured in her delirium, "I was right to send him the telegram—oh, I'm sure I was right—to send it."

Seated in a big chair beside the bed, Van Riebeck wondered what telegram it could be. For hours he sat beside her, continuously mopping sweat from her face and body and forcing her to drink water. Toward dawn the fever began to abate and her mind gradually became rational.

Her big eyes, sunken in their sockets, looked slowly around the room lit by a single oil lamp with moths clustered around the chimney, then they came to rest on Van Riebeck in the chair beside the bed.

"Funny," she said weakly, "but for a moment—I thought I was at the farm."

"You are at the farm, darling. You're in

your own bed." He was deeply relieved that her mind had returned to normalcy and bending over her he explained, "You've been in delirium for almost a week."

"Oh no . . . the war with. . . ."

"All finished. I've brought you home. By God, I swear to you you'll never have to go through anything like that again!" He kissed her forehead tenderly. "Your spirit is so indomitable that I abused it, and forced you to physically do things you weren't strong enough for. I beg your forgiveness."

"Oh, darling, don't reproach yourself ever. Everything I've done—was easy—just as long as I was able to be with you. Has Paul arrived yet?"

He regretted that her mind was wandering again. "No, Paul isn't here, darling. You remember, he's at the Cape."

"Yes, but he answered my telegram—saying he was coming."

"What telegram? You've been talking of some telegram all through your delirium."

"Oh Lord!" Katie thought, then decided that this was the time to confess to him about what she had done. The

172

words came slowly and when she had finished she pleaded, "I was right, darling, to send him the telegram in Nancy's name, wasn't I?"

At this moment in life had she upset the entire world with telegrams to all the world's Prime Ministers and Kings and Queens he would have agreed with her.

"Certainly you were right. Absolutely right." He would deal with the situation when Paul arrived. "Now do you feel you could drink some chicken broth? You've had no nourishment for almost a week."

She shook her head slowly. "Not yet— later perhaps. Tell me, did all the Mapoochis escape from those awful caverns or were they buried alive?"

It surprised him that she cared so much about the Kaffirs but he swallowed his annoyance. Because of her anxiety he lied. "Oh, the Mapoochis streaked off over the mountains to the north. They escaped from the caverns and they'll never bother us again."

"I'm glad—I'm so glad they escaped from the caverns. I'll sleep now, darling." Relieved of her horrible imaginings, her heavy lids fell shut and she soon slept.

Van Riebeck waited a few minutes, then, feeling he could safely leave her for a little while, went out to smoke his pipe on the stoep. He was deeply grateful that the worst of her fever had passed and she was recovering.

Out of all the cycle of twenty-four hours he loved this time when dawn with a mauvy greyness chased night from the world and danced as a golden wisp of light along the mountain tops until the sun rose to establish its supremacy.

Van Riebeck tamped tobacco into the bowl of his pipe with his thumb. He was anxious to go to the yard to have the servants throw water over him. He felt that he must smell gamey; he had not washed or eaten properly since before the final day of battle. The aroma of coffee on the air made him go quietly to the kitchen where Joanna was starting to prepare breakfast.

"Missus is much better," he told the black woman who smiled in relief. "She sleeps well. You've got the chicken broth ready for when she awakes?"

"*Ja, ja,* Baas. It's good that she is

better." Joanna opened her mouth in a wide smile. "Baas wants coffee?"

"Yes please, on the stoep. Are the children still asleep?"

"*Ja*, Baas—they are tired from the journey, I think."

He smiled, nodded, then going down the corridor, looked into the bedroom to check that Katie slept peacefully, then he went to the stoep to enjoy a pipe and the wonders of the sunrise.

He was mentally facing up to an unpleasant truth, which old Doctor Mayer had almost rudely flung at him. It was that Katje was not a woman to endure the hardships up here for any length of time. So they must separate again. God! How often in their lives had they been parted, but for her health's sake she must go down to the Cape, whilst he stayed up here to do his duty in the Volksraad, to help build the Republic.

A coloured girl brought him coffee and mossboletjies on a tray, then left. He sipped the coffee and started to crumble one of the spongy buns, then hearing wagon wheels turning and the sound of oxen approaching, he looked up and at a bend of the land he saw a wagon making for the house. Who the hell came to visit before dawn? He stood up as the wagon drew closer, and he recognised the big figure of a golden-haired man standing beside the driver.

"Paul! My God!"

Van Riebeck told himself to be careful not to shout lest it awaken Katje. He ran down the steps and welcomed his son.

Paul jumped off the wagon and strode forward with outstretched hand to greet his father.

They shook hands heartily and clapped each other on the shoulders whilst smiling into each other's faces—so alike as they stood eye to eye.

"By God, Paul, it's good to see you here!"

"It's good to be here, Father, but along the way I heard I'm too late to join in the fighting, that you licked the Mapoochi."

"Yes, it's over, thank the Lord." Van Riebeck said walking Paul to the house as the driver drove the wagon around to the back yard.

Paul was so excited he wanted to shout aloud so that Nancy would wake up and come out but it was too early, he warned himself. He must be patient.

On the stoep he asked, "Father, is the family still asleep?"

"Yes, it's just about five o'clock."

"How is everyone?"

"Your mother has just recovered from the worst bout of malaria that I've ever seen, but she's on the mend now, thank God."

"Fine! Fine! Poor mother, and Nancy, is she all right?" Paul hoped his voice had no sound but a brotherly interest.

Van Riebeck, knowing of Paul's love for Nancy, hesitated before delivering a blow to Paul's soul. He even pitied his son as he said lightly, "Nancy? Well, I hope she's all right. She should be nearing the Cape by now."

"The Cape?" Paul was stunned, his blue eyes stared unbelievingly at his father. "You mean she's not here!" Then fury seethed through him. Had Nancy purposely tricked him into coming up here because of some mad whim of hers?

Van Riebeck sensed how Paul was suffering. "Yes, she got tired of being up here and left—you can't blame her."

Paul was ready to tear a lion to pieces with his hands. "She's not here," he muttered then forced himself back to normalcy. "I must pay the wagon driver for the hire of his wagon and get my things out." He ran down the steps and across the garden.

Van Riebeck sipped his coffee, then looked once again into the bedroom.

"I'm awake, darling," Katie murmured. "I thought I heard voices coming from the stoep. Has Paul come?"

"Yes, a few minutes ago. I didn't bring him in because I thought you were sleeping."

"How did he take the news that Nancy had gone?"

Van Riebeck reflected a second then said, "He's either got a marvellous control of himself, or it did not upset him because he behaved quite calmly. Could you see him now?"

"Oh yes. I feel so much better. Do bring him in here."

"Right, I will." He blew the wick out on the oil lamp and opened the shutters to let fresh air into the room. "Whilst he's with you, I'll shower and change, but would you drink some broth now?"

"Yes, darling, Let Joanna bring some in. I must get my strength back."

A few minutes later Paul came in and up to the bed. The sight of her favourite child seemed to restore some health to Katie.

"Darling—Paul. Truly, it's a tonic to see you."

He smiled at her, hiding his shock at the change the malaria had made to her beauty—yet she was still so like Nancy that it hurt him.

"Why go catching malaria, Mother? That's not like my indomitable Mother." He sat near the bed.

"Stupid of me, wasn't it? Darling, aren't you excited about the gold on your land?" She forced enthusiasm to her eyes.

"Yes—yes. It's very exciting, but I don't think you're well enough for long chats yet. By the way, what made Nancy suddenly leave?"

Now was her chance to destroy his love for Nancy and she gathered her frail strength to hurt him. "Oh, you know Nancy, so flirtatious and capricious. Most of the young men in the district were infatuated by her and one day she favoured one and the next day it was someone else." Katie knotted her fingers tightly together as she continued lying and inflicting hurt whilst her searching eyes never left Paul's taut face.

"Of course she never intended to remain up here and when the parents of a young man who was courting her were trekking to the Cape, she decided one day to go with them, then the next day *not* to go. In the end she went. Of course, he was the attraction."

Katie hoped the lie would explain to Paul the contradictary telegrams he had received.

"Yes, she's nothing but an unreliable bundle of trouble." The bitterness of his voice wounded Katie as he went on. "I pity the man who gets her for a wife."

Joanna's entrance with the chicken broth was a welcome break and, glad of an excuse to get away and think about the business, Paul said, "I'll clean up, Mother, whilst Joanna feeds you your broth." He strode toward the door. "Be back later."

Impossible for Katie to know how

deeply her lies had hurt him, but no matter—all thoughts of Nancy, like a cancerous growth must be dragged from his being.

Paul went through the day spending some time at his mother's bedside telling her about each member of the family in the Cape, answering as best he could her thousand questions for, whilst the answers bored him, they brought new life to her.

"How I long to see them all," she said wistfully, "and Terence still has not fallen in love since that horrible little Louise du Toit?"

"No, I think she hurt him deeply when she broke the engagement off, when she thought we were wiped out by the disease of our vines."

"Miserable type of mercenary girl, but the way the ostrich farm has pulled us through—thanks to you—would surprise her. You were still there when John arrived?"

"I saw him for two days."

"Darling, do tell me about him."

He shrugged his wide shoulders. "Not much to tell. Of course he now speaks like an English-born gentleman, not a colonial.

He sounds damned snooty—like his father used to sound. He's not very tall; Kenneth is a head taller, which annoys John. He dresses like a lord." Laughter burst out of Paul. "When we went to see the ostriches one of them grabbed his gold watch and chain from his waistcoat and swallowed them. You should have seen his furious face."

"Oh, Paul, how can you laugh?" But Katie joined in laughing, "And when does he start working for Cecil Rhodes?"

"He must be working for him now, I imagine. Lord, he's puffed up about that, thinks Rhodes is some kind of tin-pot god."

"He's not popular with the Boers. He's already been nosing in to buy land concessions to dig for gold from Lobengula in Matabeleland."

"Ah yes, that reminds me, Mother. What about this business of re-registering my land? Did you manage to do it?"

"Yes." Katie's heart beat faster as she lied. She must face the problem. "Just before the war broke out, I went to see the Field Cornet. The deed is safe in what I call my strongbox where I keep all our birth certificates and all important papers." She forced a laugh. "But could we go into all of that tomorrow? To tell the truth, I think I really should sleep for a while."

"Of course, Mother—I've been thoughtless in keeping you talking." He immediately stood up.

"Oh no you haven't—every moment spent with you is precious to me. I suppose you'll be off soon to look over your land?" She prayed that this would be his plan and not a quick return to the Cape to find Nancy.

"Yes, I intend to take a good look around and prospect the place as thoroughly as I can. Now you get some sleep."

As she watched his tall figure quietly leaving the room she thought, "Oh God, let it be that all is now over between him and Nancy. Let Liz get Nancy on to a ship to England; let Paul meet some girl up here to interest him."

When Paul left Katie, he went to Van Riebeck who was waiting for him to ride over the farm to check up on the out-buildings, the wheatfields and herds of cattle. Van Riebeck had been away for over two months and was anxious to inspect the farm.

Without talking they rode for a while over the vast uninhabited land, their wide-brimmed hats pulled low over their eyes, long guns slung across their backs, for lion and leopard sometimes came up to the edge of the cattle enclosures.

"You've built your stock up well, Father, since the rinderpest wiped them all out."

Paul's eyes appraised the fine looking beasts. He remembered too well the awful scene three years ago when the land was filled with dead and dying cattle.

"Yes, but buying new cattle and helping to finance the war against the English have made a serious hole in my finances as you know. If you weren't running the ostrich farm so advantageously we'd be in a hell of a mess—as you know the Volksraad has no money to pay its members. It's all a labour of love."

"Don't worry, Father. I'm going to make a fortune for all of us in gold."

"You well might. Although I'm against

gold mining, you have to mix with the scum of humanity."

They were several miles from the house and riding with his father was soothing to Paul; something in his big, strong personality minimized Paul's anger, it was helping him to regain some inner calm about Nancy's dirty trick of leaving before he arrived. He supposed, after her first telegram telling him she was coming, she had expected a reply, expressing his joy but he had not sent one fearing that his mother might see it. Now his father's voice broke into his thoughts.

"I would have thought that the life of farming would suit you better than mining, Paul."

"You're probably right." He waved an arm across the wheatfields toward the mountains. "This is my kind of life really."

"Yes, I think once our Republic gets its own outlet to the sea, there will be plenty of money to be made on shipping our produce to the world. I'm anxious to know how the Zulu campaign is faring."

"I heard about it when I was trekking up. Of course, the people I met in the

Orange Free State weren't too pleased about the Transvaal fighting to make Dinizulu sole king. But everyone believed that Joubert would soon mop up the rest of the Zulus and bring them all together under Dinizulu."

"The last despatch I had from Kruger was most hopeful. I'm afraid I should ride into Pretoria tomorrow to give a full verbal report to Kruger about our campaign. Would you stay here with your mother whilst I'm gone?"

"Gladly, Father. When you get back, I'll move off to prospect my land."

"Right, and don't forget you've lots of friends up here who want to see you. After all you've spent some years up here. Why not send invitations over to the Bredas, the Hofmeyers and the du Plessis? I'll tell you what—let's have a victory celebration. Get hold of the Hottentot violinists, have the servants prepare a big supper. It would do your mother good to have music and dancing. Do me good, too, to have some gaiety—what do you say?"

"It's a fine idea, Father." He would enjoy seeing old friends and the good-looking, golden-haired girls who looked so healthy and strong. Amongst the crowd surely there would be one willing to lie in the bushes with him. They always had in the past. "I'll talk it over with Mother, then organise it. But for when?"

"Your mother should be strong enough for a party in ten days' time and I'll be back by then. Oh, and whilst I'm away, would you have Obsete and his boys take care of the tin roofs on the sheds. They've got neglected during the two months I was away."

"Right—I'll look into everything on the farm, Father, don't worry."

How good it was to have his eldest son with him, Van Riebeck thought, but hell that this young man, a replica of himself, should bear the name of "Kildare" instead of his rightful name of Van Riebeck. Damnable how some old sins, committed in youthful folly, lived on to punish a man for his lifetime.

15

"**A** VICTORY party, what a splendid idea!"

Katie congratulated Van Riebeck when he came back and told her about it. "It will hold Paul here for one thing and another thing he might become interested in some girl who'll take his mind off Nancy."

"Of course he will. He's a young bull," Van Riebeck said teasingly. "So you see, you're not the only one who had ideas about helping him over his troubles. But why didn't you tell me at the time that you were going to send him the telegram about gold on his land?"

"Darling, I know how you despise anything to do with mining, also you were getting ready to go to Zululand, so I didn't want to bother you with family affairs."

"Well, I hope Paul *doesn't* find gold on his land. I've a feeling that gold could bring trouble to the South African Republic."

"But if you sold digging concessions for big amounts, it would solve the Republic's financial troubles by putting cash into the almost empty exchequer."

"It's true, but if we start permitting mining, we'll have the scum of the world flocking here. Already we're threatened with trouble from Rhodes trying to coerce Lobengula for concessions which will mean God knows how many Englishmen will come up here. I'll learn the latest news when I reach Pretoria. But, darling, I want to tell you what I've been thinking—you'll like it in one way and in another way you won't."

"Don't be so mysterious. What is it?"

"You've got to go to the Cape for a while. You've been through too much up here. Doctor Mayer thinks it's affected your health."

"No—no," Katie murmured whilst her soul sang a Te Deum at the very thought of Abend Bloem—Capetown—the sea. "I won't leave you. My health will be all right soon."

"You *say* that, but I've made up my mind you must go—just for a few months."

"But I won't leave you! Not another separation—we've had too many!"

"Now don't let's make any real decisions at the moment, when I get back from Pretoria we'll make our plans."

Later Doctor Mayer arrived and after he had examined Katie, he privately told Van Riebeck that, though she was almost over the malaria, he could not say she was in good health. Hearing Van Riebeck's idea to send her to the Cape, he heartily endorsed it and Van Riebeck, though upset about the idea, made his decision to soon arrange it.

Just after dawn the next day Van Riebeck rode off and later Paul came to sit beside Katie's bed where he started writing notes bidding their friends to the party. Katie was so happy to have him there and to believe that he and Nancy had been saved from each other, that she felt her health returning.

During the next few days she busied herself making out menus with Joanna who immediately started the kitchen maids in peeling and stewing fruits for tarts, jellies and sweetmeats and conserved fruits which could be prepared ahead of time.

"We've invited about one hundred friends, Joanna," Katie said, "so many animals and fowl must be slaughtered. Of course the guests will make their own breakfasts beside their wagons, but we will give a big supper and a dance the first night, a mid-day meal the second day, then another supper and dance, and on the third morning the wagons will trek homewards."

"*Ja, ja,* Missus, we have already started. We will be ready in time." Joanna laughed, she was not at all worried by the tremendous work ahead of her, for not only must she cook for guests, but for all of their servants, but like all Kaffirs she loved the excitement of a party when they met their own old friends who served the white guests.

Paul enjoyed the activity, it took his mind off Nancy, and he worked with the Kaffir boys in building long wooden trestles to act as supper-tables and many more for benches. Also they constructed a small raised platform where the Hottentot musicians would be seated. Then Paul attended to the hanging of the candle lanterns on trees in the cultivated gardens.

They would be lit just before the party began.

The sixty odd wagons of their guests would be outspanned a small distance from the house, for it was, of course, impossible to accommodate them in the house.

Paul next worked with the farm hands in smoothing out a big area for dancing. Stones were removed, bumps flattened, holes filled up, then with big brooms made of thorn bush they swept the space and stamped it as flat as possible.

Van Riebeck, held up in Pretoria upon political affairs with Kruger, was shocked one morning when news arrived that Grobles, the South African Republic's special adviser to Lobengula, who was to live in Matabeleland, had been murdered just as he crossed the border.

"It's that damned scoundrel Rhodes who arranged it," Kruger told Van Riebeck, "I swear it is. He has spies all over the place. He must have heard that Grobles was going to settle in Matabeleland with Lobengula, so decided to stop our plans. He's determined to get the Chief to sign the land concessions to him to dig for gold." Kruger spat out into a nearby spittoon. "And of course the English missionaries are all working on Rhodes' behalf."

"Damn Rhodes with his greed for power, he's worse than any of the English we've had here."

Van Riebeck had previously decided to leave unsaid that one of his stepsons was working on Rhodes' staff, but now he decided to divulge it; one day the connection might prove useful.

After he had told Kruger, the President combed his fingers through his long grey beard and smiled slowly as his heavily lidded brown eyes peered into Van Riebeck's blue eyes.

"Ach, Van Riebeck, so you think that we might have a spy in Rhodes' camp. That would be useful."

"It might help us if we knew ahead of time what he was planning, just as he gets to know our plans and so had Grobles murdered—the bastard!"

"*Ja, ja*, he is a bastard—but how can you get your stepson to act as spy? A young honourable Englishman—he will not do it."

"No, I'm sure he wouldn't, but I might

write to Van der Byl, my brother-in-law, who runs my place in Stellenbosch, to see what he can pump from the young man. He might get news 'out' of him without John realizing he's disclosing anything."

Kruger nodded. "The plan is good, it could be helpful if it worked."

"Well, I'll try it. Have you another man in mind to replace Grobles?"

"Not yet—not yet. I have only just got the bad news but we must choose another man to go to Lobengula as soon as we've finished off the Zulu campaign and the Volksraad meets. We have many problems to discuss."

"This growing talk of gold being found on the Witwatersrand disturbs me." Van Riebeck thought of his conversation with Katje and said, "But if we sell our concessions for digging for a big fee that would help put money into our exchequer."

"Of course but better still, when Joubert finishes off the Zulus who defy Dinizulu and we get Saint Lucia Bay to use as our port to send our produce all over the world, that will put clean money into our exchequer. Now I know you are

194

anxious to be off—your wife was struck by malaria I heard."

"She's better now and we're having a Victory celebration on the farm; I must be back for that. I wish you and Mrs. Kruger could come but I realize you cannot leave government affairs."

"But next time you and your wife come to Pretoria, we'll celebrate here when we have got Saint Lucia Bay."

The men shook hands and Van Riebeck left the stoep of Kruger's house where the President, in his dark suit and black top hat, liked to sit smoking and drinking coffee whilst conducting his governmental affairs, and the Boers liked Kruger's informal type of ruling their affairs.

Van Riebeck returned home a day before the guests were expected and was delighted to find Katie up and waiting for him on the stoep.

She went into his outstretched arms. When they had kissed he held her out to examine her.

"Thank God you look almost like your real self." But he saw the dark circles beneath her eyes.

"I'm splendid." She lied lightly for she

still felt weak and tired too easily. "And look, we have everything ready." She waved toward the lanterns in the trees, the dance space, the wooden benches and long trestles for tables. "Almost everyone we asked is coming. We'll have fun."

"Good, good, and where is Paul?"

"Gone into Lydenburg to buy lots more wine and brandy and he's taken Franz and Adrian with him. But, darling, come and sit down, you look tired and dusty." She gently pushed him on to a reclining chair. "Brandy and coffee?"

He nodded, running his fingers through his thick golden hair to loosen it from his moist scalp. God, he thought, he was going to miss her when she left for the Cape. His eyes watched her figure going into the house. Lovely, despite having borne ten children, her waist was slim as a girl's and her body had never thickened.

Late in the hot afternoon, in a clearing in the bush beyond the cultivated gardens, fifty-four wagons, each with a team of sixteen oxen, had gathered and were outspanning. About a hundred whites, with adults and children, had poured from the wagons with fifty or sixty black servants. There was much activity as the Van Riebeck servants helped the wagons settle into comfortable positions. The air rang with jovial shouts as neighbours from far off farms caught sight of each other.

In her bedroom, Katie was dressing for the dance when she and Van Riebeck would welcome their guests. She wore a six-year-old lavender satin gown with a deep Alençon lace collar falling over her bare shoulders. She smiled to herself as she smoothed the bodice around her waist. It still fitted beautifully.

She peered into her dressing-table mirror, rubbed a rice paper over her face, darkened her eyes with Malay kohl, and lightly reddened her lips with cochineal. Not too much artifice, she warned herself, for Van Riebeck hated it. Then she piled her red-gold hair atop her head in a bunch of ringlets.

"Not bad," she thought, "for a forty-five year old who's just been laid low by malaria." Then she went on to the stoep where Van Riebeck and Paul, both dressed in tight grey buttoned-up jackets and tight trousers, stood waiting for her.

The three of them went down to the garden lit by candles in lanterns and there they welcomed their guests. The Dutch women were transformed from the big women in voluminous cotton dresses and wide-frilled sun bonnets, who cooked at the fires near the wagons at the battle with the Mapoochi. Now they were decked out in old finery of brightly coloured satins and silks and their abundantly thick golden hair was plaited and twisted becomingly around their heads.

The men were scrubbed so that their sun-tanned faces shone. They looked uncomfortable in jackets too small for them and trousers too short. Most of the suits had come with them from the Cape thirty years ago when they had first trekked—but no matter, Katie thought, these men were valorous conquerors.

There was loud laughing and compliments and much kissing between the women, hearty handshaking and back-slapping between the men. Then the Hottentot violinists let loose a bedlam of screeching sounds on their violins and with roars of laughter, the people started to choose partners and to move into the dance space.

Paul swiftly assessed the crowd and, seeing a couple of young men approaching Herta Vostler, he stepped up to her and slipping his arm about her waist, he almost lifted her on to the dancing space.

"What a lovely young lady you've grown into, Herta."

Paul smiled down at the pale-faced girl —who had never failed to wear her goatskin mask in the sunlight to preserve her skin. Now she looked up at Paul with round blue eyes, wide with delight at his compliments and because he had chosen to dance with her as she had determined he would when she had deliberately stood near him. When he had lived up here for a few years, her three older sisters had all been secretly in love with him, but he had only lightly flirted with them.

"How are your sisters?" Paul asked as he twirled Herta around in the fashion of the dance.

"All married now." She was glad to say, knowing they could not compete with her for Paul's attention. "Are you married yet?"

"No, Herta, who would have me?" He grinned down at her remembering how hot her sisters had been and how they had tried to marry him.

"That's stupid talk, Paul. You know very well that most girls would marry you and perhaps they'd be making a mistake. Just because you are so big and handsome, doesn't mean you're a good man—or clever, or that you'd be a good husband."

"Well, well, Herta, you don't think like a Dutch girl, do you?"

"Yes, I do, but I want a man like your father, or President Kruger—a man who is educated and clever."

"Well, I went to University in Amsterdam to study law. Would that make you call me educated?" He wondered if she were still a virgin and held her away at arms' length to glance down at her breasts, tight and urgent looking, stretching her blue satin bodice. She would be good to lie with. But would she consent?

"Yes, I remember when you went to Holland. I was a child then. Why did you come back now to the Transvaal?"

"I was ceded land on the Witwatersrand

instead of money when I fought for the Afrikaner Korps. Now they say there's gold on it." He glanced around examining the other girls to see if he had chosen the prettiest, and decided he had done well. In a little while he would suggest that she might be too hot dancing and might like to go for a walk in the cool air of the bushes. She seemed very encouraging the way she pressed her body up against his.

He saw his mother dancing with Piet Cradock and he laughed inwardly knowing how bored she must be.

"Piet, I'm so sorry I feel the heat so much—I must sit down—forgive me," Kate was saying.

"*Achja*, it's too much exercise for you after the malaria. I'm sorry, Katje," and he led her to the benches to sit down.

"Don't stay with me, Piet. Find someone else to dance with."

"All right, Katje, perhaps Cecile is not too heavy with child." He laughed and went over to his wife.

Katie's eyes searched among the couples for Paul. Eager to know who he was dancing with she could not find him. Strange, it was absurd to imagine for a moment that Paul was the type of person to be moping alone in the house. She got up and went towards the house.

Paul and Herta had already slipped away from the dance and were walking hand in hand in the shadowy bush just beyond the fires where they could still hear the squeaky violins. He was surprised that the suggestion had not come from him but from her.

She had said, "It's so hot—let's go and sit somewhere cool and talk." So they had slipped away.

"You're not afraid of lions out here?" he teased.

"Silly, remember I was born up here. Not many things frighten me."

"I know you were born here. How old are you now?"

"Seventeen and old enough for anything." She said with significant emphasis. She was so excited at being with him alone out here that she wanted to let him know the truth; it always seemed the easiest way out of all difficulties. "All the times when I was a child and my sisters made eyes at you, Paul, I used to think if only Paul would wait a little while for me and I watched my body growing into a woman's and I knew that if you waited for me I would please you more than my sisters. I have waited for you to come back to Lydenburg."

Well used though he was to swift success with women since he had been no more than a tall boy, Herta's boldness surprised him. Was it just naïveté—or was she really offering herself to him?

"I always liked you, too, Herta. Even when you were a child I could see you'd grow into a lovely young woman."

She stopped walking and stood before him, looking up at him. "Well, Paul, in the Lord's name kiss me! I never thought you'd waste so much time in talking."

She grasped his forearms in strong hands and stepped up to press her body against his body, raising her face to his she murmured.

"I've dreamed of this happening one day."

Swiftly excited by her, he caught her in iron-like arms and kissed her passionately. His hand went to her breast and as he fondled it she unhooked the front of her bodice so that he could hold her bare breasts which she knew were so beautiful.

She was on fire to lie with him. It was a climax of several years of longing for him and she was hot like all the women of her race. Seeing him tonight she swore to herself that she would have him. He laid her down on the earth and in the moonlight he saw her lift her wide satin skirt and pull down her long calico drawers. She half moaned.

"Oh, I'm longing for you, Paul! Hurry —hurry!"

He slid on top of her murmuring "But I dont want to take your virginity."

"Don't be mad, I'm not a virgin."

After a few minutes they lay side by side, panting and she said, "Lovely, heaven couldn't be so wonderful. You are just as I imagined you would be. Oh, let's lie together every night whilst you're up here."

He would certainly like to have her to lie with for quite a while and he said. "But your family leaves day after tomorrow to go home."

"Don't worry, I won't go with them. I'll get around your mother somehow so she'll invite me to stay on. No one is going to stop me making love with you—it's our right."

Her determination and self-assurance were a bit irritating, but what did it matter to him? If she wanted him that badly, it suited him and if she could arrange it for the few days he would be staying up here, so good.

"I think we'd better get up, Herta. There are fleas around here and you'll get bitten on your bottom."

"I don't care. I'm not afraid of fleas or snakes either if they come along."

She was so utterly different from girls he had known that she started to interest him.

"You're a funny girl. Tell me, who were those other men you used to lie with? Where did you meet them?"

"Not men. Only one of my brothers but he got married last month and my five other brothers are too young to lie with and I miss it terribly."

He had never met with such honesty. He was amazed. He sat up remembering how he and Nancy had suffered such agonies of remorse because of their sin of incest and Herta spoke so lightly of it.

"But don't you think it's wrong to lie with your brother?" he asked.

"Wrong? Wrong? You tell me what we were supposed to do? We live such lonely lives on our farm; sometimes we don't meet outsiders for a year. We didn't hurt anyone by taking pleasure from each other's bodies. It happens in lots of families on lonely farms."

Her frankness and freedom from shame appealed to him; she excited him and in addition he liked her, but he felt that they had been missing from the dance for long enough.

"I think we should go back, Herta, to the dancing."

"All right, but let's do it just once more. You like it, too, don't you?" Her greedy hand caught hold of him and started to caress him and he gladly turned back to make love to her again.

16

EVEN though she sat talking to a group of pregnant and old women, Katie was aware when Paul slipped back amongst the dancers and her eyes flew to see who was the girl with him. She recognised Herta as one of the Vostler family. Herta was surely not more than a beautiful child. Could a kiss and light embrace from her help Paul forget Nancy?

Later Paul danced with other girls and young married women but mainly he danced with Herta, then when the festivities ended and the guests started for their wagons, he walked her back to her wagon.

"Would you like to ride around the farm with me in the morning?" he invited her.

"Yes, of course." Then she whispered, "Come early so we can do it before the mid-day meal."

He laughed at her frankness. "It's three o'clock now. I'll come about ten."

With the first light, servants started quietly to clean up the debris of the previous night, then they spread clean white cloths on the trestle tables in readiness for the mid-day meal.

Inside the house in their bedroom Katie stirred in Van Riebeck's arms and he murmured, "Are you awake so early, darling? Are you feeling all right, or was last night too much for you?"

"Oh no, it's just that I didn't feel strong enough for dancing."

"Well it's the Cape for you, my love, and very soon too."

"Please—no talk of a separation—it upsets me. Last night was a success, wasn't it?"

"It certainly was and you organized everything beautifully."

"Oh, I couldn't have managed without Paul. By the way, did you notice all the attention he paid young Herta Vostler?"

"I did and it pleased me. She's a beautiful girl—a perfect specimen of a Boer female and the Vostlers are a fine family. It would be a good thing for Paul if he married her and settled down."

"Oh no, darling! The girls up here may be good-looking and fine characters but Paul needs a more educated wife."

"My darling Katje, why? A girl like Herta will run his home perfectly, bear him healthy children. You know how I have wanted him up here. He would be an asset to the South African Republic. We need young men like him and he loves the rough life up here. I think he prefers it to the Cape."

"I don't agree with you. He has told me that most of all he loved studying law at the University in Holland."

"Yes, it's one of my regrets that I took him away before he got his law degree, but I thought he could study in Pretoria—it turned out that he didn't want to. But that's past. I think it would be wise to encourage his interest in Herta. Even if he doesn't stay up here, Herta would make a good wife for him in the Cape." Van Riebeck waited a second then added with a quiet decisiveness. "Such a marriage would certainly squash Nancy's interest in him."

"Yes, yes, that's true." Katie clung to the thought that anything was preferable to that terrible affair. "But Herta leaves tomorrow with her family. Should I invite her to stay on for some days?"

"A good idea; I would."

Paul rode up, with a spare horse, at the Vostler wagon at ten o'clock. He dismounted and immediately Herta came out and he lifted her off the wagon. She looked very pretty and fresh in a white calico dress patterned with sprigs of yellow flowers, a wide-frilled yellow sun bonnet covered her mass of golden hair. Her demure air amused Paul who now knew what a hot little animal she was.

"Hello, Herta, you look even prettier by daylight."

She smiled her thanks and at that moment Vrou Vostler came out to stand on the wagon board with a light shawl half covering the baby suckling at her breast.

"Good morning, Mrs. Vostler," Paul pulled his wide-brimmed hat off.

"It's good to see you, Paul," she answered, enjoying the sight of this splendid young specimen of manhood. Then her eyes moved approvingly over the long gun slung across his back. "That's wise, Paul, to take a gun; hungry lions often come close to our herds. See you at the mid-day meal."

He smiled and nodded, then lifted Herta

on to a horse and slung a leg over his own animal. They moved slowly out of the vicinity of the wagons toward the wide vista of wheatfields.

For a while they rode in silence, then she burst out laughing and said, "Mother hopes you mean to marry me. I hate that about our women; the moment a man looks at one of their daughters they start to plan the wedding feast. Is it like that in the Cape?"

Once more her total frankness astonished and pleased him. He said, "No, in the Cape everything is done quite subtly. You've never been there, Herta?"

"No, but I'm longing to go. I met your sister Nancy when she was here. Her clothes were beautiful and also her grand manners, but I didn't like her much, she seemed very affected to me, not friendly like your mother. I think Nancy will make a man a bad wife. She used to flirt and lead a man on one day, then the next day she wouldn't come out of her room to even say good evening to him. I think she is unfair to men."

Infuriated that she dared to criticize Nancy, Paul then calmed down, for much

211

that Herta had said was true. He was thinking of Nancy's telegram bringing him up here and her then not waiting for his arrival.

"I think Nancy's beauty has made her too sure of herself. Are all the Cape beauties like that?"

Paul burst out laughing. "I don't *know* all of them but I can only say that girls you meet at Government House and at high society homes are not as frank and honest as you are and, believe me, that is meant as a compliment. I don't like deceitful, primping young misses."

She laughed with delight, showing all of her pretty, white pointed teeth. "I'm glad you said that. And are they much prettier than I am?"

"No, they're not! They look at all the fashion magazines that arrive from London each week and try to copy London and Paris clothes. They also powder and paint a bit too much."

"I would never do that."

"You might if you lived down there."

"I wish you would fall in love with me and marry me because I've loved you for almost all my life. I'd take great care of you as a wife."

He was so astonished that he reined his horse in to stare at her and at first he had no reply. As she also reined in and stared at him he said, "Herta, I like you very much, but I still feel you're a child."

"After last night? That's silly talk. Come, there's not another human being within miles. Let's lie under that Tambouti tree and make love. For me that's one of the finest pleasures in life."

Paul felt he was making a mistake in being with her when he had no intention whatever of ever marrying her and she seemed so set upon it. Still he turned the horses towards a tree, tied them and spread out a blanket he had packed in his saddlebag; then they lay on it. It amused him that today Herta had come prepared for love-making and wore no long drawers. The sight of her with her dress bunched up to her waist to show lovely bare white legs spread out wide for his admiration was very exciting to him.

"Are my legs pretty? Do you like my body, Paul?"

"Of course—you're lovely." Her extraordinary honesty was having a strange effect upon him; her mixture of childishness and womanliness was very appealing.

They made love as they had on the previous night and afterward she wriggled out of her dress and lay naked on the blanket with her golden hair spread around her. She watched his face to see if the sight of her like that pleased him.

"My God, you're lovely, Herta—like a Grecian statue." He knelt beside her planting kisses all over her as she almost purred with joy.

"That's what God made women for to delight the man they love. Kiss—kiss—oh, keep kissing me." She held his head to her breast.

For two hours they stayed making violent love. He had never known a female with Herta's physical health.

Now as he lay resting beside her he said, "When did you and your brother start making love?"

"When I was thirteen and he was nineteen. He said I was better to lie with than any woman he had ever had. Do I please you that much too?"

"You please me a hell of a lot, Herta. I wonder if your brother misses you?"

"Oh no, his wife will please him now. And you, Paul—you please me much more than he did—because I love you."

"You didn't love your brother—that way?"

"No, no, at first I did it just because he explained how badly he needed a woman and I was sorry for him like a bull who needs a cow. Then afterwards I grew to like it so much I did it to please myself, but it's all more wonderful with you because I love you."

"And your parents never found out?"

"No, but if they did, what could they say? The Old Testament is full of fathers and daughters lying together. I would rather lie with my brother than an old man like my father."

"You really have no mental or spiritual feeling about the whole thing." He laughed, still astonished by her frank attitude.

"But what's mental or spiritual about men and women coupling any more than there is in four-legged beasts coupling? It's as natural as being hot or cold, hungry or thirsty."

"So that means you wouldn't be faithful if you married?"

"Ach, but I would be faithful. With my husband only I would make love, but it is still a bodily thing, is it not?"

"I suppose you're right. Come, my funny little philosopher, we must go back for the mid-day meal. Tonight we'll go to the bushes again if you want to."

"Oh yes! Tonight, but it seems a long way off."

Later as he lifted her on to the horse's back, with her long hair rolled neatly up into a bun, she looked at him with great appealing eyes.

"Paul, do you love me a little?"

He did not laugh or quickly tell her not to be absurd, instead to his own surprise he murmured, "I'm damned if I know. It's all a bit of a shock to me. Certainly you are quite different from any woman I've ever known, but I tell you one thing, Herta, I don't want the usual Boer wife with twenty children and a baby always at her breast! I don't want a woman who gets so fat she can barely walk by the time she's thirty."

"I would only have the number of children you want and I would never eat so much that my figure changed."

"For God's sake, Herta! I didn't say I was going to marry you!"

"But why not?"

"Because I don't want to marry anyone! Come on, this thing has got out of hand."

He furiously galloped off, but being a fine horsewoman she caught up with him and when they reached the house, he carefully avoided her and spent the day shooting with a party of men.

In the evening when the music began for the dance and couples started waltzing she came up to him in her blue satin gown and said, "I made you angry today. I'm sorry. You don't *have* to marry me. I will be sorry, but I won't break my heart."

Her nearness was unsettling and this in itself made him furious with himself. A little Boer girl in the Lydenburg district was not going to upset him. He, who could marry any of the Cape beauties he might snap his fingers at.

"Let's forget the marriage talk, Herta. I

217

like you very much but I'm leaving soon to prospect for gold in the Witwatersrand."

"I know, your mother told me about it this afternoon. She also invited me to stay for a few days."

There was absolutely no sound of triumph in her voice nor any look of it on her lovely face.

He stared at her, then asked with surprise, "How did you manage to make her invite you?"

"I didn't do anything—she just said, 'Herta, why don't you stay on for a few days and keep Paul company before he leaves for the Witwatersrand?' I was surprised and told her I was sorry but I could not stay on."

Suddenly her refusal infuriated him and he snapped, "Well you can go and tell her that you've changed your mind and you'd like to stay."

A wide smile chased the seriousness from her face and she murmured, "So— you want me?"

"To stay? Yes, why not? We have fun in the bushes, don't we?"

She nodded and gave him a little wink.

"I think you like me more than you want to admit to yourself, Paul."

"Oh let's stop talking and dance."

Not long afterwards they lay in the bushes at a spot where he had earlier hidden a blanket. He did not want fleas and ants to bite her. He tried to shake off the strange hold she had on him and he could not understand it himself. Even out shooting with the men, her face and voice had pestered him. Absurd! Damned ridiculous! He could not be falling in love with her. But he also knew that, since last lying with Nancy, Herta was the first female who had driven the longing for Nancy from his mind.

Love-making with the seventeen-year-old girl was all satisfying, exciting, wonderful.

As they lay side by side, catching their breath, he said, "You're very quiet tonight, Herta?"

"I was thinking I would like to go to the Witwatersrand with you."

"But damn it, I haven't invited you!"

"I know, but two years ago a Malay fortune teller visiting Lydenburg told me I would marry a man I loved since a child and I'd dig for gold with him. I remembered that when your mother told me you were going to prospect on your land."

He began to feel uncomfortable as if Fate were playing games with him.

"Thousands of men will soon be digging for gold, so why think the Malay woman meant me?" he muttered.

"Because you're the man I'm in love with."

"Aren't you ashamed to admit all this to me?"

"Ach, Paul, why should I be ashamed of the truth?"

"But when I say I don't *want* to be married, surely you feel ashamed?"

"Not at all, you are the one to be ashamed not me," she burst out. "I would make you a fine wife. I can cook, sew and shoot straight. Also I play the piano and speak German which the one-legged German taught me and I'm pretty and you like to lie with me." Words were pouring from her and he listened almost fascinated. "I am willing to live in the Cape with you, the Transvaal or the gold mines or anywhere in the world. What more do you want in a wife, Paul?"

He felt almost hypnotised for he was beginning to feel that what she said made sense.

He did not want to marry any of the affected Cape beauties. In fact he had never felt like marriage at all before Herta suggested it. Marriage to Herta would cure him for ever of all thoughts of Nancy, except as a sister.

"Well, Paul, what do you think about our marrying?"

He chuckled. "Haven't you ever heard that it's the man who's supposed to propose—not the girl?"

"That's silly. You might go off and not ask me, so I'm asking you to marry me, Paul." Suddenly her practical voice broke on an unexpected sob and that went straight to his heart.

He murmured, "Darling, funny little Herta. It's madness—I'm sure, but will you marry me?" The words had suddenly burst from him.

"Paul—Paul—oh, Paul," and she collapsed sobbing in his arms.

Hours later when the festivities ended, Paul went to find his parents in their bedroom. He knocked and his father called, "Come in."

As he entered Paul blurted out, "I came to tell you that I've asked Herta to marry me."

Katie swung around on her chair and stared at him. She did not know if she was going to laugh or cry, but Van Riebeck slapped him on the shoulder with one hand whilst pumping his other hand.

"I'm delighted, Paul, you've chosen well. Herta will make a fine wife."

"I'm sure she will." Katie forced herself to say, although she liked the girl after having spent some time with her during the day.

"I don't know what's happened to me," Paul laughed as he sat on the foot of the bed. "It's Malay magic or something, but I would have bet my land with gold on it, that I'd never fall in love so quickly." He shrugged, "but I have within two days and I feel like a . . . I don't know what to say —a dog with two tails—I suppose."

Paul and Nancy were saved. Thank God, Katie silently prayed with half her mind as she got up to go to kiss Paul's cheek.

"Oh darling—I'm so happy. Have you asked her parents yet?"

"No, I came to tell you two first."

"They can't be in bed yet. Hurry to their wagon and ask for her hand, then bring the three of them over to the house for a brandy to celebrate with us."

"Thank you, Father."

Paul stood up, deeply satisfied by his parents' reaction to his news.

He had started for the door when Katie called, "Wait—wait a second!" She went swiftly to her little leather jewel case on her dressing table and plucked out a ring with a small ruby. She held it out to Paul. "An engagement ring, darling. It belonged to your great-grandmother. I hope Herta will like it."

"Mother, you're wonderful!" His blue eyes bathed her in love.

"Go! Go quickly and bring them."

As the door closed on Paul, Katie went into Van Riebeck's arms and he held her tightly as she asked in an agonised voice, "Is it right. Is it right? It's all so sudden. How can he know if he really loves her? Or she him? She's only just turned seventeen."

"Katje! Katje! You of *all* people to ask such questions when you and I fell in love the first hour we met. And don't forget *you* were only seventeen like Herta."

"Yes, yes," she tried to convince herself. "You're right," but she did not consider the comparison was comparable. She had been a famous beauty, well born, well educated. "But the Vostlers themselves—they're rather rough people, aren't they?"

He was annoyed by such a reference to his old friends. "His ancestors in Holland were well known lawyers. Two hundred years ago a younger son settled in the Cape and started the South African Vostler branch. Her family were quite famous Amsterdam medical men—fine Dutch stock. Of course with eighteen children and very little money they haven't been able to give Herta a fine education such as Nancy and Mary have had."

"I'm not worried about that," she lied, for it rather riled her that her wonderful Paul should marry such an uneducated girl and she would have to arrange something so that Herta would receive the right

224

additional polish. "Come on, we must light the lamps in the living-room, they'll be arriving soon."

17

EARLY the next morning before the wagons pulled out, Van Riebeck announced Paul and Herta's engagement which caused great jubilation for the Boers always rejoiced at a betrothal amongst their people. It meant another family would be formed and later the birth of many children. It was a worry to all of them that their Boer population was so small.

All the women and girls gathered around Herta who proudly showed her engagement ring, and many cast envious eyes, not because of the ring, but because Herta had caught Paul. Not only was he big and handsome but his reputation as an elephant hunter and a fine fighter was well known.

When the last wagon pulled out and the occupants had been waved on their way by the Van Riebecks, they turned into the house, for the Vostlers had stayed on to discuss the wedding arrangemnts.

Seated in the living-room Paul swiftly told them, "Herta and I want to be married next week, very quietly, because she's coming with me to the Witwatersrand and I want to start without delay."

"Paul!" Mrs. Vostler declared. "And no wedding celebration!" Her moist full face twisted with disappointment.

"Mother—what's another wedding celebration to you?" Herta demanded in her forthright way. "You've given three for my sisters' marriages and you've four more girls coming up after me—you'll be able to give parties for all of them." She turned her big blue eyes on to her father. "Please, Father, we would like to marry quietly in Pretoria—with just you and Mother and Paul's parents. Paul is going to buy a wagon and oxen and we'll trek to the Witwatersrand after the wedding. Please say you think it's a good idea."

Of his eighteen children, Herta was Vostler's favourite. He admired her forceful character and she had always had her way with him.

Now he nodded, then looked toward Katie and Van Riebeck saying, "I think their plan is good. Do you agree?"

Katie's stomach felt awash. Paul's marriage to be so lightly decided upon. She forced herself to smile and nod as Van Riebeck said, "It's the best idea. It's splendid. It pleases me very much that Paul will go to the 'gold' country with his lovely wife. It is not good for a man to be alone in mining towns."

"Good! Then it's settled." Paul laughed with relief and catching hold of Herta's hand said, "When do you want us to leave for Pretoria?"

"Next week, if that pleases you. I must go home with Mother and Father to get my 'kist'." She smiled delightedly as if she had spoken of her dolls.

"Ach, Paul, for years she has been embroidering such lovely sheets and pillow slips for her 'kist'." Mrs. Vostler spoke proudly. "None of my other girls made such beautiful linen as Herta has, you will be surprised and I must give her a well-fitted hussapotheck with all the right herbs and medicines, in it. She is a very well trained girl, Paul—cooks and sews better than I can and she knows much about caring for sickness."

"*Ja, ja,*" Vostler was enthusiastic. "And

my wedding present will be half your span of oxen. Eight of my finest beasts." Frikkie Vostler looked at Van Riebeck. "I shall send them over so you can match eight of yours to them. Paul must have a fine matching span. A Boer is often judged by his fine oxen. He can also have some of our Kaffirs—a reliable driver and two lead boys."

As they went on making plans Katie thought such a man as Paul could have married an English or French titled heiress, and now they could have been discussing castles and thousands of English acres, but such was Fate, they must discuss oxen.

"Have you decided to remain up here? Or will you return to the Cape and the ostrich farm?" she asked Paul.

He frowned, not having yet answered that question to himself. "I'm not sure, Mother, but I don't want to leave the ostrich farm until Ken or Stephan are ready to take over. Uncle Chris is too busy in the House of Representatives to shoulder the job all the time."

Inwardly Katie rejoiced. Even if his land yielded much gold she did not want Paul to become a permanency in the Transvaal. It was enough that she and Van Riebeck were stuck up here and of course Van Riebeck would insist that his young sons Franz and Adrian would become true South African Republicans. At that moment Hendrik came in and handed a bundle of letters, newspapers and a telegram to Van Riebeck.

"Baas, I just get back with these from Lydenburg."

"Thank you, Hendrik." Van Riebeck smiled at the Vostlers' surprised expressions. "Oh, Katje sends for all of this from the Cape—newspapers and magazines. Ah, Katje, here's a telegram for you."

She took the orange-coloured envelope from him. "Excuse me," she asked the Vostlers who nodded and went on talking to Paul and Herta, whilst Katie slit the envelope open, unfolded the message and read.

"Nancy and entourage safely arrived but absolutely refuses to sail for England all love Liz."

Of course! Nancy refused to go because she thought Paul would return at once to the Cape. She handed the telegram to Van Riebeck, then told the others.

"It's to say that my daughter arrived safely at the Cape."

"Ach, good. It is welcome news to hear that a traveller has arrived safely," said Mrs. Vostler.

Katie was wondering how Paul felt upon hearing about Nancy, but he was entirely absorbed with Herta who was saying how she longed to see the Cape and Table Mountain. Suddenly a thought flashed to Katie of how she could help Nancy to decide to leave for England. She turned to Van Riebeck.

"Darling, later we must send into Lydenburg to telegraph the good news of Paul's betrothal to the family. Now if you'll excuse me a moment I must see Joanna—our cook—and tell her that her daughter has arrived at the Cape. She's Nancy's maid."

At the mid-day meal, the plans for the wedding continued. It was decided they would all meet at the Blesbok Inn in Pretoria in a week's time, then there would be a quiet civil marriage. Mrs. Vostler was all for a Predikant to perform the marriage but Herta, having been primed by Paul, who knew his mother would later want a Catholic marriage, ruled her mother out and Mr. Vostler agreed with his daughter.

When the Vostlers had left and Katie had gone to the bedroom Van Riebeck and Paul left for Lydenburg to look for a wagon. In Boer fashion, Van Riebeck felt that for him to give Paul a fine wagon as a wedding present was almost as good as giving him a house, for a wagon was a Boer's second home.

In Lydenburg news had just been telegraphed from Pretoria that the Boers and Dinizulu had won the war over the spurious rulers and Dinizulu was now the sole King of Zululand.

In the main street people had gone half-mad with joy, shouting and laughing, men slapping each other on the back, pumping each other's hands. Women were hugging each other and over all the hilarity were the magic cheers.

"We have a port!" "A way to the sea!" "At last our own port!"

Overjoyed Van Riebeck and Paul were

shaking hands with friends and strangers all the way to the end of the street and to the market that sold wagons and carts.

They were lucky in finding several wagons to choose from, for Lydenburg boasted the best wagon builders in the Republic and people came from all over to buy there. Van Riebeck settled on a robust twenty-foot wagon with high wheels. The big bed ran across the width of the wagon behind the driver's box, the canvas hood fitted perfectly over the strong rounded roof slats.

"We'll buy this one," Van Riebeck told the wagon merchant who nodded. "*Ja*, Commandant—you've chosen well. It's the best we have."

"It's a splendid wagon, Father," Paul pulled him aside, "but very expensive—that second-hand wagon would do nicely."

"No, we'll start you off with the best and strongest," Van Riebeck chuckled, warmed by his love for Paul and the triumphant news that Saint Lucia Bay was now a Boer possession.

Turning back to the merchant he pulled a wad of English banknotes from his pocket.

He counted out the price saying, "We'll send our Kaffirs with a span of oxen in for it tomorrow morning."

"Oh, Father—I'll come with the oxen myself." Paul was delighted to own such a sturdily built new wagon. When they left the merchant he said, "Father! What a wonderful wedding present! But I don't believe you can afford it. I know how low your finances are."

"To hell with that. You're marrying a fine Boer girl and we've got a port of our own at last, man—oh man—that's going to put money in every Republican farmer's pocket."

The following day Van Riebeck was working at his desk in the living-room, when a rider arrived with a letter from Kruger which Van Riebeck eagerly tore open and read.

"Dear Van Riebeck,

You will have heard that thanks to the Lord, we have been victorious in Zululand. Representatives of the Volksraad must be present when Dinizulu with a bodyguard of 10,000 warriors is crowned king.

For this mission I am not choosing you, for a Volksraad member is required to go to the Cape to register with Queen Victoria's High Commissioner, the deed from Dinizulu granting our Republic sole rights to Saint Lucia Bay.

I consider you to be the best man to go. You were born in the Colony, have a home and fine connections there and your education in Holland is also a help in dealing with the English.

When you were here last you told me your wife had been ill and you were sending her down to the Cape to recover, now you can trek with her.

Please come to Pretoria to see me as soon as possible.

Your friend
Paul Kruger."

Van Riebeck was so elated he jumped up and strode to the bedroom hoping Katie was not asleep but reading. He quietly opened the door and went into the shadowy room, tiptoeing across the lion-skins covering the floor.

"I'm not asleep, darling, just resting,"

Katie said looking up at him. "Anything wrong?"

"No! No! Everything is wonderfully right! I'm going to the Cape with you!" Then he read Kruger's letter to her.

She jumped off the bed and flung her arms about him. "I can't believe it! I just can't! We've never had such luck. Oh darling. I feel better already. I'll rush and start packing." As words were bursting from her she was pulling on her shoes and buttoning them, then bundling up her hair. "I must make preparations at once. Oh God, I thank Thee for letting us go together!"

He was amazed by the metamorphosis in her. Wonderful how just the knowledge that they were going to the Cape together had already revitalized her.

But then a bitter thought speared him like a dagger: her tremendous happiness and relief to be leaving the Transvaal highlighted how deeply she hated being there. Bloody unfair when she knew that his life's work was up here and always would be. He suddenly was filled with resentment at being made to feel like a bastard for keeping her here.

236

She sensed something of his thoughts but too late realised she had exposed her true feelings. She went and caught him by the arms. Looking up at him appealingly she hoped to be able to explain how she felt.

"You do understand, darling, why I'm so happy by the news. Firstly—it means we don't separate and I'm absolutely longing to see all the other children. I . . . I can't help it—I miss them so much! I haven't seen them for two years and John not for six years. Then I miss my beloved sister, I so often long to talk to her, and I want to hear Mary sing. I want to see Abend Bloem, lovely, lovely Abend Bloem, Table Mountain—the sea." She laughed happily. "Oh, if only I could go to sleep and wake up to find myself in the Cape."

He was flaming with jealousy by all of her deep longings. He could not bear to see the love in her eyes for all the things in the Cape. He caught her roughly by the shoulders, his fingers digging into the flesh.

"Oh yes, I understand how you feel," he spoke coldly, "but tell me when you're at the Cape do you think of the South African Republic and long to be back *here*? Do you worry how it's progressing? No need to answer me. I now know how you loathe everything up here. You haven't deceived me over the years with your hypocrisy. Also in the Cape there are all the handsome English officers at Government House to pay you compliments. You're still beautiful enough for that."

Had he struck her she could not have been more astounded. Her big eyes widened with astonishment as she stared up into his cold hard face. Then she wriggled her shoulders to be free of his hands for her own temper was mounting by his injustice.

"God, you haven't changed. What a brute you can be. You're right! I *do* loathe everything up here." Now she would punish him. "It's raw and crude—almost barbaric, but I've tried to hide my loathing from you and to be a helpful wife. I've worried over the Republic's troubles and God knows they're never ending. Living in the wagon during the war with the

English. Living in the heat—the stench whilst you fought the Mapoochi!"

"You don't have to give me a detailed list of your martyrdom." His voice was thick with sarcasm. "Strangely enough I can sense it from you. I know that you feel you're superior to all the Boer women, that Herta is not good enough for Paul!"

"That's a lie! I'm just sorry she's so poorly educated, knows nothing about paintings, art of any kind, travel, great authors, poets!"

"My God, that would be useful for a Boer's wife! By your standards, she's poorly educated, but I prefer women like Herta to women with your type of education. Herta will make Paul a damned good wife. She knows all the things she should to *help* him. She'll be satisfied to be with him wherever it is, not like you, always aching to leave here. Doctor Mayer kindly pointed out to me what a mistake I'd made when he said, 'Your wife's not meant for this rough hard life.'" Van Riebeck sneered, "'Not a delicately born lady like her. She is too fragile—not like these great strong women of your race.' Now I realise I was a fool to marry you,

Katje, and you were a fool in London when I was in hospital with my broken legs, not to be the Duke of Rotherford's mistress so that. . . ."

She reached up and slapped him with all her strength across his taunting face.

"How dare you! Damn you! You insulting swine! Rotherford wanted to marry me and you know it!"

For a flash of time she thought he would strike her, his eyes went dark with an insensate rage but then he grinned in the old infuriating way that made her want to strike him again.

"I see, we're back where we started," he said. "In the past you always settled our arguments by slapping my face. School-girl tactics—you're far too old for them. I want you to know that I'm tired of feeling obligated to you because you so kindly reached down from your aristo-cratic pedestal to share my life up here. When you get to the Cape, you can stay there unless you forget all your nonsense and make up your mind that as my wife you belong up here, otherwise I'm better off without you!"

He spun around and strode out of the

room leaving her drained of physical strength. She sank on to a chair and tried to sort out the confusion in her mind. In God's name what had made him suddenly turn on her like that? Because she had so openly enthused about her love for the Cape and her family there? But how could he be so jealous of that? Of course the Doctor's opinion had riled him. The great Van Riebeck considered any woman should be honoured to share his life were it in a snake-infested cave. Oh, damn him to hell!

Well, after nine years she had told him she loathed the place. That had stung him and she was glad of it. What an unappreciative swine he was not to realize how deeply she had loved him to have lived up here. Oh God! She dropped her face into her hands. She could not believe they had again quarrelled so violently and what now? She knew how hard and implacable he could be. How would this quarrel ever be repaired? How and when?

18

THE wedding in the magistrate's stuffy little office in Pretoria was over. Herta, lovely as a ripe peach, in a full-skirted pale pink dress, with pink oleander flowers tucked into her thick golden plait encircling her head, was now Paul's wife.

As she looked up at him her big eyes shiny with joy and Paul leaned down to kiss her, Katie felt a surge of satisfaction in her belief that Herta adored Paul and in a womanly way would always care for him. Henceforth Katie would feel safer about Paul now that Herta was beside him.

The marriage brought a double relief, for Liz, telegraphing congratulations to Paul and Herta, also said Nancy was sailing for England.

Poor Nancy, Katie thought, was she suffering? But thank God that dark episode was finished.

The wedding party left the magistrate's office and walked the small distance to

Pretoria's smartest restaurant. "The Burgher" where they toasted Paul and Herta in champagne.

"My marriage is still like a dream to me," Herta laughingly told them all quite unashamedly. "It's so wonderful that I'm Paul's wife. I'm the luckiest girl in the whole Republic."

"Paul's damned lucky to have caught you for a wife, Herta," Van Riebeck said in what Katie considered was a voice loaded with meaning for her.

Since their quarrel they had not spoken to each other except in other people's presence. At nights on the farm in the big bed they lay at the extreme edges to be sure they would not touch each other. The very least he owed her was an apology, no matter how perfunctory, but sad experience told her he could maintain his anger for months. Early in their lives it had been for years, but then there had been no marriage bond. Katie wondered if they would trek all the way to the Cape with this anger festering between them? Certainly she would not relent until he apologised for his insults.

After lunch, the Vostlers, Katie and Van

Riebeck walked Paul and Herta across the wide, dusty road to an open space where Paul's new wagon with the fine span of matching oxen stood waiting for the newly wed couple.

Now after all the goodbyes, kissing and handshakes, the young couple climbed aboard their wagon anxious to start on their way. Herta wanted to change into a simple dress and Paul longed to peel off his tightly buttoned jacket and tightly fitting trousers and be in comfortable cotton shirt and moleskin trousers.

They stood on the board at the back of the wagon and Paul called to his new driver, a trusted servant of Vostler, *"Voorwarts! Voorwarts!"*

The Kaffir's eighteen foot long whip cracked out over the lead oxen's heads and they bent low straining their arched backs. The wagon creaked as the great wheels started turning and Paul and Herta were on their way. Happy in their marriage and excited that they were going to find gold. Suddenly his mother looked so like Nancy that Paul sickened for her, but he put his arm around Herta and hugged her to him and his unhappiness faded.

"Goodbye—goodbye! Good luck!"

The Vostlers and Van Riebeck called out but Katie only waved. Holding back tears she stood until the wagon turned a bend and was out of sight, then they all shook hands with each other and the Vostlers started for their wagon to return to their farm.

Van Riebeck went to Kruger's house for a last few hours of conference with him, whilst Katie went to the Telegraph Office to telegraph to Liz that they were leaving almost immediately for the Cape. They had arranged to join up with a Mr. and Mrs. Niekerk, a family of Cape Dutch, with three grown up offspring, who had been visiting relatives in the Transvaal. All told there would be five wagons. Three of Niekerk's and two of Van Riebeck's. There was livestock for eating, and good Kaffirs for servants and to help hunt for meat along the way and eight riding horses.

As Katie had feared would happen, she and Van Riebeck had been trekking for a month with the quarrel still dividing them. Van Riebeck shared her bed only for appearances' sake before the Niekerks, but he seldom returned to the wagon during the day so when the children slept in the hot afternoons Van Riebeck and the other trekkers hunted for meat, she was free to read.

From where he rode, Van Riebeck reined in so that young Niekerk could catch up with him. "Would you like us to hunt for a while?" he asked.

"Would I? Oh yes, Commandant Van Riebeck! It's been such a quiet trip; we've only seen giraffe, springbok and blesbok and lions too far off to hunt." Niekerk's suntanned face smiled with eagerness at the thought of hunting.

"There's not much game on the wagon trail nowadays, too many humans travelling the trail have driven the animals off. Let's ask your father if he minds if we halt the wagons for a while. I've spotted some swamps to the left down there." Van Riebeck pointed at shiny dark patches ahead just showing through the surrounding shrub. "It's likely we'll find big game there."

The elder Niekerk gladly agreed to outspan and the women did not object. It was a good spot to halt for a few hours and prepare the mid-day meal. Katie secretly rebelled against the smallest delay in getting to the Cape, but she said nothing. It was a relief for her, of course, to sit on the ground on a folding chair and be free from the wagon's rocking and swaying.

Franz and Adrian delightedly ran about, avoiding the oxen which glad to be freed of the yoke wandered off a little way to chew at what greenery they could find. The chickens were freed from the coops which were slung beneath the wagons and went pecking around.

"Don't go too far away, boys," Katie called to Franz and Adrian and Maarje wandered off to watch over them.

Van Riebeck took Hendrik with Niekerk and himself for he knew how Jantse's young son loved to hunt. He had taught the Zulu as a boy to shoot and he could be relied upon. The wagons were well guarded by the elder Niekerk and all of his Cape boys, who were good shots.

Now Katie glancing at Van Riebeck, Niekerk and Hendrik riding off in the direction of the shiny dark blobs which meant waterholes, told herself she felt no concern about him as she usually did when he went hunting; he was too cruel and implacable.

Seated in the shade of the wagon she forced welcoming smiles when Mrs. Niekerk and her two daughters came up carrying their folding chairs and sat down to chat. Mr. Niekerk and his two teenage sons who had longed vainly to hunt with Van Riebeck, went not too far off to see if they could raise some birds for the pot.

Riding in the direction of the swamps, young Niekerk asked Van Riebeck.

"What do you think we might find, Commandant Van Riebeck?"

"Not elephants, but lion perhaps, hippopotami, rhinoceros—buffalo." Van Riebeck's eyes narrowed to slits as he scanned the dusty earth in between the patches of scrub bush they were travelling over. "Don't see any spoor, do you, Hendrik?"

"No, baas—I see no spoor, but I see lion droppings."

"*Ja*, but old, several days I should think, Hendrik."

The sound and scent of the horses flushed a flock of koraan from the bush, and with their white bellies visible, they rose up and darted away.

"Don't shoot!" Van Riebeck swiftly ordered Niekerk. "We don't want to alert big game if there's any around and I've a feeling that there is. Perhaps a hippopotamus near the waterholes."

"Hippopotamus! Lord, I'd like to bag one of those great brutes!" Niekerk murmured.

"Well, look into the bushes over there." Van Riebeck pointed to a special spot where a great weight had flattened down some bushes. "That's made by a big animal, perhaps buffalo. When we get to the water I think we'll know more."

They now rode slowly so the horses made little sound and no one spoke. As they entered dense bush, Van Riebeck felt the shiver that ran through his horse and at the same moment his sharp eyes spotted two huge dark bodies—rhinoceroses evidently sleeping.

He quietened his horse and immediately pulled up murmuring, "Rhinoceros there! See them—a bull and cow in the bush. Their eyesight is bad but their hearing and scent are very keen. They may be asleep; anyhow I don't think they've spotted us."

At that moment the tick birds, picking lice off the rhinoceroses' huge bodies, sensed danger and started flapping their wings and screeching warnings so that the rhinoceroses started to rise heavily to sitting positions with their little eyes staring straight at the three horsemen, all with guns aimed at them.

Van Riebeck muttered, "They may run off or they may charge right at us. You take the cow, Niekerk! Hendrik, we'll take the bull."

Young Niekerk excitedly fired but his aim was poor and his bullet merely grazed the cow's shoulder. Bellowing with rage she got quickly to her feet as Van Riebeck and Hendrik each put a shot into the bull who turned and started to rush off into the bush, Hendrik spurring his horse to follow.

At that moment the cow came charging at Van Riebeck but he, wanting to give Niekerk a face-saving shot broadside at the animal, whirled his horse and cantered swiftly off. Then suddenly the horse's foot caught in a hole, it fell and threw Van Riebeck as Niekerk's gun jammed.

As Van Riebeck tried to rise from his back the cow was already straddling him —snorting madly, ready to trample him to death. Her evil bloodshot eyes were staring into his as she lowered her head with its horrible tusk to rip him open. He had just time to pull his long knife from his belt, then using both hands and all his strength he drove the knife upwards to the hilt deep into the cow's heart and her tusk slipped sideways, ripping his shoulder open.

She coughed and smothered him in blood, then rolled over dead. Niekerk rushed up. He was terrified by the sight of Van Riebeck covered in blood but relieved that the rhinoceros was dead.

"My God! I'm sorry, Commandant, my bloody gun jammed. Are you badly hurt?"

"Get this bitch of a cow off me, man— I can barely breathe."

Niekerk pulled, Van Riebeck shoved and at last he was free of the stinking smelling weight and Niekerk helped Van Riebeck to his feet.

"The bitch has gored my bloody shoulder, but at least she missed my heart." He swayed for a moment, then strength flowed back into him. "Where's my horse?"

"He's here, Commandant, but I think he's badly injured," Niekerk muttered.

The animal had broken a leg in its fall and would have to be shot. It was one of his favourite horses, and this bothered Van Riebeck more than his wound. He looked around for Hendrik who at that moment broke through the bush and came riding up.

"I followed the old bull, Baas! He's ready for the cook pot. *Magtig*! Baas!" He swore as he saw Van Riebeck's wound. "You're badly hurt!"

"No, no, but give me your horse, Hendrik, I must get back to the wagons and get disinfectant on this. Take care of everything here, Hendrik." He nodded toward the injured horse. "Too bad. I'll send help from the wagon. Stay with Hendrik," Van Riebeck ordered the abashed Niekerk, whom he could have gladly strangled. Silly bugger—couldn't shoot straight! Then he started riding toward the wagons. The wound was agony, he felt shaken and only hoped he could stay in the saddle.

Everyone had heard the shooting and their eyes were fixed on the veld where it had come from. Then they saw Van Riebeck cantering in and as he neared the wagons, Katie spotted that he was covered in blood and her heartbeat seemed to stop.

Mr. Niekerk and the coloured boys ran to help him off the horse. As he stood on his feet he swayed a little from loss of blood and Katie rushed to him.

"In God's name! Your shoulder!" With horror she saw the white of the bone showing. "I must treat it. Come and lie down."

"I'll lie on the ground. Get turpentine." He looked at Mrs. Niekerk's harassed face. "Your son's all right, so is Hendrik. Katje, send boys and a horse out to them. We got two rhino."

They helped him to stretch out and put cushions under his head whilst Katie knelt beside him to pour turpentine into the terrible wound.

"Don't worry, Katje, it's not too bad. The brute might have ripped up my hard heart."

He managed to give her a little wink to try to relieve her fears, then gratefully swallowed a full mug of brandy the Niekerk girl held to his lips.

As the turpentine soaked into the raw blood vessels and flesh, he winced at the sting but knew that hopefully it would stop blood poisoning. Mrs. Niekerk gave him more brandy and Katie said, "The blood vessels must be tied up to stop the bleeding." She called to the harassed looking Maarje, standing nearby, "Bring me sewing thread quickly."

"Can you tie up the blood vessels yourself?" Mrs. Niekerk asked in amazement. "Because I don't know anything about such things. There's always a doctor at hand in the Cape."

"I can do it—I've done it before." Katie spoke with great deliberation to give herself courage. It was years since she had first seen this done.

"She's a good doctor," Van Riebeck forced himself to say. "I'll have a couple more brandies, Mrs. Niekerk, please."

The Niekerk girl rushed to get it from their wagon whilst Katie took the thread from Maarje then dousing it and her hands in turpentine, she carefully picked the purple-blue vessels out of the messy gore of Paul's shoulder and tied the thread around first one vessel and knotted it, then another and knotted it. The cut blood vessels seemed endless but at last the profuse bleeding was being stemmed and all the blood vessels had been tied up, then Katie tied pieces of blood vessels to what she thought were their corresponding halves. Sweat was dropping down into her eyes; someone mopped it away, for she dare not stop until all the severed parts were tied to their own ends.

"Finished," she murmured at last. "I can't sew the flesh and skin—a doctor will have to, but I'll hold the sides together until they meet. You bandage the wound, Mrs. Niekerk—tightly—as tightly as you possibly can to make the flesh grow together."

As Mrs. Niekerk bound pieces of torn up sheets around Van Riebeck's wounded shoulder, under his arms and over his chest, Katie pinched the flesh and skin together so that the two sides met and held with the tight binding.

"Thank God! He ought to be all right

until we can get him to a doctor," Katie murmured.

Then she let strong hands lift her to her feet. Her hands and forearms were covered with blood and she felt sick and faint. She caught at Maarje's arm for support whilst she looked down at Van Riebeck swallowing his sixth mug of brandy.

He looked up at her with a grin. "You've done a fine job—thank you, Katje. We'll celebrate tonight with a roast of the rhino's hump—it's the best part."

Then his eyes fell shut and he slept. Leaning heavily on Maarje's arm, Katie stumblingly went a small distance off where she fell on her knees and retched and retched until she thought her stomach lining must come up, whilst Maarje lovingly held her head.

19

FROM then on, the wagons travelled as fast and for as long a time as possible, stopping only to give the oxen necessary rest periods for Van Riebeck badly needed a doctor's care. Whilst there was no blackening which would mean gangrene in the wound, the flesh was not growing together.

He no longer rode his horse but travelled in a wagon. He spent hours reading Goethe, for he always carried several volumes of his favourite writer in his saddlebag.

Katie's terror at seeing him wounded had swept away her anger with him and her solicitude and devoted care had restored his love for her, but despite their good feelings, they were both utterly weary of the trek.

Then at last the day came when the wagons' wheels were crashing over the stark red earth of the Karoo with its ugly stunted bushes. Patience—patience, Katie silently upbraided herself and finally they entered the Western Province, an Eden filled with fruit trees, greenery and flowering bushes. The sight of it was balm to the trekkers' sunscorched eyes.

Here the Van Riebecks said goodbye to the Nierkerk family and knowing it was only a matter of days before they reached Stellenbosch, Katie had to fight herself to hide from Van Riebeck her almost unbearable excitement.

When they reached the lovely little University town of Stellenbosch, with its avenues of great oaks, its grassy plots and tidy white houses, Van Riebeck sent Hendrik on horseback to advise Liz and his old friend Christopher Van der Byl that they would soon be with them.

Within an hour, the Van Riebecks reached the great spreading, white homestead where all the family awaited them on the stoep. When the kissings and huggings were over, Christopher ordered a coloured boy to bring the Cape cart out from the stables and said to Van Riebeck, "I'm driving you into Doctor Fraser's surgery at once. You mustn't waste another minute."

"Yes, yes, Chris, his shoulder needs immediate attention," Katie said.

She was relieved that Van Riebeck was to have proper care and also relieved that he would not be there to watch her so she could give her emotions their way. She laughed and cried whilst again and again she hugged and kissed her children and her beloved sister, Liz.

After greeting the line-up in the hall of smiling coloured house servants, she and Liz and the children went into the drawing-room that Katie so loved. The glossy tiled floor of red merging with rose, the pale grey walls, long green satin curtains with draped pelmets, crystal chandeliers, great mirrors—how she had revelled in choosing the decor over twenty years ago, but all looked fresh and beautiful for Liz had revered things.

"Mary darling, you've grown so beautiful," Katie told her second oldest daughter who smiled shyly and squeezed Katie's arm as Katie went on, "And I'm longing to hear you sing." She pulled her third daughter into her arms. "And you Eileen—you too look wonderful and you've grown so!"

Eileen planted an extra kiss on her mother's cheek, "I haven't seen you for a hundred years it seems, Mama darling."

"I know—I know, my pet." Katie felt penitent. "But you know that you have to stay in the Cape for the sake of your education."

"Yes, but Papa Paul should live down here so we can have you with us."

"Ah—that would be wonderful—but I'm afraid it's not possible. Anyhow I'm here now."

"Katie, I'd better send messengers to Terence and John in Capetown telling them you've arrived. John's working with Cecil Rhodes as you know, but lives with Terence behind his consulting rooms. I know they'll come racing home, also I'll send a boy on horseback to the University to get Kenneth from Stellenbosch."

"Oh do—do, Liz darling—I'm so longing to see them all!" Eileen and Mary were playing with their youngest half-brother Adrian whilst Franz was running around the big room declaring that he could remember everything.

"So Nancy left," Katie murmured to Liz. "Was she happy?"

"No—no." Liz answered thoughtfully. "I can't say she was happy. It was all so odd. At first she was determined not to go to England—then after a few days she suddenly burst out with 'I'm going to England!'"

"It's far better for her in England than out here. Where is little David? Did Nancy care about him?"

Liz shrugged a little sadly and murmured so that Mary and Eileen should not overhear her, "Not really. She helped the family when she fell in with our plan and let him replace her dead child; also she made him legitimate, that was important. Anyhow the little angel looks upon me as his mother. But now, why don't you have a little rest? Your room is all ready for you if you want to go up, whilst I arrange to send the notes off to the boys."

"Good, darling." Katie stood up. "I'm absolutely longing for a bath, Mary," she called to her daughter, "do tell the maids to bring a bath and hot water up to my room."

"Of course, Mother, and would you like some tea or coffee?"

"Tea, darling, would be lovely."

"I'll bring it up myself, then help you unpack."

"Thank you, my love—oh, how glorious—glorious it is to be home again!" Katie sang out as she flung her arms around the smiling Liz and gave her an extra hug; then she went swiftly from the room, up the great staircase, loving the fresh smell of wax and polish that seemed peculiar to Abend Bloem.

In her big bedroom she looked joyously around. What wonderful nights she had spent here years ago with Van Riebeck when he had lived on his adjacent estate. She smiled as she gazed down at the huge four-poster bed, resting her forehead against one of the carved posts. She was tired after the exhausting trek and would catch a little rest until Mary came with her tea. Unbuttoning her shoes, she eased them off and pulling the hand-made crocheted bedspread back, she lay down with her eyes on the open window, framing the soft blue sky and the purple-blue of the mountains. Would that she might stay here for the rest of her life. Happily like a child come home—she fell asleep.

"Mama—here's your tea. Oh, I've woken you—I'm sorry." Mary stood looking penitent as Katie smiled up at her.

"Darling—I only had my eyes shut—daydreaming. I'd love the tea. Sit down on the bed and tell me about your singing."

"I'll just put the tray down." Mary walked over to the table.

"I've made up my mind," Katie said as she propped herself up with pillows, "that I'm going to send you to the best professor in Milan, but first I'll have to find a proper family there for you to stay with."

Katie was surprised at Mary's reaction. No joy—no gratitude—only a sad face as she poured the tea.

"Mary, aren't you glad that you'll go to Italy?"

Mary came and handed Katie her tea, careful to avoid looking into her mother's eyes. The girl knew so well that they were such perceptive eyes that they had often seemed to read people's thoughts.

"Oh yes, Mother—I'm glad, thank you. You don't take sugar, do you?"

"No, I gave it up years ago for Lent and never went back to it." Katie took the cup and saucer from Mary and sipped her tea sensing that Mary was nervous of her. But why?

"Mary, you mustn't be afraid of going to Italy. I'm going to write to your father's cousin, the Duke of Rotherford, and ask him to find a suitable family for you to stay with and. . . ."

"Mama! Mama! I don't *want* to go!" Mary burst out violently. "I want to stay at Abend Bloem! Please don't send me away!"

Katie was amazed, not only by Mary's plea, but by the tragic look in her long grey eyes.

"Mary, whatever are you so afraid of? Being alone in a foreign country or what?"

"Yes, yes, that's it!" Mary grasped at the excuse whilst her tortured mind longed to toss the truth at her mother's feet. But impossible—for ever impossible! "I'd be too afraid of being in a foreign country. You remember that awful man Vasco Argarve in Lorenzo Marques—the way he wanted to marry me." She paced the floor restlessly eyeing the door as if longing to get away.

"Of course and you only a child of thirteen. It was preposterous! But why let that

264

experience influence you about going to Italy? When you wrote to me six months ago you were so eager to go."

Katie's look was glued to Mary's face in an attempt to reach the truth. Mary stopped pacing and trailed her slim fingers across her forehead as if trying to wipe her bewilderment away but her eyes held their frantic look.

"Yes," she murmured, "at first the idea of one day singing in the world's great opera houses seemed wonderful," her voice dropped to almost a whisper, "but . . . but now I don't want to go—I *can't* go!"

Deep uneasiness stirred in Katie but she decided not to push the subject with Mary at the moment. Later she would find out what had caused this amazing change in this frail, delicately beautiful daughter. Forcing a light tone in the hope of aiding Mary, she said, "Well, we needn't think about it now. We've plenty of time to discuss it later."

Instant relief brought the colour back to Mary's cheeks, and her eyes lost their frantic look. "Oh, thank you, Mother— thank you. Shall I pour more tea for you?"

"Yes, please."

Mary came and took the cup and saucer. She adored her mother and it would be heaven to be with her but for this terrible secret which she could never divulge. She poured the tea and handed it to Katie who saw how her hand was shaking but did not remark upon it. She suddenly decided, "Mary's in love and too shy to talk of it. She'll tell me about the man later."

"Tell me, darling, how often do you go into Capetown for singing lessons?"

"Oh, three times a week." Mary's face went taut again.

"It used to be twice, didn't it?"

Mary gave a curt little nod. "Yes, then Madame Visele suggested I came three times a week." She hated lying about it for it was she who had invented the story of a third lesson, in order to get out of the house more often.

"Madame Visele is so anxious to develop your voice I suppose. You go by train and a maid always accompanies you, of course?" Katie hoped her questions might produce some light upon who the man was.

"Of course." Mary moved toward the

window to avoid looking into her mother's eyes. "Mainly Sannie drives me in the Cape cart or carriage—it's much nicer than the train, the countryside is looking so beautiful now."

"Oh what a glorious change all the greenery and flowers make to the dryness of Lydenburg. Tell me, darling, is there anything worrying you? You seem so nervous? You know you can tell me anything; I'll always understand and help you."

Mary spun around defensively. "Of course nothing's worrying me! What should be worrying me? What do . . . ?"

A knock on the door interrupted her and she went to open it.

"It's the maids with your bath." She flung the door wide to admit two coloured girls in stiff white dresses carrying an oval-shaped copper bath and three more coloured girls holding big flagons of water.

"I'll come back later, Mama," Mary said and with relief slipped away. She was trembling as if with malaria and her mother's love and sweetness had almost brought her to tears. She went to her room to be alone and bolted the door. Had anyone ever been in such trouble as she was in?

A few minutes later Katie was soaking in warm water scented by some lavender cologne made at Abend Bloem which Liz had thoughtfully sent up. Katie was agitated and annoyed. Surely she should have been allowed one happy hour in Abend Bloem without a new problem being tossed into her lap? Lord, oh Lord, she thought wearily, did worry over one's children ever end? Not long ago she had killed the terrible monster incest between Paul and Nancy—now Mary had tossed some unknown, evil-smelling mystery at her, for she sensed by Mary's whole demeanour that it was no ordinary affair that was plaguing the girl who had always been so open and tractable.

20

REFRESHED by her bath and changed into clean clothes, Katie went to find Liz. She was in the small drawing-room which she used as an office and busy on the accounts for the ostrich farm. She looked up as Katie came in.

"Ah, Katie darling, now you look more like your beautiful self."

"I'll feel better tomorrow when I've washed my hair. The men haven't come back yet?"

"No, probably Doctor Fraser decided to stitch Paul's wound immediately."

"I hope so—it's been terrible the way it stayed open—the sides almost touching but not quite and scabs forming over the edges."

Liz shuddered. "How horrible, but don't worry about it any more. Old Fraser will take care of it. I think Chris and I will move back to the Van Riebeck homestead. It will give you more space here, especially as Terence and John will want to stay a few days."

"Oh, darling, must you go?"

"It's no hardship. All Chris's papers are there, he prefers working there and most of our clothes are still there." Liz laughed gaily. "In fact, we really live between the two estates and so there's loads of room for both our families."

"Good—good, whatever you've arranged. Do tell me how the vines are doing. I'm longing to see them."

"Don't be disappointed; they're only small, but what a relief to have vines growing again near the house instead of seeing those hideous ostriches strutting around. Still thank God for them, the feather business is doing well."

"Thank God is right. It's so important for all of us." Katie sat down and spread her wide skirts out around her feet. "I suddenly started to think what would happen if ostrich feathers go out of fashion before our vines give grapes? You know, Liz, I had an idea when we were trekking. Why not grow huge groves of fruit trees and ship our konfyt—our wonderful dried peaches and apricots and conserved fruits, to England? I'm sure they'd travel well in steamships that now only take three weeks to make the trip. I never came across such sweetmeats in England—did you?"

"Never—it's a brilliant idea." Excitement brought Liz to her feet. "It's absolutely brilliant. Let's start shipping as soon as possible. Our trees are heavy with apricots and peaches and we know all the ropes about exporting and can use our wine and feather exporter."

"Why not? Of course it might be very expensive on account of the weight of the fruit, but let's make enquiries soon. Also we could conserve pineapple and melon rind. Shall we try it? But don't talk about it to the men in case they pooh-pooh the idea."

"Chris wouldn't, I'm sure, it's so brilliant and why should Van Riebeck not agree for heaven's sake?"

"I don't know, but he sometimes resents the success of some of my ideas. Oh Liz, I wish I could be more modest and retiring —like you are—I so often aggravate him quite unwittingly."

"But, darling—I don't have your

wonderful brain or I would have thought of the konfyt to send to England."

"Nonsense. Anyhow, will you get the gardeners going on picking and drying the fruit in the sun. Perhaps we'll have to buy more drying trays and plenty of sugar, of course. If we really get going we'll have to buy much more fruit, and plant more trees too. How wonderful if we start up another export trade. Let's go into Capetown soon and see our shippers and discuss costs and get a timetable of steamships carrying cargo. I suppose the ostrich plumes still go by sailing boats?"

"Oh yes, it's so much cheaper."

"But with fruit it must go the fastest way so it won't spoil and we must start at once to make contacts in England to dispose of the fruit."

"Katie—you're wonderful; there never was anyone like you."

"Liz—Liz, it's your wonderful confidence in me that inspires me. I'll write tomorrow to Fortnum and Mason in Piccadilly and offer our conserves, they stock. . . ."

"What's the excitement between you

two?" Chris asked as he and Van Riebeck came in. "You look as. . . ."

"Darling, your shoulder," Katie swiftly interrupted going up to Van Riebeck, "what did the doctor do?"

"Oh, stitched me up of course, but he said you'd done a good job of sewing the blood vessels together, I should have the use of my arm in a month or so."

He gave her an intimate little wink. "Now I want the biggest brandy in the Cape Colony and then a long soak in a bath."

"Both will be ready in no time," Chris laughed at his boyhood friend and went to a cupboard to take out brandy and glasses. "My God, you had a lucky escape, man— that bloody rhino just missed your heart."

Van Riebeck sank into a big chair, long legs stretched out before him; he looked tired and travel stained. "You don't know how lucky I was, Chris, because until Katje saw me covered in blood she hadn't spoken to me for a month."

"What utter rubbish!" Katie burst out as she felt her face colouring. She didn't want Liz and Chris to know that she and Van Riebeck still quarrelled violently. Her sister and brother-in-law had endured so much of their quarrels over the years.

Van Riebeck took the glass of brandy Chris handed him then raised it as a toast to Katie.

"Well, Katje—my apologies for all of that."

She felt she could strike him. What a time to choose for so long overdue an apology and before other people—how ungenerous of him and how typical of him. She turned to Chris.

"May I have a brandy, too, please, Chris."

"I'll be back to have a drink with you," Liz said moving to the door, "but first I've got to give some orders to the gardeners."

The men politely rose and Liz shot Katie a secret look and lifting the hem of her wide skirts she hurried out. Katie's new idea had brought great relief to her. For some time she had been worried about both Katie's and her own family. Counting all of them, it meant nineteen of them were mainly dependent upon the ostrich plumes. What if they should go out of fashion and become an unwanted product? With a shudder Liz recalled how they had stared into the ugly face of poverty when the vines died and they had no more wine to ship to England. And it was not only Katie's and her own family, it was all the coloured families—more than a hundred people who were dependent upon Abend Bloem and must be cared for. Exporting conserved fruit might work into a big business.

Liz had just left the room and Van Riebeck and Chris were about to re-seat themselves when Kenneth bounded in.

Seeing Katie he shouted, "Jumping Jerusalem!" and lifted her from the chair, wrapped her in his arms and swung her around planting kisses on her cheeks.

Laughing delightedly, Katie thought, "How Irish Kenneth is—none of his English father's stiffness," and as she clasped him around the neck, she kissed his cheeks.

Then he replaced her on her feet and she sank breathlessly into a chair, her hands going up to tidy her hair.

"Is it wonderful to see you, Mother? Oh, is it?"

Then he turned to Van Riebeck with a

wide grin and hand outstretched, "And you too, Father!"

His bright grey eyes lit on to the bandanged shoulder and arm in a sling. "What happened? Argument with a lion?"

Van Riebeck laughed, "No, a rhino— but I got the last word in."

"I'd wager you would—tell me about it."

Van Riebeck quickly told him then said, "Lord, Ken, you've shot up."

Van Riebeck liked Kenneth best amongst Katie's children whom he had not sired. He admired Kenneth, who as a little chap had shown much courage during the Batlapin attack in Lydenburg; he also liked his frankness and good humour.

"I've shot up, Father . . ." With admiration Kenneth eyed Van Riebeck who was inches taller than himself. ". . . but I'll never reach your six foot four, or have your build."

"You'll do, man, as you are," Van Riebeck smiled. "I'm delighted with the look of you, Ken. Tell me, do you like studying law?"

"Truthfully—it's dull." Kenneth moved to the table to pour himself a brandy. "But

Uncle Chris and I often discuss my future. We wonder if I should chuck law and come on to the ostrich farm, especially now that Paul has gone gold prospecting. Tell me about Paul's wife. What's she like?"

"Lovely and very pretty." Katie smiled.

"She's a fine girl, you'll like her, Ken," Van Riebeck said, then Katie told him more about Herta.

"I hope Paul brings her down here soon," Ken said, "but perhaps he'll stay up in the Witwatersrand and make a fortune in gold. Mother, I'm entered for the rowing match in the Capetown Regatta next week. Will you come and watch me?"

"Of course—how lovely."

"He's got a good chance of winning," Chris told Katie.

"And I'm starting to get up a cricket team at Abend Bloem; we've got Uncle Chris, Jan, Stephan—when he's not praying—he wants to be a priest you know, then there's me and also Sannie—he plays well—just like a white man and I'm hoping that John and Terence will join us on week-ends."

"That sounds splendid. Do you play in

top hats as they did years ago when I watched a game in Capetown?" Katie laughed. "Oh, the men looked so funny."

"No, Mother, we're more informal out here."

"But Sannie is coloured." Van Riebeck threw a puzzled look at Chris, "Doesn't anyone object to him playing in a game with whites?"

Chris took his pipe from his mouth and spoke slowly, knowing that Van Riebeck was amazed and annoyed. "No, not really —a few friends have told me when they've been over for dinner and cards that it's not a good idea—but I don't see it that way. Sannie was born at Abend Bloem—his parents have worked here for twenty-three years. He's a fine boy, a lot better than many of the whites I know."

It pleased Katie that in the Cape the strict Transvaal line of colour separation was not observed.

"Hmm," Van Riebeck spoke thoughtfully, "there really are a lot of differences between the Cape Dutch and Republic Dutch. I wouldn't have this damned wound if the Cape Dutchman with me could have shot straight." He stood up.

"Well, I think I'll go and have that bath. I'll see you all at dinner."

"Too bad about Father's arm," Ken said. "Probably he has quite a lot of pain with it and won't say so."

"*Ja—Ja*," Chris nodded in agreement, "it's a bad wound. Doctor Fraser gave him some morphine before he stitched it. The effect must be wearing off now. Anyhow, he has some morphine to take if it pains too much. You know Van Riebeck, he never complains and he's determined that the arm will not stop him going to see the High Commissioner; he's going to register the deed of sale from Dinizulu of Saint Lucia Bay. Of course he's got to write in for an appointment."

"Well, tomorrow is Friday, so he can't see Sir Hercules Robinson," Ken said. "I believe he always goes hunting until Sunday night so Father will have to wait until Monday which is a good thing—he'll be feeling better by then."

"I certainly hope so," Katie said. "I wonder where Mary is?"

"Probably mooning around or lying down," Ken said, taking his cigarette case out of his pocket. "Lately she's always got a headache and she even bolts her bedroom door so that little David can't get in and worry her. She's behaving like a prima donna already." He chuckled, "Isn't that true, Uncle Chris?"

Chris smiled benevolently and pulled gently at his blond beard. "Oh, she's all right—she's just a bit different from most girls. She's quieter, then perhaps she's listening to some secret music that only she can hear that she's going to sing."

The phrase caught on to something special in Katie's mind and made itself appear important. She repeated it.

"Listening to some secret music that only she can hear that she's going to sing. Yes, Chris, I suppose that's it."

But Katie did not mean any music Mary learned at Madame Visele's; she thought of it as a music of love—but with *whom* was she in love? Ken might know, she must speak to him alone. She stood up.

"Who will come with me to see the vines?"

"I will of course." Kenneth sprang to his feet.

"All right, then I'll work on the accounts; take some work off Liz's shoulders." Chris nodded to the piled up desk.

"Poor Chris—always so much work—but I'll soon be helping with it," Katie promised as she and Kenneth left the room.

Outside Katie linked her arm through Kenneth's as they strolled away from the house toward the orange and lemon groves where the scent of the fruit sweetened the air, on through orchards of peaches and apricots which Katie now looked at with commercial eyes. They were going to help with Abend Bloem's new export but there were not nearly enough; more must be planted.

Walking in the shade of pepper and loquat trees Katie said, "It's funny about Mary, with all your friends at the University. Haven't any of them fallen in love with her? Or she with them?"

"Oh, they've all been smitten with her, but you know she's not a bit flirtatious—she never encourages anyone. She's the opposite of Nancy who wants every man to fall over because of her beauty. Mary is very stand-offish and lately she's grown worse."

"Of course she's always been shy but now she seems to me to be so nervous as if something is worrying her."

"I haven't noticed that, Mother, but then we're never alone together."

"The funny thing is that she doesn't want to go to Italy to a singing coach. In fact, she pleaded with me not to send her to Italy. It's extraordinary and. . . ."

Katie broke off and stood to stare at the low grape vines planted over a year ago, in long neat rows with chalky white paths stretching on to the mountains' base. They covered the earth as far as she could see.

Lovely, lovely sight, it made her weak with emotion and her fingers tightened on Kenneth's arm. He seemed to understand how she was feeling and remained silent.

In a few moments she murmured in a shaky voice, "One of the loveliest sights I've seen—oh how I've longed for this."

"I know, Mother, how you feel. I must admit we all felt as if we were getting a conducted tour into heaven when we came to watch the vines being planted. In fact, we didn't just watch, Terence, Paul and I, Uncle Chris, Jan and Stephan—we all helped plant vines. God—what a wonderful day it was! Aunt Liz broke down and wept."

Katie nodded toward the low white building. "I remember years ago—long before you were born when I had just bought Abend Bloem, that the Kaffirs had to hack away vines and tree branches covering the doors of the vat and inside, the stone chambers smelt of years of disuse and tarantulas and scorpions were nesting everywhere."

"Abend Bloem was very neglected, wasn't it?"

"It had been for about twenty years. Only a very old woman lived in the house with a couple of half-dead servants. All her family had left in the great trek after the Dutch freed the slaves. In the end she had to sell and I kept thinking as I was buying it, 'Her end is my beginning.' That's the shape of life—someone's beginning is someone else's ending."

"You were all alone then."

"I had Terence and Paul, but they were tiny boys. I'd just come down after existing for five years in the wilderness of Hoffen, but I had my lovely gold nuggets to buy Abend Bloem with, but, oh what work it was to restore it."

"Don't sound so sad, Mother." Kenneth couldn't bear the thought of her early struggles alone in Hoffen. "You have Father and four grown sons to care for you now and as far as I'm concerned, I promise that I'll always care for you—you'll never be alone again."

"Kenneth, what a marvellous son you are and I'm a lucky woman. Thank you for caring so much about my welfare. Come on, let's go back to the house, Aunt Liz will be looking for us and you've not seen your little brothers yet."

She stood on tiptoe and pecked at his cheek. Always she had believed that Paul —her lovechild was her favourite, if favourite she had. Now she knew it was Kenneth, with his frank nature, his sense of humour and the approval he had always felt for her.

21

THE following day whilst Chris, Van Riebeck and Ken rode over inspecting the Van Riebeck and Abend Bloem estates, Katie asked Mary, "Darling, help me wash my hair." It hung so long she could sit on it and was very thick. "It's such a job."

Mary hesitated, "Oh, Mama, I'd like to, but I promised to ride over and see the Coftzee girls. I always do on Friday. I'll tell them you've arrived then I can be back for lunch."

"Let *me* help you, Mama." Eileen burst out. "I'd love to wash your hair. When I was in Lydenburg you said I rubbed your scalp just the way you liked it."

"It's true, too—I've asked the maids to take up the basins and hot water, so shall we go up?"

They climbed the big staircase together, Eileen's arm around Katie's waist, Katie embracing Eileen's shoulders. She had the uncomfortable feeling that Mary had swiftly invented the lie of going to the Coftzee girls to avoid being alone with her again, she prayed she was wrong.

A little later as Eileen was towel-drying Katie's hair, Katie's mind was struggling to discover something hidden in Mary and she asked, "Is it always the same maid who rides into Capetown with Mary when she goes for her singing lessons?"

"Always Cillie—she's Mary's favourite. You remember her, Mama; she's one of Sannie's sisters, and Sannie always drives Mary."

"Do you ever go with them?"

"I wish I could but I'm usually in school."

"What about school holidays? I know you used to love going into Capetown."

"I still do, but Mary won't take me; she says she doesn't want to be bothered with a little sister and that I talk too much."

Katie turned around laughing to hug Eileen's plump young body. "You *are* a bit of a chatterbox. Well, I'll take you into Capetown soon and we'll have fun and you may talk as much as you like. All right, darling, I think I'll go and sit on the back stoep and finish off drying my hair in the sun and you go off and play with your cousins."

When Katie was settled in a wicker chair on the back stoep with her long hair hanging like a damp cloak drying in the sun, she heard men's voices floating through the open back door. They were coming out on to the stoep. She quickly pulled her hair to the back of her neck and excitedly jumped to her feet as Terence and John strode on to the stoep.

"Mother!" Terence hugged her and fondly kissed her cheeks. "How marvellous that you're here."

"Darling—darling Terry." She kissed his cheek, then turned swiftly to John. The likeness to his dead father had developed amazingly in the six years since she had last seen him.

"John darling." She slipped her arms around his neck. "It's too wonderful to see you—you're a man now!"

"And wonderful to see you, Mother." He caught her by the shoulders and they exchanged kisses on the cheek.

"Shall I get some hair pins or combs or something to put your hair in order?" he asked primly. "You can't sit out here like this before the coloured domestics." He waved at a maid on her knees polishing the far end of the stoep tiles.

His reprimand quelled Katie's emotion and turned it into laughter, just what his father would have said.

"Her hair is fine—she's just drying it, John, you idiot," Terence said as they all sat down. "I like it like that—reminds me of when Paul and I were little kids and first came to live here."

"My hair's not quite dry, John," Katie said, "but if it upsets you like this I'll go and bundle it up."

"Absolutely no!" Terence ordered. "I'm the doctor in the family and you can't roll damp hair up, even in the heat." His dark eyes examined her. "You don't look too well."

"Actually I'm splendid—had malaria like you often have." She glanced at John. "At last I can congratulate you in person on getting your Oxford degree—you're almost a fully fledged lawyer. I'm so proud of you."

"Just a couple of years articled to a law firm, then I'm it, but, Mother, it's so exciting working for Cecil Rhodes instead. What a genius that man is."

John's clipped English accent sounded almost affected she was so used to the slow colonial accent but Katie knew the English accent was now natural to John after three years at Eton and three years at Oxford.

"Everyone seems to think Rhodes is a genius," she said, "especially after he formed the De Beers mining syndicate. That made him many times a millionaire, didn't it?"

"Yes and he was not even thirty. The De Beers syndicate means protection for thousands of people because it keeps diamond prices up, no matter how many are found."

"Why don't you introduce him to Mary?" Katie teasingly suggested. "How lovely to have such a man in the family."

"That's a funny thing about him." A puzzled look came into John's grey eyes. "He can't stand women, won't even have one working in his house."

Terence coughed, very obviously to shut John up. He did not know if Rhodes was a pedarist or not, but it was not a subject for discussion with their mother.

"I hear he's very good to his staff," he said.

"He's wonderful, especially kind to all the young men working for him, but mind you, they've got to be intelligent. I'm one of his secretaries and I've got to keep my wits about me—he's such a swift thinker. He sends such long telegrams to Kimberley it's as if they were letters."

"How does he feel about the Boers in the Transvaal?" Katie asked.

At that moment Mary came riding up to the stoep and a coloured boy ran from the house to help her dismount and to take her horse. She looked beautiful in her green riding habit with the long skirt. Terence and John stood up as she climbed the steps and joined them.

"How's our Ophelia today?" John asked teasingly. "Pale and serious and ready for the scene 'Oh woe is me to have seen what I have seen'—see what I see."

"Know your Shakespeare—don't you, John?" Mary snapped, then smiled at Terence. "How's the medicine man?"

Terence pulled up a chair for her and she sank into it. "Whew, it's hot riding today, but isn't it wonderful to have Mother here?"

"It certainly is and now that we've got her here I vote we keep her here." John looked seriously at Terence and Mary. "She's lived in the wilderness quite long enough—too long."

"I feel the same, but there's nothing we can do about it," Terence gave a hopeless little shrug, "short of kidnapping Father and chaining him down here."

"Mother must go where her heart is."

Mary's voice sounded so dramatic, that they all looked at her in surprise.

She jumped up crying, "Don't stare at me for heaven's sake. I'm going to get out of my riding things." She hurried through the back door.

"What is the matter with her?" Katie's big eyes were filled with apprehension as she turned them on Terence. "She seems so strange."

"It's just that she doesn't care much for John's teasing. Don't forget that Paul and I and Kenneth, too, have always handled her with kid gloves. She was such a sensitive kid and dramatised everything."

A sad realisation shook Katie that for

the past nine years as Van Riebeck's wife she had grown away from her older children, seeing them for short periods and only at intervals. Of necessity they had not lived long in Lydenburg with her because of the lack of suitable education up there.

"Well cheer up for heaven's sake, Mother," John said laughingly. "Mary's not your only child. Think of me now. By the way, Grandmama sent you all sorts of loving messages and so did Cousin Howard." John turned to Terence and winked. "Howard used to be in love with Mother you know."

"John, you've grown into an impossible tease. Thank goodness Terence knows you're talking nonsense but how is your Cousin Howard?"

"Splendid. Of course you haven't seen him for four years; he's changed very little and still not married."

"Well, perhaps he might really fall in love with Nancy now that she's in England." Terence remembered the Duke's flirtation with his sister that caused her so much grief. "It would suit Nancy to a 'T' to be the Duchess of Rotherford."

"Mama—Mama."

Adrian came running from the house pulling little David by the hand. They rushed up to Katie who had only seen David for a few seconds the previous night.

"Yes, my little loves, what is it?"

Adrian started climbing on to his mother's knee whilst Terence picked David up and started tossing him in the air above his head and the little boy squealed with delight.

Katie's eyes flew to Terence's face, thank God he obviously loved his son, supposedly his nephew, for Terence's face was alight with devotion for the child. Katie almost sighed aloud in relief.

"John," she said, "you don't know Adrian—your latest little half-brother."

"He's another Van Riebeck all right— hello, Adrian." John perfunctorily leaned over and tousled Adrian's golden hair. "But I must say little David doesn't look a bit like Nancy or that wet husband of hers—Eric Preston."

"David is the image of *my* father—so Irish looking," Katie swiftly explained. "Grandchildren often take after grandparents more than parents."

Then Maarje appeared, nodding respectfully to John whom she had last seen in England, and he gave her a friendly smile.

"Hello, Maarje—are you still seeing ghosts and foretelling the future?" John remembered how she had predicted the shipwreck they were in on their way to England. "Tell me my fortune quickly."

Words suddenly burst from Maarje.

"Master John have much gold—much diamonds! Man buried high in rocks on mountain."

"Not me I hope?"

"No—no, other man! Give much money to Master John."

"Good, that's a fine bit of fortune telling. Thanks, Maarje."

She giggled shyly and told Katie, "I've come to take them for lunch and sleep." She nodded to Adrian and David.

Terence kissed David's cheeks then Adrian's, gave them a little spank on their bottoms and Maarje shooed them into the house.

"My hair's dry now so I'll go and do it up," Katie said. "Shall we meet on the front stoep for a sherry before lunch? It's cooler than here."

Her sons followed her into the house and as she climbed the stairs Terence called out to a maid who was dusting in between the thickly carved banisters.

"Cillie, would you bring sherry and glasses to the front stoep?"

"At once, Master Terence." The pretty coloured girl gave him a wide smile.

As the half-brothers settled into deep wicker chairs on the stoep with the long avenue of beautiful tall oaks stretching out before them, John said, "By jove, Cillie has grown pretty. She's nothing like the kid we all used to play with and Sannie's a good looking fellow too."

"Their whole family is good looking; I think it's a mixture of Zulu and white blood, but don't you start making eyes at a coloured girl for God's sake."

"Have your wits left you, Doctor," John sneered. "Give me a cigarette. I left my case in the suit in my portmanteau."

Terence dug in his jacket pocket, pulled out an ivory case and held it open to John. "Sorry, if I sounded potty but you've only been back in the Cape a few months and you've made eyes at every pretty white girl you've seen."

"What's wrong with that? Anyhow, Cillie looks almost white."

"Yes, it's funny the girls in her family take after the white side, the boys like Sannie, are dark with marvellous physiques—like Zulus. That's from the mother. She is Zulu, supposedly of royal stock; the father was a Dutch sailor, he's dead now. Strange how the mixed blood has turned out. Of course Cillie's children could be black as Zulus."

John shuddered. "God that stops me thinking that she's even pretty. Of course I remember her mother—a strapping woman, used to work in the vineyards. By the way, Terry, I want to learn Zulu. It's the same as Matabele, isn't it?"

"Yes, the Matabeles are a Zulu offshoot, but why the devil do you want to learn the languauge?"

"Rhodes is besotted about going north, I'd probably have to go with him, it would be a feather in my cap to be able to speak Zulu."

"Well, we'll have to find you a teacher —male—don't bring coloured girls back to my consulting rooms."

"Good God—you're as rabid on the

colour question as the Transvaal Boers. I've grown out of it after six years in England. At Oxford we had black chiefs' sons from Ethiopia and Indian Maharajahs' sons—black as the ace of spades, but good chaps most of them."

"I'm sure all the fellows working for us at Abend Bloem are good chaps only you don't want them in the family."

At the sound of a carriage approaching they peered down the long avenue of oaks and recognised Van Riebeck, Christopher and Kenneth in the open carriage.

"Why the devil are they in a carriage and not riding?" John asked.

"I'm damned if I know." The half-brothers walked to the steps of the stoep as the carriage drew up, then they saw Van Riebeck's bandaged shoulder and arm in a sling and went down to greet him as he left the carriage.

"John!" Van Riebeck held out his right hand. "It's very good to see you, man."

As John shook Van Riebeck's hand he fought against his years of resentment and jealousy on behalf of his dead father, but against his will admiration swept through him for the big magnificent looking man. Even more handsome than John had remembered him.

22

AT dinner that night Katie revelled in a couple of the happiest hours she had known for years. All her children were in Abend Bloem, excepting for Paul and Nancy. Van Riebeck, Liz, Chris and their children, Stephan, Jan, Cornelius and Theresa were also there. Marie alas was in England.

Around the great table spread with a Brussels lace cloth and lit by candles in silver candelabra that shone on crystal glasses and fine china, everyone was laughing, chatting, disputing as they ate excellent babootie. The wine was good; it was some which Chris had put down before the disease had destroyed the vines, and he kept it for very special occasions.

The table was so wide that Liz and Van Riebeck sat together at the head and Katie and Chris side by side at the other end.

Soon the conversation became political when Van Riebeck said, "This is a night for me to celebrate. You young men might as well know, although it's not been officially announced, that the South African Republic has got its own port at last!"

"It's splendid, Uncle Paul. We've read rumours in the newspapers," Stephan said, "that Dinizulu has given you the land at Saint Lucia Bay, but never read of anything definite."

"Dinizulu didn't 'give' it to us, Stephan; it was his payment for the fighting we did for him and for putting him back on his throne."

"I think it was a just thing to do," Liz said. "He is the rightful heir."

"But you must be prepared, Paul, for trouble in getting Dinizulu's contract to work," Chris warned. "In the House of Representatives we heard that Germany has her eyes on Saint Lucia Bay. Because of some German traders living there, she has an excuse to come in to protect them and claim Saint Lucia for Germany just as she claimed Angra Pequena."

"Bismarck certainly stole a march on the British there, but that should help us," Van Riebeck said. "The British would undoubtedly rather sanction the South

African Republic in Saint Lucia than Germany."

Chris nodded. "I would imagine so, but of course Cecil Rhodes might oppose you. He's a true Imperialist—wants everything in Africa to be British—isn't that right, John?"

"He's marvellous!" John burst out defensively. "He even wants England to get America back under English rule . . . don't laugh." John turned around on his cousins who were chuckling at the absurd idea. "I tell you, Rhodes is far-seeing. It's a dream of his to have a road from the Cape to Cairo. That's his cry—'My road to the North!' Then my road through to the Mediterranean!"

Van Riebeck was listening attentively: this would all interest Kruger. "Rhodes certainly has grandiose ambitions," he said hoping to spur John on to talk more but Chris said.

"I'm afraid that the fight to rape Africa —the whole continent—has started—it's an international exploitation. All the world seems to want the products of tropical Africa and what England fears very much is that Germany will join hands with the Transvaal."

Van Riebeck shook his head. "We don't want that. We want to stay an independent Dutch Republic, but, John, what does Rhodes think about Matabeleland and the rumour of gold being found up there?" Van Riebeck went on eating his babootie with an assumed indifference.

"He's most interested, of course. Matabeleland will be part of his road to the North. I want to learn the language—all of his staff want to. The men he's just sent up to talk to Lobengula know very little of the language."

Van Riebeck was furious—so the Boers' suspicions were confirmed. "I hope his men will be safe," he said, "because our man Grobles was murdered just as he was going into Matabeleland."

Van Riebeck's eyes were on John who, flattered by the attention he was receiving, burst out, "Yes, I know about Grobles; the message reached Rhodes."

Van Riebeck felt dangerously angry. How could Rhodes have received the news had he not engineered the murder? There was no other way, for the Boers had kept absolutely quiet about Grobles' death.

"That was a rotten thing to happen." Chris shook his head and poured wine into Katie's glass. "Grobles was a fine man—I met him years ago."

"He *was* a fine man. We shall miss him." Van Riebeck looked back at John. "So Rhodes is interested in the Matabeleland gold—strange when he has bottled up most of the diamond fields."

"Rhodes wants digging concessions in Matabeleland—not for himself but for British diggers—miners to go up there—he wants more English in the North."

Katie was suddenly filled with the horrible conviction that Van Riebeck was pumping John and John, in his youthful pride at being attached to the Almighty Rhodes' staff, might be spilling secret information. She held no brief for Rhodes but John must be protected against himself.

"I'm longing to hear if Paul has actually found gold on his land," she said. "Just imagine! He wanted to know what we will all choose as presents if he becomes a millionaire."

"Gold could make the Republic rich," said Jan, Liz's second son, who always served with Kenneth in the Cape Militia. "Look at the fortunes made on diamonds."

"By people like Rhodes—it's the big syndicates who've become so immensely rich," Van Riebeck said. "Our people in the North don't look at money the way their relatives do down here. It's land and cattle they count as wealth."

They were nearing the end of dinner and when everyone had finished the sweetmeats and tarts, Katie caught Liz's eye.

"Shall we all go into the drawing-room together. If we leave the men here to drink brandy and talk politics, we won't see them for hours." She stood up.

"Yes, you're right. Already we're late and the maids will want to clear away." Liz stood up and everyone rose with her.

"In the large drawing-room, where Katie had many times given most successful balls, they all gathered to the side where french windows led to the stoep and a light breeze was drifting in.

"Mary, will you sing something for us?" Katie asked.

"Please, Mama, don't ask me tonight. I've one of my awful headaches."

"She does look pale," Katie thought and decided not to insist, then Kenneth started to organise everyone for games.

"Cards, Mother, or dancing, what's it to be?"

"I'd quite like a game of whist, but first, Franz must go to bed. Look, he's half asleep already; I'll go up with him."

"I'll put him to bed, Mother." Mary swiftly volunteered. "And if you'll forgive me, I'll go to bed, too. I think a thunderstorm's on the way, I always get these headaches before one breaks."

When she was gone Katie said to Liz, "Mary looks quite delicate; perhaps she needs a tonic."

"Perhaps. These last few months I must say she's become very touchy. That's another reason that I'm so glad you're here, added to all the others." Liz squeezed Katie's arm. "After all the trouble we've had with Marie and Nancy we don't want any trouble with Mary."

"Really our daughters are very difficult."

Katie felt ridiculously depressed for a

moment, then Kenneth called her to the whist table and for the remainder of the evening the family played whist, back gammon or chatted.

Hours later a thunderstorm broke and on her way to bed Katie looked in on Franz and Adrian lest the storm should awaken and frighten them, but they were sleeping peacefully.

Passing Mary's room, she thought she would pop in to see if she were asleep but with surprise found the door bolted, then remembered Kenneth had mentioned that Mary bolted her door against the younger children.

On Sunday, all the family, excluding Van Riebeck and Van der Byl, piled into the two carriages and a Cape cart to drive to the tiny Catholic Church in Stellenbosch where they attended Mass.

The rest of the day was filled with happiness for Katie. A crowd of family and neighbours for lunch, afterwards in the big space in the back garden, an exhibition of Kenneth's attempt at a cricket match, then came dinner, cards and bed.

At daybreak, Katie, Van Riebeck and

Liz were dressed and downstairs ready to breakfast with Terence and John and to ride into Capetown with them, for Terence had early appointments at his consulting rooms and John was due at Cecil Rhodes' office on the Herrengracht.

When they neared Capetown, Katie grew joyously excited but hid her feelings from Van Riebeck lest they pointed up her loathing of the Transvaal.

She loved the double and treble storied white buildings with big Dutch gables, with in between them a sprinkling of plainer English architecture. The wide main thoroughfare, the Herrengracht, was flanked by great oaks and beginning at the sea with an old pier it stretched up to end in Table Mountain's base. A centre canal at intervals was crossed by decorative little bridges and flanking the sidewalks well stocked fashionable shops displayed their wares. Shiny carriages and barouches pulled by fine high-stepping horses moved along side by side with red omnibuses drawn by teams of six horses. Under a wooden clock tower a long row of coloured women sold brilliant flowers from great bunches kept fresh in zinc tubs of water.

"Whilst Capetown's not London, Mother," John joked, "it certainly has a charm of its own. If you put me down at Terry's place I'll leave my portmanteau and walk to the office. I'll be back home for the week-end."

The carriage turned into a side street that was abustle with street sellers, and half naked Kaffirs driving cattle to the market in Loop Street were yelling at their beasts in Swahili.

"All the good old Capetown smells, Mother," John laughed as the carriage drew up and he and Terence got out.

"You can inspect my consulting rooms when you pick me up for lunch, Mother." Terence said.

"I will, darling, and John, what about you?"

"Sorry, but the staff lunches with Rhodes. He can't bear to ever be alone."

Then the carriage went on to drop Katie and Liz near the Standard Bank on the Herrengracht, they got out leaving Van Riebeck to be driven to Government House, where he must present his credentials to Sir Hercules Robinson's aide and make an appointment with the High

Commissioner. He then intended calling at the offices of the Afrikaner Bond—a growing society amongst the Cape Dutch to forward the Afrikaans language. He arranged to meet Katie and Liz at four at the Traveller's Rest, which had always been a favourite coffee house with them. Katie loved its swinging wooden sign that stated:

"Genuine coffee, not wheat, served as early as morning gunfire."

Arm in arm Katie and Liz strolled down the Herrengracht stopping to gaze into shop windows. "I think I should buy some clothes, Liz. I've not had a new rag since I was in London six years ago."

"But fashions out here are years behind London, so you still look lovely in your dresses, but Madame Harles is not far from here if you want something made."

"Well, perhaps I'd better save the money. I've so many dresses that I've never worn in Lydenburg or Pretoria, they're too 'fancy' as my Boer women friends would say. Ah, here's the Bank." She stopped before a new, well constructed building. "How much monthly allowance do you think I should send

Nancy? Of course Lady Eaton would be offended if I offered to pay for Nancy's upkeep."

"Naturally any grandmother would be, but Nancy doesn't need an allowance, she's going to sell those two big diamonds —they're worth a fortune."

Katie stared in amazement, at Liz. "Diamonds! What diamonds?"

"Didn't you know? Someone gave them to her in Kimberley. Then because of Rhodes' De Beer Syndicate and some kind of official regulation forbidding diamonds to leave the country, she got nervous about taking them abroad."

"It's the first I've heard about the diamonds. I'm very upset, why didn't she tell me about them? My God—she's developed into a strange girl."

Liz secretly agreed with her sister but she said, "Don't be upset. She knew you'd question her about how she got them. She only told me about them at the last moment when she wanted me to take them aboard her ship—she was afraid of taking them and getting into trouble."

"But what about you? Supposing the

officials had caught you? She didn't care about that?"

"Yes, but I wasn't a passenger, anyhow it worked out quite well."

"Oh Lord! Lord, Liz! I don't want to even think about it—or how she got them." Katie suddenly became furious. "Well she certainly won't get financial help from me! No need to go to the Bank now. Let's go to the shippers and talk about exporting the konfyt."

At the shipping office, Katie and Liz snapped their parasols shut and went in and the bell above the door tinkled to announce customers. The grey-haired English manager, Mr. Berk, came forward with a smile to meet them. He shook hands with Liz who had upon occasions called upon him about exporting the ostrich feathers, then his face lit with remembrance of Katie.

"Why it must be twenty years ago, Madame, when you first came in to arrange the export of wines from Abend Bloem—you haven't changed at all."

"Thank you, Mr. Berk—that's an extravagant compliment."

After the handshaking and friendly

greetings were over and Katie and Liz were seated with cups of coffee beside them, they asked Mr. Berk his opinion of their idea of shipping konfyt and conserved fruits to England.

His response was enthusiastic. "It sounds an excellent idea and you'll be the very first to do it, so you should capture the English market. I'll show you our list of exports which represents everything that's exported from South Africa." He dug amongst a file of papers on his desk, picked one out and handed a sheet of paper to Katie. "Now just look at that."

When she had finished reading Katie looked up excitedly at Mr. Berk.

"No fruit! Fresh or conserves! Splendid! Now about space in the holds of the steamships? Our fragile products can't go on a slow sailing ship."

"Of course not. I don't believe it will be too expensive to ship because it won't take too much space. Shall we handle it as we always handled the wine—18% of your selling price?"

"Perfect, Mr. Berk." Katie and Liz stood up.

"We'll soon be writing to tell you how we're progressing," Liz said.

There was more handshaking, then the sisters gathered up the hems of their wide skirts and passed through the door held open by the smiling manager.

They unsnapped their parasols and walked out. They were pleased and excited by their visit and with what they had learned.

"We must start in earnest to get the fruit ready," Katie said, "We'll need light-weight wooden boxes to pack it in and . . ." She broke off. "Oh, aren't we near Madame Visele's studio? Do let's go in, I'd like to talk to her about Mary's singing—hear what suggestions she may have about Milan."

"A good idea, darling—the studio's just down the street."

At a door with a brass plate engraved with the words "Madame Visele—Theatre Francais Paris," they rang and a coloured maid admitted them then went to inform Madame Visele that they were there. They settled on red plush and gold chairs and looked around at the over-lavish decor.

Madame Visele did not keep them

waiting but swept in wearing a theatrical-looking flowing garment, bringing with her the scent of heavy perfume. Her dark hair was wound about her head in Grecian fashion; a long white arm and hand was dramatically extended to Katie.

"What a pleasure this is, Mrs. Van Riebeck."

"Indeed it is for me too. This is my sister, Mrs. Van der Byl."

The woman shook hands. "Ah yes, Mrs. Van der Byl, I received your letter and I hope that Mary has recovered?"

"Recovered!" The word burst simultaneously from Katie and Liz.

Madame Visele looked from one sister to the other. "Yes, yes, a month ago I received your letter saying she was confined to bed with fever."

"But I didn't . . ." Liz murmured in confusion and Katie interrupted.

"Madame Visele, you mean you've not seen Mary here for a month?"

The Frenchwoman shook her head, "No—but you seem so surprised—If you didn't write the letter, then who did?"

Pulling on her store of resilience Katie said, "I'm afraid that Mary must have written it herself. I'm quite shocked. But why should she play truant when she loved her singing lessons?"

"Yes, but I'm sorry to say about three months ago I began to feel she was losing interest."

"Losing interest? But she told me you had advised her to increase her lessons to three a week." Too agitated to remain seated, Katie rose and paced the room. "It's extraordinary! Most upsetting! For a month she's been leaving home three times a week supposedly for lessons . . ." she shot an enquiring look at Liz who nodded vehemently, "but she hasn't been near here! So where has she been? What has she been doing for those three mornings a week? With whom has she been?"

"Don't be too upset, Mrs. Van Riebeck —I think the answer is quite clear. It's not the first time I've had young girls do this. Mary has obviously fallen in love," Madame Visele smiled and shrugged. "I'm sure you'll find that is the answer."

"But why should she have lied and been so deceitful?"

"Shyness perhaps," Madame Visele suggested.

"That's it, Katie—nothing serious to worry about." Liz forced a consoling smile although she was shocked. "Come on, we have to meet Terence for lunch."

"Mary really has an exceptionally beautiful voice," Madame Visele said, "I assure you. I do hope she'll have a chance to study in Italy."

"Yes—I actually came to discuss that with you, but I'll have to wait for another day."

The women shook hands and the sisters left.

23

THE next day, alone in her bedroom with Mary, Katie pleaded, "But, Mary—trust me—tell me where you've been going. I'm your mother as well as being your best friend. For God's sake confide in me!"

"No, no, you simply couldn't understand." The girl's eyes looked agonised. "You're the very last person I could confide in about this."

Mary's distraught condition drove Katie's spiritual hurt away. "But why can't you say where you've been three times a week for an entire month?" she asked. "I obviously think you're in love and won't tell who the man is. Why not? It's natural at your age to fall in love—no one's going to blame you, but say who he is."

"I can't." Sobs burst from Mary and her clenched fist thumped a bed post, "I can't! That's what's so hard. I can't—I can't—I can't!"

"But *why* not, in God's name?" Then a terrifying thought struck Katie like a stomach blow. "He must be a married man I suppose."

Mary despairingly shook her head as tears streamed down her pale cheeks. "Mother . . ." she murmured, "Mother, I beg you—if you love me, stop questioning me—just . . . *please* stop questioning me —just leave me alone!"

Trembling with agitation, Katie forced calmness on herself. She must find some other method to deal with Mary.

"Don't be upset, Mary, just remember you are my beloved daughter—most precious to me and I want to help you, not to criticize or judge you—whatever has happened."

Suddenly Mary burst out crying and dropping to her knees beside Katie buried her face in her lap, as convulsive sobs shook her fragile body.

"Oh, Mama—I'm so lost . . . so lost."

Deeply upset, mystified by Mary's sorrow and secretiveness, Katie's hands caressed the girl's head and shoulders. "My poor, poor darling, but things are never as bad as they seem to be—troubles have a way of sorting themselves out, you will see—don't upset yourself so terribly."

A few minutes later, Mary calmed down, kissed and thanked her mother and left.

After dinner, which Mary did not attend, excusing herself because of a feverish headache, everyone went to the drawing-room, and the men sat talking politics, whilst Katie spoke confidentially to Liz, telling her about the scene with Mary.

"There's something very strange going on in her life; she was in a dreadful state of distress. I discovered nothing about where she had been when she was supposed to be at lessons and she refused to tell me anything about this man."

"Obviously she's been meeting him when Cillie was with her and Sannie driving her, so they must know who the man is." Liz said. "Naturally you can't demean Mary by questioning them. But of course you won't allow her to go on any more trips."

"Of course not. Oh, Liz—I keep hoping that possibly she's dramatising the whole business. Let's go and listen to what the men are talking about."

Van Riebeck, Chris and Kenneth sat drinking after-dinner coffee and sipping brandy. They stood up for Katie and Liz and as the women settled into chairs the men reseated themselves.

"I was telling Chris and Ken about my appointment next week with the High Commissioner," Van Riebeck said. "It annoys me that he's decided to keep me waiting seven days. It's the same rotten treatment we got in London years ago from Carnarvon. The High Commissioner should show more respect to a member of the Republic's Volksraad."

"I shouldn't think that he intends to be rude to you, Father," Kenneth spoke placatingly. "I imagine he knows why you're calling on him and he's cabling to London for Parliament's advice on the subject."

"That's it!" Chris nodded in affirmation. "I told you I thought it would be no easy job for the South African Republic to get England's sanction on the occupation of Saint Lucia Bay."

"But, God, man! We fought for it!

Zululand can pay her debts even though she's under the Queen's protection." Van Riebeck tossed some brandy back, wondering furiously when the damned English would treat the South African Republic with respect.

"It's a tricky problem for England, Paul, with Germany breathing down her neck." Chris spoke with quiet authority. "It would have been better had the problem of the Republic claiming Saint Lucia Bay arisen whilst the House of Representatives was sitting. There are enough Cape Dutch representatives to have voted for your cause."

"But we want the ratification at once! We fought to get it and want to start work on building a dock at once to make it acceptable for large ships to put in there."

"But, Father, why couldn't the Volksraad start the work?" Kenneth asked with the enthusiasm of youth, "without waiting for England's ratification?"

"We'd like to, but it would be stupid: we could be putting our money and labour into the scheme and then have England veto it and claim it. It wouldn't be the first time that happened. No, I must await the

High Commissioner's pleasure." Van Riebeck stretched his long legs. "But I was pleased to see what progress the Afrikaner Bond is making. The idea of using the Afrikaans language as well as English is obviously spreading in the Cape."

"But I think it will cause separation." Liz spoke gently yet firmly. "It's making the Cape Dutch feel that they're different from the Cape British, when actually they're all South Africans. It would be the best thing if all whites would unite as *one* country—*one* people!"

"Oh, oh, darling—you really have put the cat amongst the pigeons," Chris laughed at her, "especially as you know how Paul feels about the South African Republic."

"We don't mind if you people wish to become citizens of the South African Republic and be ruled by the Volksraad," Van Riebeck said with his blue eyes dark with seriousness, "but there is no hope that we'd ever subject ourselves to the Cape Government. The same applies to the Orange Free State and Natal—they can come under our flag—but the Vierkleur must fly supreme—that's the *only* way union would be acceptable to us." Van Riebeck's shoulder was aching and for some reason he was weary of discussing politics. He stood up, "If you'll excuse me I want to write to Kruger to get the letter off in the morning."

After he had bidden them goodnight, they all decided to retire. Liz and Chris, with Stephan and Jan, went off in the Cape cart to the adjoining estate and as Katie and Kenneth saw them off he said, "It's such a wonderful night." He gazed up at the purple-blue sky with stars that seemed ready to burst out into showers of silver. "Let's take a turn—down the avenue, Mother."

"I'd love that." She called out to the coloured butler, "Put all the lamps out, Joseph, but one, and go to bed. We'll lock up."

Arm in arm, they strolled slowly under the giant oaks that flanked the avenue and Katie breathed deeply of the warm air sweetened by Abend Bloem.

"Oh how I love the scent of Abend Bloem," Katie said, stopping for a second to enjoy a bush heavy with the big, bell shaped flowers of a magnolia-whiteness, that opened only at night.

"It's a good name for the estate," Kenneth said, as they again started walking.

Then he suddenly stopped and pulled her in between the darkness of the oaks. "There's a horse coming, who the devil is it?"

A horse and rider cantered by toward the house, then around to the back of it.

"Who is it?" Katie asked.

"God, it's Mary!" Kenneth muttered. "Where the hell has she been?"

Katie clutched at his arm. "To meet some man! She's in love with someone but refuses to say who he is. If she's been to meet him, it means he lives near here."

"What a rotter! Letting her ride home alone at this time of night."

"Perhaps he rode to the top of the avenue with her—wait! Listen!"

Nearby came the sound of cantering hooves dying out on the country road. "I suppose that's Mary's swain, I'd like to get my hands on the so and so. Why the devil won't she produce him? This is carrying shyness too far."

"Of course it is, God knows, but she grew hysterical when I persisted in questioning her." Katie told Kenneth about the scene with Mary. "In the end I thought it wisest not to continue to upset her."

"Well, I'm sure it's nothing serious." Kenneth did not want to add to his mother's anxiety, but he was furious and determined to watch Mary and find out who the man was.

The upset over Mary had made Katie suddenly feel drained. "Darling, I think I'll go in now, I'm feeling tired."

The next day, the timber and sieve wire which Katie and Liz had ordered when in Capetown, arrived to be made up into drying trays for fruit and for this work Liz asked Chris to loan her some of the coloured boys from the ostrich farm. Kenneth, glad of an excuse to stay home from the University supervised the building of the trays.

Katie enlisted the help of the younger children in picking apricots and peaches to fill the old baskets, previously used to carry grapes to the vats. Later everyone would help in stoning the fruit.

That morning Katie had arisen with the

determination of putting Mary temporarily out of her thoughts. It was stupid to enlarge upon something which was undoubtedly a concocted drama of Mary's.

Katie's first enthusiasm for exporting the delicate conserved fruits had now grown into an assurance that the product would become popular and she wrote about the fruit to Fortnum and Mason of Piccadilly in London, who dealt in rare delicacies. Then she wrote to the Board of Trade asking for a list of English importers dealing in sweetmeats.

For a few days Van Riebeck was away travelling around the nearby countryside, calling on prominent Dutch men who had sent money and arms to the Transvaal to help the Boers in the recent Anglo-Boer war. All were delighted to welcome him— a true Dutch hero. He returned to Abend Bloem on Friday just after Terence and John arrived from Capetown.

When all the family was in the big drawing-room, John burst out excitedly, "Uncle Paul, I've an invitation for you and Mother from Cecil Rhodes to lunch at his home—Groot Schuur—on Sunday."

"But I thought he hated women," Katie said.

"Oh, as luncheon guests he doesn't mind them," John laughingly assured her, "and when I told him you both were down here he said, 'I'd like to meet Van Riebeck.'"

"Very gracious of him," Van Riebeck said dryly but he was secretly eager to meet Rhodes and take his measure. He turned to Katie. "Would you like to go? I believe you would."

She knew such a meeting might be advantageous to him. "Yes, of course I'd like to meet him and to see his supposedly wonderful home. Thank you, John, we'd better send a message of acceptance, hadn't we?"

"I'll take care of that, Mother," John said. "I'll send a boy with a note at once. It won't be a long lunch because Rhodes' chest has been bothering him again and he has to rest a good deal."

Later as Katie sat with Liz in a shady corner of the big stoep, they discussed the forthcoming lunch and Liz said, "I don't like the fact that Rhodes abhors females and is surrounded by only young men."

Katie pulled a grimace at Liz. "I wonder if he's perverted as Nancy's husband was? I hope John's safe working for Rhodes?"

24

"GROOT SCHUUR" was a great, spreading white two-storey house with big Dutch gables, large small-paned windows and wide shutters. White pillars supported the ceiling of the wide stoep.

"It looks huge," Katie remarked to Van Riebeck and John as their carriage approached the house.

"It's fairly big, Mother—thirty rooms, fifteen bedrooms and two bathrooms and lots of reception rooms and studies. I like it when I have to work down here."

The Van Riebeck carriage pulled up before the house where coloured boys in spotless white sprang forward to hold the horses' heads.

Van Riebeck left the carriage and helped Katie down, then John followed and they climbed the wide steps to the stoep. At that moment Rhodes came out of one of the french windows to welcome them.

In a swift glance Katie was surprised to

see that he looked more like a man in his forties than early thirties but he exuded a feeling of bottled-up power. He was big and thickly set. His hands were clumsy looking, his mouth hard and his grey-blue eyes like ice as he bent to shake her hand.

"Charming of you to have come, Mrs. Van Riebeck."

She bowed her head with a smile hiding her surprise at the shrillness of his voice. Then his eyes darted to Van Riebeck's face.

"Commandant Van Riebeck, I've looked forward to our meeting." The swift measuring and weighing of Van Riebeck was obvious but Rhodes had evidently no intention of any pretence.

"Thank you, Mr. Rhodes," Van Riebeck grinned sardonically at the Englishman's appraisal of him. "I've been interested in meeting you, too." His whole demeanour was one of almost impertinent "don't-give-a-damn-for-you-Rhodes."

Rhodes clapped a hand on John's slight shoulder. "One of my favourite boys John is," he told Katie. "Let's go in."

He led the way into the spacious hallway empty but for two mahogany, colonial

Dutch commodes, the work of Batavian slaves. In the high ceilinged library, with delicately panelled walls and floor to ceiling bookshelves, they all sat near a french window that gave a view of fields and, in the distance, the blue of the sea. A coloured butler set down a silver tray with an assortment of bottles, decanters and glasses.

"What do you drink before lunch, Mrs. Van Riebeck?" Rhodes' shrill voice asked.

"Sherry, thank you."

"Commandant?"

"Brandy for me."

"And for me." Rhodes glanced at the coloured butler, then at John. "Dear boy, you'll choose for yourself, of course." As he smiled at the young man, Katie noticed that his eyes changed from ice to fire and she felt uneasy.

"You've a fine looking library, Mr. Rhodes," Van Riebeck said eyeing the books.

"Yes, yes; I don't care for novels but I've an interest in architecture." He waved at a row of books on the subject. "Someday, quite soon, I intend to build the perfect town."

"And where have you chosen your site?" Van Riebeck's voice was casual.

"I'm not sure of that as yet but God knows Africa is so huge—I'll certainly find the perfect spot."

"There should be some place that doesn't interfere with established governments."

Rhodes laughed, "I've no wish to upset the Transvaal, if that's what you're warning me about."

"I don't believe you do wish to upset our Republic, unless the rumours of gold grow; then Mr. Rhodes, I'll be expecting you with the millions you've made in diamonds to start buying claims in the South African Republic."

"Three cheers for your honesty, Commandant. Your prediction is faultless."

"Meanwhile we hear you are interested in Lobengula's land?"

"An exaggeration—I assure you."

"Liar," Van Riebeck thought but said, "I'm glad to hear it."

"When I was at Oxford," Rhodes went on, "I was most impressed by a lecture of Ruskin's, when he said, 'England must found colonies as fast and as far as she is able; formed of her most energetic and worthiest men; seizing any piece of fruitful ground.' I entirely agree with Ruskin, England *should* establish a power so great as to make wars impossible—she would establish the best interests of humanity. Various men have various ideas of happiness. For some its marriage and fatherhood—others great wealth—each works at this, his life long. My desire is to advance my country's greatness. I believe the English are the finest race in the world and the more of the world we inhabit, so much the better for the human race."

"My God, man, if those are really your ideas," Van Riebeck burst out angrily, "let me warn you to keep your English hands off the South African Republic unless you want another war!"

"Commandant, forgive me! I believe I've upset you." Rhodes seemed to be genuinely surprised. "My idea is not for immediate practice—it's merely a dream. Some more brandy—"

Trying to control his anger, Van Riebeck held out his glass, "Thank you, I'd like some."

The butler poured brandy into his glass

and Rhodes went on. "You must not be offended by my outspokenness—I'm a dreamer, accustomed to talk aloud." Then in a low tone as if to himself, he murmured, "A sick man must hurry—so much to do, so little time."

The beating of a gong came as a relief to Van Riebeck and Katie. Rhodes smilingly announced. "Lunch! Do follow me!" He started to move swiftly from the library.

The high-ceilinged dining-room had white-washed walls with old mahogany furniture polished to a mirrorlike gloss. Rhodes indicated the chair on his right hand to Katie, his left to Van Riebeck and waved to John to occupy any other chair that he wished to. As they were being seated, two young men joined them. They were colleagues of John's whom Rhodes introduced and they sat down.

As three coloured butlers in spotless white brought in plates of hot soup, Rhodes started to talk again.

His eyes on Van Riebeck's face, he said, "I approved of the Boers' move in forming the Zulus into one race again—all little kingdoms must be abolished. Some day, when I have the Cape Premiership, I'll do the same down here." Rhodes hastily spooned his hot soup into his mouth in between sentences. "I'll give the natives self-rule in tribal affairs, but everything will be under an English umbrella. Don't you agree, Commandant?"

Having told himself Rhodes was a madman, Van Riebeck said, "We think like that in the South African Republic. The Kaffirs, if they are to live in peace side by side with whites, must submit to the whites in all major decisions."

"Splendid! I'm glad we're in agreement."

"But, Mr. Rhodes," Katie broke in, "if you want them to live peacefully, why in heaven's name do you pay them with guns when they work on the diamond mines?"

"It's obvious," came Rhodes' swift reply. "They only come to work in the mines to get guns. If we refuse them guns and ammunition they won't flock to the mines! De Beers would be brought to a standstill. Without the Kaffirs who would do the work in South Africa? One must be practical about these things."

"I sometimes wonder if the diamond

mines have benefited the country," Van Riebeck said.

"It depends what you want," Rhodes shrugged, "a country of farmers, or a country that can also become industrialised and independent. We're in the nineteenth century, Commandant. We must open the country up to the world, as America has, but I know that this is not your President Paul Kruger's view—am I not right?"

"Kruger feels—as a very religious man —that the Boers live happily on their land with their cattle and wheatfields. He believes gold and diamonds only bring trouble in their wake."

"And you, Commandant? Do you agree with Kruger?"

"No, I've wider views, but what troubles me is that so far the riches of the country haven't gone to the Dutch. Take the case of the De Beers farm where some of the first and finest diamonds were found; the old farmer sold his farm for six thousand pounds. It was worth six million! Alas, he was no match for London's buyers and to give you an idea of how he felt about it, when someone said how he had been swindled, he asked. 'What would we have done with the money? We've a living-room and bedroom and kitchen. Of course we could have a new wagon and Cape cart, but we can afford to buy them out of the six thousand pounds.' I told you that tale, Mr. Rhodes, to show you how the vast majority of Boers feel about money—it is not their God. Cattle and land is what they value and they fear that there will be more gold finds."

The coloured butlers removed the soup plates and returned with huge platters of game.

"An interesting story, Commandant—the Transvaalers are a strange people, they do not realize that money spells power—that's the only reason I wanted it and still want more. Not for myself, you understand, but for England! I dream of a giant cartel governed by the English aristocracy where only the strongest rule. What a fine world we would make of it." The expression in his strange eyes was joyful as if he visualized this new world of his dreams.

Van Riebeck threw a secret look across the table to silence Katie whom he sensed was ready to denounce Rhodes.

"As you remarked earlier," he said, "each man has his personal dreams—I must say that yours and Paul Kruger's are far apart. Kruger is worried lest there be a great discovery of gold in Lobengula's Matabeleland. He thinks that this gold will cause our country to be soaked in blood."

"How very pessimistic—how absurdly melodramatic." Rhodes' voice was particularly shrill. "A blind man can see that gold will make your country rich, Commandant —pay your debts, put cash in your exchequer."

"Perhaps it would be possible, but to change the subject—I'm curious to know your feelings on Saint Lucia Bay. Would you vote in the House of Representatives to uphold Dinizulu's contract with the South African Republic?"

"Why not? The English don't need it as yet."

The impudence of the answer brought a derisive laugh from Van Riebeck. "Well, Mr. Rhodes, you are outspoken to the point of rudeness."

"I believe in speaking the truth, even to the point of rudeness. I hope you'll forgive me."

Rhodes smiled and looked down the table at John and the two other young Englishmen. "The truth—that's what I emphasise to my boys. Truth is ever simple—isn't that what I say, boys?"

The young men smiled and nodded and it infuriated Katie to see how they obviously hero-worshipped this madman.

"One must never waste time—it's too precious—not enough of it." Rhodes turned back to look at Van Riebeck. "The great fault of life is its shortness. Now you surely understand what I meant about Saint Lucia Bay? I've explained my dream for Africa's unification, so naturally Saint Lucia will some day also come under the English flag."

"Our dreams conflict," Van Riebeck said with quiet slowness. "The future will see which of us is granted realization of his dream."

"I like you, Commandant, you're an honest man. I like your outspokenness. But you haven't told me yet what your dream is."

"To ensure that the South African Republic remains free, to build a fine city of Pretoria, to have our own port operating

—Saint Lucia Bay—to pay our debts; to produce a fine Boer culture; to scrap the Pretoria Convention and rid ourselves of your Queen's Suzerainty. But above all and I emphasize *this*, that the South African Republic should continue to be free."

Rhodes had never taken his eyes off Van Riebeck's strong, determined-looking face, and now for a moment their eyes locked dangerously. It was as if Van Riebeck had slapped a gauntlet across Rhodes' face and challenged him to a duel.

Silently Katie applauded Van Riebeck for throwing the challenge. With knife and fork held quiet she waited as did the young men, all eyes on Rhodes.

Then his shrill voice burst out. "Yours is a very insular dream, Commandant. It would have a short life, but then everything in life is too short: life, fame, achievement. From the cradle to the grave what is it? Three days at the seaside."

With an obvious effort he shook off his depressed thoughts and said, "And the Queen's Suzerainty, why in the Lord's name do you want to shake that off? It can benefit you."

340

"Well, to quote Kruger, 'If you're ill and a strong man knocks you down and steals your purse, watch and clothes, leaving you naked, then later returns your clothes, would you accept them?'"

"Naturally," Rhodes laughed. "Better than being naked."

"But you'd still want your watch and purse back and that's our position. Mr. Gladstone returned our clothing only; we want our watch and purse. The Republic wants all of its land back and to be free of the Queen's Suzerainty. Some of our farmers are living under Kaffir chiefs' rule, because of England's land grab in the Pretoria Convention. It must be changed."

"But those matters are for Lord Derby, Secretary of State for the Colonies, to decide."

"Yes, we intend sending a deputation to see him in London."

Suddenly Rhodes obviously lost interest in the subject and said, "Well, we've all finished lunch so let me show you around my grounds."

Without apology to Katie he scraped back his chair, stood up and made for the door and there was no choice but to follow him out of the house with Katie thinking, "We're obeying him like children, the man is a monster."

"Let us walk a little way up the mountain to see the spot where the two oceans meet."

Katie thought with Rhodes' ideas of grandeur, one ocean is not enough! Afterwards he perfunctorily took them around his private zoo including caged lions, and two spreading paddocks where zebras were feeding and where springbok roamed.

"You see I have my own small Africa gathered around me."

"It's all very interesting, Mr. Rhodes, and you've been most kind," Katie said dryly. "But now I think we must be leaving. Perhaps you might have time to visit us some day?"

He gave his sudden warm smile that lightened his cold grey-blue eyes. "I should like to come, thank you." Then he glanced at John. "Don't go yet, stay and make a fourth at whist. I'll loan you a horse to ride home later."

He saw the Van Riebecks into their carriage and bowed stiffly.

As soon as they were out of his hearing,

Katie said to Van Riebeck, "A monster! He's power drunk for England. Such Imperialists destroyed Ireland—I loathe them yet somehow he has a certain charm."

"Where? How?" Van Riebeck demanded angrily. "He's a bloody madman, as Napoleon was. This Rhodes will cause us all trouble. Just as well he's a sick man. Better for Africa if he hurries up and dies."

"Darling—what a horrible thing to say."

"Why? I'd put down a berserk beast and that's what he is. Well, I must write Kruger a full account of all this. It won't come as a complete surprise to him, nor did the maniac come as a complete surprise to me. I'm glad I've met him. Now I know what to expect."

25

"WHAT a commotion is going on in here!" Van Riebeck said gaily with a smile of approval as he stepped through the door of the wine hall, where Katie and Liz, with three coloured women were picking out the finest fruit from piles of peaches and apricots and setting them aside for conserving.

"I really think we might be starting something that will build into a paying affair," Katie laughingly told him; then fearing that he might resent another project from her, she swiftly added. "It's Liz's idea as much as mine."

"I think it's a damn good venture. Chris and I were discussing it last night. Pity that you didn't think of it on our farm in Lydenburg."

The reproach in his voice was obvious and stung her, as if she cared little for the welfare of the farm. Damn him! She straightened up, her back was stiff from a long period of bending over.

"Surely the idea would not have worked up there? It would cost a fortune to transport the konfyt from Lydenburg to a port, whereas here we pack the boxes on to carts and drive directly to the docks to load them into the ship's hold. The expense of transportation is an entirely different proposition."

For a second their eyes clashed, then he said. "Yes, it's just another instance of how badly the Republic needs its own port. Well, I'm off to spend a couple of days with Hofmeyer. I want to be well briefed about the Afrikaner Bond. Later in the week I'll ride in to Capetown to see the High Commissioner."

He strode over to give her a perfunctory kiss, then remembrance swept over him, of how deeply they had been in love twenty years ago in this very spot when sorting grapes for the wine-making. Now he kissed her with added tenderness which she immediately sensed and, rejoicing at the fact of love revived between them, she reached up and took his face between her hands. She gazed up longingly into his wonderful blue eyes that could be so cruel, kind, cold and warm.

"I'm sure the High Commissioner will endorse Dinizulu's grant of Saint Lucia Bay," she said. "There can be no question of it!".

"Let's hope you're right." He put his mobile arm around her and squeezed her to him. "Don't overwork, darling."

Then he lightly kissed Liz's cheek and strode out into the sunlight.

"He's worried, I know," Katie murmured to Liz. "He feels the High Commissioner might not sanction Dinizulu's land concession without permission from London. Oh Liz, I hope he won't have to go to England to put the affair before Lord Derby and Parliament. These long separations are awful, and we can't afford for me to go with him with the small children and Maarje and Philip. That damned war with the English and the rinderpest wiping out our cattle really made a deep hole in our finances."

"But the ostrich feathers are selling well, you'll soon be making good money again, Katie. Don't worry, Chris and I have also money put aside which is at your disposal—it's from our half of the feathers which you so generously gave us."

"Gave you! What nonsense! Where would Abend Bloem be without you and Chris? Oh well, if Paul *has* to go to England, at least it means I'd have more time down here."

"If only the railway to Pretoria would soon start, it would mean you could come down regularly at least twice a year." Liz went on automatically sorting the peaches, trying to shake off an unexplainable depression. "Now that we're all growing older, you simply must make some such arrangement."

"God knows how I'd like to but Van Riebeck would never tolerate me leaving the Transvaal so often."

"It seems to me, darling, that after that attack of malaria you had, that he'll *have* to tolerate it!" Liz loved Van Riebeck but felt he was terribly selfish. "You've been through so much physical hardship in your life." Liz noticed how pale Katie had gone and grasped at her arm. "Stop working now! You've done more than enough for today. The worst of the heat is over so the fruit won't spoil in here, it's nice and cool. Come and have a rest."

"Yes, I think I might."

They pulled their deep frilled sunbonnets on and left the coloured women with instructions about the sorting, then arm in arm they strolled through the vineyards where the baby bushes, to Katie's impatient eyes, seemed painfully slow in growing. When would the grapes come and restore their wine trade?

"It's a pity that Paul is still so jealous of Howard," she said, "because the Duke of Rotherford with such an honoured place in the House of Lords, could be helpful with Paul's problem of Dinizulu's concession, but of course I dare not even suggest to Van Riebeck that he write and ask Howard to help."

They had tea in the small drawing-room, then Katie went up to rest and Liz drove herself in the Cape cart to the adjoining estate. She would return with her family to Abend Bloem for dinner.

Up in her big bedroom Katie dozed for an hour, then awakening feeling strengthened she was also filled with restlessness, so she got up and changed into her riding clothes. She would ride alone down a favourite route which long ago she and Van Riebeck had called "Lovers' Path".

There were only some maids around as she passed through the house and out to the back stoep, then to the stables where she told a coloured boy to saddle a horse for her. He gave her a leg up and thanking the boy, she rode through clumps of wild gladioli, through woodland to a beautiful leafy tunnel where trees met and their branches intertwined overhead.

She revelled in the quiet, nothing but the sound of her horse's hooves and the creak of its saddlery. She breathed deeply of the aroma of rich damp earth. Then nostalgia swept over her as she reached tall trees with bunches of silver leaves soft as velvet. So long ago Paul had picked some for her—she still had them pressed in a book of poems—the Cape Colony was supposedly the only place in the world where they grew. She loved Paul as she always had. Nothing must ever alter that.

Now the horse was quietly leaving the tunnel and stepping out into a wide vista of land dropping down to the unlimited Atlantic.

Day was gently dying, spreading its

chiffon-like shroud of mauvy haze over the world. God how she loved this view—this time of day. Here she and Paul had made love on the daisy strewn green sward that rolled down to join the beach. Lovely, lovely days those had been. Wonderful! They had been young—so deeply in love.

She sat her quiet horse, staring at the sea, clasping her memories to her heart; then soft nearby voices reached her.

"For us there is no chance of happiness," a man's deep musical voice lamented. "We're cursed."

"Don't say that, darling! How can love like ours be cursed? We've hurt no one."

Katie's heart thumped and she tightly grasped the reins. That was Mary's voice!

"We've hurt ourselves and we will hurt the people who care for us."

"That's not true!" Mary cried. "I'll go away—somewhere up country—after a time you'll forget me."

"I'll never forget you! Never! Never! But promise me you won't go away!"

"I promise you anything—anything, darling! I would die for you—I would. . . ."

"Sssh—sssh . . . don't talk of death, but

350

wait—I thought I heard the stamp of a horse's hoof. Someone may be near. Let's go deeper into the woods."

Silence! More silence—leaving Katie trembling with shock, ill, too agitated to think clearly. She waited a few minutes. Then trying to calm herself, she turned the horse around and walked it slowly down the leafy tunnel as her eyes searched the shadowy woodlands on either side for a sign of the man and Mary but she saw nothing. An ill-foreboding took hold of her —made her shiver and pray, "God take care of Mary."

She was glad when she reined in at the house and saw Kenneth on the back stoep coming down to help her dismount.

"You look very pale, Mother." Kenneth's grey-blue eyes swept anxiously over her.

"I've had a shock—nothing serious. Let's sit down and I'll tell you about it."

He held her elbow steering her to a group of wicker chairs and as Katie settled into one she murmured, "It's Mary! I didn't see her, but I'd swear I heard her voice in the woods."

When she had repeated the conversation

to Kenneth he said thoughtfully, "I think that proves that it's a married man—undoubtedly from the district. Probably a friend of the family's. What a rotter!"

"Ken—oh, my dear—how can we put a stop to the affair?"

"Don't worry, the first thing I must do is to discover who this swine is. I'll follow her when she doesn't know it. I swear I'll find out who this damned married man is and thrash the life out of him!"

"Ye . . . es." Katie loathed violence but decided Kenneth's way would be the only course to take. For some unexplainable reason she did not want to bring Van Riebeck into this. "I suppose that's the first thing to do—find out who he is."

"No need to worry Father about it." Kenneth seemed to read her thoughts. "He's busy enough. Mary's my sister and it's up to me to take care of her."

"Yes, I think that would be best. We had so much trouble with Nancy in Lydenburg, with all of her moods and sulks, that I'm ashamed to have to admit that Mary's being so troublesome too."

"Now don't worry so much—go up and

change for dinner and please put your faith in me to take care of all of this nonsense!"

"Yes, gladly." She squeezed his arm. "What a comfort you are, Ken."

Dinner as usual on the surface was a happy affair, attended by Liz, Katie and their husbands and children. Katie forcibly shook off her depression and when dinner was over, as usual the family gathered in the big drawing-room for music and cards, and Mary, anxious to please her mother, sang whilst Katie accompanied her on the grand piano.

When the song finished and the whole family applauded, Mary's cheeks turned pink. She gazed at Katie with wounded looking eyes and Katie saw in them the appeal for help. God how she longed to help this flowerlike daughter of hers.

"That was beautiful, darling." She smiled at Mary.

Katie was carrying on with her plan to deal gently with Mary, believing it would eventually induce her daughter to trust in her.

"Would you sing another song?"

"Please not tonight, Mother." Mary's pale face looked like a Botticelli painting of a girl pleading and Katie's heart ached for her.

"Of course, darling, but you're feeling well?"

"Oh yes, Mother, don't worry about me."

"Shall we walk on the stoep? It's cooler out there," Katie asked and they went through the french windows and strolled slowly over the tiled stoep lit by candles hanging in hurricane lamps.

"The air *is* cooler out here, thank goodness," Mary said then as if she had prepared the words in her mind she asked, "What was the *real* reason that Nancy went so suddenly to England? I felt there was something mysterious behind it all."

Fear and surprise momentarily dominated Katie and she asked herself had Mary guessed at the truth?

"Nothing mysterious. It seemed the wisest thing for Nancy to do," Katie managed to say. "You know how restless Nancy is. She never took to any of the eligible men out here so I thought the best place for her was in England where she would have a great choice. After all her divorce from Eric has finally come through."

"Oh, *why* must people marry? Not everyone wants to! I think one is better off without marriage."

An extraordinary remark coming from an eighteen-year-old and it set alarm bells ringing in Katie's ears.

She said with a casualness she did not feel, "But marriage is a normal state. In Ireland I was taught by the nuns that motherhood is the reason and triumph of every woman's existence."

"Don't! Oh, don't! Please don't, Mother! I won't believe it!" Mary stamped her foot in agitation. "Life has so many things besides breeding. Oh Lord—I've one of my headaches coming on. Will you forgive me if I go to bed?"

Mary planted a swift kiss on Katie's cheek and rushed into the house leaving Katie standing in amazement, staring into the house and watching Mary in her long white skirts flying up the wide staircase.

"What now? What now?" Katie asked herself, distressed by the scene and determined to find out what was torturing Mary. Katie hesitated long enough to regain her calm and then went into the drawing-room and managed to make a secret sign to Kenneth who was deliberately seated watching the stoep whilst simulating reading the *Cape Argus*, when in reality his eyes had been on his mother and Mary. Now he went out to join Katie who in a low voice told him what had happened.

"I'll wager she intends slipping out to ride again and meet that swine!" Kenneth muttered. "I'll go around to the side of the house and watch her window. When she puts the light out, I'll race around to the back door to wait for her and follow her. Tonight I'm going to find out who the bastard is and I'll thrash him within an inch of his life."

"Go, darling. Mary desperately needs to be rescued from herself and this man."

Katie watched him saunter down the steps of the stoep into the surrounding darkness to go to keep watch amongst the bushes where he would have a view of Mary's window.

26

BACK in the drawing-room, whilst trying to behave normally, Katie's unhappy thoughts clung to Mary. She had a creeping terror that the girl might do something fatal to herself. But never! Brought up in the Roman Catholic faith, as Mary had been and always so devout—it was impossible to think for a second that she would commit suicide.

Forcing herself to join in a game of charades with the family, Katie was secretly upbraiding herself, for she felt herself to blame for Mary's circumstances. Had Mary been with her, this unknown man could not have gained such a hold on her.

When at last Liz suggested that it was time to retire, Katie could have sung out with relief. Goodnight kisses followed and Liz and Chris with their family rode off in the Cape cart to the adjoining estate, whilst Katie and Eileen, leaving servants to lock up, went up the wide carved staircase, then on to Eileen's room where Katie sat chatting to her youngest daughter as she undressed.

In her voluminous cotton nightdress, Eileen knelt by Katie's knees and devoutly said her night prayers with an addition that surprised Katie.

"And dear God let me live with my Mama again. In the name of the Father, Son and Holy Ghost."

As she listened, tears sprang to Katie's eyes, and on her way to her room, she realised that Eileen's prayer had emphasized her guilt that she had chosen a life with Van Riebeck to a life with most of her children.

In her bedroom as she lit her candle, then slowly prepared for bed she struggled with her nine-year-old problem of how she could somehow induce Van Riebeck to spend more time in the Cape. Her children needed her and were so scattered; Paul now in the Transvaal, Nancy in England, Terence, Kenneth, John, Mary and Eileen in the Cape, only Franz and Adrian with her when she was in Lydenburg.

Brushing out her waist-length hair she told herself impatiently that she was too well aware that Van Riebeck would always make his home in his beloved South African Republic—nothing would ever induce him to relinquish his seat in the beloved Volksraad.

Some devil made her think of how different life would have been for her had she left Van Riebeck when he lay with his broken legs in St. George's Hospital in London following the shipwreck, then later accepted the offer of marriage of the Duke of Rotherford. With his immense wealth he could have cared for her and all her children on his Cumbria estates described by his aunt as, "62,000 acres of God's most beautiful land!" There would have been seasons in London for her at his beautiful Belgravia house, operas, theatres, balls, Ascot races, lovely clothes, magnificent jewels, carriages, thoroughbreds for hunting, trips to Paris and Italy. Her sons would have been educated at Eton and Oxford as John had been. Mary would have met eligible men and not be in this mysterious and dreadful dilemma.

Then she got into bed, blew the candle out and lay watching the moonlight casting its shadows on the ceiling whilst wondering if Ken would succeed in his plan to follow Mary and discover who the man was who was causing her such unhappiness?

Although fighting against it, her mind once more returned to the Duke and how he had followed her from England to the Cape, still pursuing his hope of taking her from Van Riebeck who was then in Lydenburg. Distrustful of her own feelings Katie had immediately arranged to trek North.

"My God, Katie," Rotherford had said, "I've come all the way to see you and I think you owe it to me to give me a little more time."

"Please, Howard, I've got to go to Paul —you know that."

"If Van Riebeck really loves you why does he drag you up to that hell of the Transvaal?"

"He's not dragging me up! I'm going because I want to."

"You can say what you like, Katie darling, but I don't believe a woman of your birth, your beauty can be happy in that kind of world. You belong in *my* world—you belong with me."

"Howard, be sensible. I'm eight years

older than you are. Even if I didn't love Paul, I'd be mad to fall in love with a man younger than myself. You should marry a young woman—have an *heir*."

Without warning he caught her in his arms, then bending her head back kissed her roughly, passionately, then some devil in her let her return his embrace—return his kisses.

The voice of one of her children calling to her from a distance returned her to sanity.

Six years ago, it had been six long years ago, since all that had occurred. Why in the name of heaven was she remembering Howard like this tonight? It must be seeing John again, with his splendid London clothes, his style, his accent, that had brought Howard so vividly to mind.

Now alone in the big four-poster bed, Katie turned and turned around again and again, trying to find a comfortable position and to free her mind of Howard. She was Van Riebeck's wife—he was the man to whom all her love was given.

"Dear God, please let me sleep," she

prayed. "Let me forget about Howard" and eventually she fell into oblivion.

For what had seemed to be half of his life, Kenneth had been standing hidden in the bush, his eyes on Mary's window that showed a light. He slapped out angrily at the pestering mosquitoes and came to the conclusion that Mary was not going to sneak out tonight. She must be lying reading, then suddenly she came to the window and placed a lighted candle on the sill.

"Jumping Jerusalem! Good God!" Kenneth swore to himself as in the moonlight he clearly saw her in the window standing in her nightgown with her long golden hair hanging down well past her waist.

What the hell was she doing? The candle? Of course! It was obviously a signal to someone. He stood absolutely still as he heard slight crackling sounds in the bushes and at the same time Mary pulled up her window sash and she let out a rope ladder to snake down against the side of the house to the ground.

In a swift flash a man's tall figure sprang

from the bushes. He streaked across the gravel path, caught at the ladder and skimmed up to the window, threw a leg over the sill and stepped into the room. The rope ladder was pulled up, the candle was removed, the window shut, the curtains drawn.

It had all happened so swiftly, so smoothly that Kenneth could barely believe he had watched it all. Then he started to shake with an insensate fury. What a bastard the man must be! And Mary! Had she turned into nothing worse than a harlot? God, Kenneth felt he would kill that man as he had killed men in the Basuto war.

He moved swiftly around to the back of the house, found a key for the door in his pocket, for since the Basuto border wars, the house was always securely locked up against chance invaders. Inside Kenneth moved to the gun room where he struck a match, held it to a candle then by its light took a gun from the rack. With a key on his belt he opened a locker and grabbed at some bullets and loaded the gun.

Now he was ready to kill to avenge his sister's innocence—her good name! Gun in one hand—candle in the other, he silently moved to the staircase and took the stairs three at a time, then went down the long corridor past his mother's room to Mary's door where he blew the candle out and put it on the floor. Forcing himself to be calm, he stood listening.

He heard the murmurs of voices—but in his enraged state, Kenneth could not understand what the words meant. He knocked three times then said.

"Open this door, Mary! I insist upon coming in."

Silence! Of course, she would pretend to be asleep.

"Open the bloody door!" Kenneth ordered in a louder voice.

Still silence, then Kenneth told himself that the bastard of a man would disappear by the window and rope ladder. Without wasting a second Kenneth blew the lock open, put his shoulder to the door and burst into the room ready to kill.

In a flash, he saw by the bed Mary—distraught looking, standing naked but for her long hair that hung about her and the man naked—a big black! Kenneth went mad and pointed the gun, then he saw the man's face. Oh God! It was Sannie!

"Don't shoot him! Don't! Don't!" Mary screamed.

At the same moment Sannie sprang at Kenneth and taking him absolutely unawares, wrestled the gun from him, pointed it at his own heart and pulled the trigger.

The gun fell to the floor as Sannie collapsed in a heap at Kenneth's feet and Mary, screaming in hysteria, threw herself on to him.

"Don't die! Don't die!" she implored, "Oh, Sannie. . . ."

"Master Kenneth . . . I glad . . . I saved you . . . from . . . murder. . . ."

Sannie's broken words came softly followed by a great sighing sound, then Sannie was dead.

Katie came rushing down the corridor crying frantically, "I heard shots! Is Mary all right?"

Then she stood in the doorway staring with tortured eyes at Sannie's body and Mary sprawled over him.

"Mary's all right," Kenneth muttered.

"I came to kill—Sannie—he was the man —but he saved me the trouble."

"Sannie! No—oh no!" Katie moaned feeling she was going insane—that naked girl was not her daughter Mary, with arms clinging around the black boy's dead body. "God help us! Help us!" Katie prayed as Mary's sobbing filled the room.

"Mama! Mama! I heard shots." Eileen's frightened voice in the corridor poured strength into Katie and she sprang from the room shutting the bedroom door behind her.

"Everything's all right," she called assuringly to Eileen. "Kenneth let his gun off by mistake. Don't let Maarje or Philip come here—if they awaken—tell them the shooting was outside."

They were the only servants who slept in the house—the others were accommodated in quarters some distance away— with the farm hands.

"All right, Mama, I won't let them come. I'm glad everything's all right."

"Now go back to bed, darling, and don't worry."

"All right, Mama."

When Eileen had disappeared into her

room, Katie raced back to Mary's room where Kenneth was standing as if turned into stone, just staring at Sannie and Mary who was now absolutely silent.

"We've got to get Sannie's body out of this room, Ken!" Katie shook his arm. "He can't be found here. It will ruin Mary's reputation! Now lift Mary up and put her on the bed, she's fainted I believe."

Moving like a machine, Kenneth scooped Mary up into his arms and laid her on the bed, he wanted to spew at the sight of her white breasts and stomach dark with Sannie's blood.

Katie felt Mary's wrist. "Her pulse is all right, thank God. Now let's wrap a sheet around Sannie. We mustn't have blood dripping from that wound all the way down the stairs."

She covered Mary's nakedness with a blanket and dragged the top sheet off the bed and crunched it up onto Sannie's deep wound to staunch the blood.

"For God's sake, Ken—don't just stand there! Help me!" Katie lashed out at him to bring him out of his state of shock.

x

367

"Yes, yes, Mother. I'm dumb with disgust. How could she with a. . . ."

"Sannie's colour doesn't matter! We've all loved him for years. Can you carry him downstairs alone, or shall I help?"

"No, no, I can manage. Where do you want me to put him?"

"In the back hall, not the stoep—dogs might get to him."

She helped Kenneth to hoist Sannie's big body across his shoulders saying.

"You've been splendid, Ken—absolutely splendid." She encouraged him as he took the full weight of the tall black boy. "Now just go slowly." She threw an anxious look at the still unconscious Mary, then taking one of the two candlesticks, she said, "I'll light you on your way," and going ahead of Kenneth, she held the candle high, to the back hall where Kenneth laid Sannie down in a corner.

"The sheet! Bring it!" Katie ordered.

Then holding the hem of her nightgown up so that she would not trip she raced up the stairs with Kenneth at her heels.

Back in Mary's room she said, "Take Sannie's clothes down and dress him, then put the gun in a natural spot from where he could have committed suicide. Then come back. Hurry, for God's sake, in case Maarje or Philip come downstairs to go to the lavatory and see you."

When Kenneth had swept up Sannie's clothes with the gun and left, Katie swiftly wiped the blood off Mary, then dipping a corner of a towel into the water jug on the mahogany washstand she bathed Mary's temples, arms and wrists whilst murmuring, "Everything is all right, Mary— everything is all right." Katie repeated it like a litany but Mary remained unconscious.

When Kenneth returned she sent him to her room for smelling salts and when he had brought the bottle, Katie held the ammonia to Mary's nose and she began to stir, then to moan.

"I'll get some brandy," Kenneth said and raced downstairs for a bottle.

"He's dead! . . . he's . . . dead!" Mary moaned. "Sannie . . . dead."

"No! No! He's not dead but badly hurt," Katie lied. "He'll be all right, don't worry—he'll be all right."

Kenneth returned and held out some

brandy and Katie put the glass to Mary's lips. She drank it, then lay back moaning.

"Now . . . you understand, Mother . . . why I couldn't tell you. Is he mortally wounded?"

"No, no, he'll be all right, won't he, Ken?" Katie threw him a warning look.

"In a month or so. The bullet missed his heart."

Kenneth handed Katie a glassful of brandy, then put the bottle to his own lips and drank and drank.

"Stay with Mary a moment, Ken," Katie ordered and sped to her room to get some of the morphine which Doctor Fraser had given Van Riebeck to counteract pain in the rhinoceros wound. She knew the correct dose for inducing sleep.

Back with Mary she insisted Mary swallow the morphine saying, "You've had a shock, darling, but if you go to sleep, I promise, I'll sleep here with you in the big chair all night."

When Mary fell into almost delirious sleep, Katie murmured to Kenneth, "I had to pretend that he wasn't dead, otherwise the shock might have been too much for her."

370

"I suppose so," he said grudgingly. "That and the shock of her being discovered with him."

"You must swear to me, Ken, on all that you hold sacred that you'll never ever tell this terrible thing to anyone—not to Terence, Paul—not to anyone!"

"Don't worry, I swear I'll never tell it! All I want is to forget it!"

"If Van Riebeck ever found out I think he would want to kill Mary."

"Yes, I can . . . understand that."

"I can't!" Katie flared defensively. "Sannie was a wonderful boy. Now get out of those blood-soaked clothes and hide them with that stained sheet in a portmanteau. Later we'll find a place to dispose of them where they won't be found."

"Yes, Mother. God, what a bloody awful mess it all is."

"It is . . . but you've always got to remember that Sannie wouldn't let you kill him . . . he preferred to kill himself because he realized that had you shot him —later you would have hated yourself. What Sannie did shows that he had the spirit of a noble man—never forget that."

"My God, Mother! I don't know how you can be so forgiving."

"Ah well—falling in love is not a crime," Katie said with infinite sadness. "Sannie was very young—Mary is, too, and it's sometimes difficult to help yourself, even when you know what you're doing is all wrong. Poor, poor Sannie—I think he shot himself really to help her out of the whole mess. God have mercy on Sannie's soul."

27

SANNIE'S death, which was considered by everyone an accident, was mourned by his family and all the black and coloured people working on the estate. Katie went to commiserate with Sannie's mother and told her that his sister Cillie must not come to work in the house until she had recovered from shock.

Now that Katie knew the truth of Mary's secret, a load was lifted from Mary and with Katie's deep love and understanding, Mary now felt that her sin had not been too unforgivable. Whilst she still loved Sannie since she had not been told of his death, the shock of the whole affair seemed to send strength to her to help herself and she agreed when Katie insisted that she must go into Capetown to stay with Terence and so get right away from Abend Bloem.

"From there we shall sail to London." Katie very firmly told Mary. "Of course you cannot carry on as you have done."

Whilst Katie abstained from reproaches she made it plain that the affair was ended.

"From London we'll make arrangements to go on to Milan for you to continue your singing training. Don't look so miserable about it, Mary. The entire change will help you in every way. The whole world is open to you and God has blessed you with a fine voice—you're lucky."

Later when they were in Capetown, Katie booked a cabin for two on a steamship leaving within a week. After deep contemplation she had decided on accompanying Mary alone—without anyone else. Later she explained to Liz and Van Riebeck.

"I've discovered Mary is in love with a married man," she lied, "really desperately in love with him. Don't ask me his name—she simply won't tell me. She was in such a terrible emotional state, ready to run off with him, so to save her from herself I've decided to take her to Europe to continue with a fine singing coach—get her away from the temptation of this man."

"I'm quite in accord with her going,"

Van Riebeck said, "but why must *you* take her, Katje?"

"Darling, she's far too young to travel alone." Katie had still not recovered from the shock of the Sannie-Mary affair.

"But Nancy did. She came out here alone from England and went back alone," Van Riebeck said.

"Nancy was a young married woman, four years older than Mary and far more capable of caring for herself."

"I don't approve of your going, Katje. There must be someone else who could chaperon her. What about one of your sisters, Moira or Sheila?"

"They can't leave their own families," Liz said gently. She was anxious that Katie should get away and enjoy the stimulus of Europe though only for a short time. It would be the first time since her seventeenth year that she would know freedom from children and household affairs.

"Yes, yes, Liz," Van Riebeck said impatiently, "but I'm against Katje going."

"Darling, please let me go with your blessing. Mary is in a terribly upset state, even though she doesn't show it. She needs me! The trip by steamship will only take three weeks going and three weeks returning. A week should be sufficient in Italy to arrange suitable accommodation in a good family and lessons with a coach. I won't be gone more than seven weeks."

"I don't like it. It means you'll be in Europe when I'll be due to return to Pretoria."

"But you said that your government business could hold you here for a couple of months before Sir Hercules Robinson receives an official reply from the London Parliament, so it won't be as if you're alone on the farm in Lydenburg. You'll have all the family here—because this time we can't afford for me to take Franz and Adrian with Maarje. It would mean two cabins."

Come what may she was determined to accompany Mary and when nearing England to tell her that Sannie was dead.

"Well, I know from experience that Katje does what Katje wishes." Unhappily he shrugged his great shoulders. "I have no choice but say 'Yes, go', Katje."

"Thank you, darling. You must know that I don't *want* to leave you. Separations from you are what I loathe and alas we've suffered through so many of them. Also whilst I'm in London I will see importers of delicacies and can surely receive orders for the konfyt."

Actually she cherished the idea of a little freedom from the South African Republic's problems. Also it would be good to be alone, but for Mary—then entirely alone for the three week journey back to the Cape. Then she upbraided herself for her selfish thoughts and went off with Liz to help organize the drying of the fruits in sugar.

Sick at the thought of leaving Sannie without even a goodbye, Mary decided that she dare not ask her mother's permission to do this. She vowed to herself that she would write to him from England, then even against herself a certain excitement started to creep into her being at the thought of seeing England and above all Italy for, next to Sannie, her love was for music and singing.

The night before sailing Katie lay with Van Riebeck in the big four-poster bed, her head on his good shoulder, his arm around her holding her body close to his.

"God knows how I hate letting you go

—I've always been the one to leave you behind, now I don't like the reverse side of the coin."

She chuckled and reached up to kiss him, "Oh yes, how well I remember lying in this very bed and weeping for days till I was almost blind, when you went off to Holland after a quarrel and didn't even say goodbye."

"I was a bloody fool in those days, I suppose."

"How lovely!" She felt triumphant. "After all these years to hear you admit it. Still—looking back on the quarrel I suppose I provoked you."

"You bloody well did. You've always been a bewitching provoking devil—it's one of the things that keeps me so in love with you. When you're in Europe—just remember that I love you and don't go flirting with that cousin-in-law of yours."

"Howard? Darling, don't be so absurd."

"But you've cabled Lady Eaton that you're coming to stay—so of course he'll turn up."

"Rubbish." Yet she felt a thrill of excitement at the thought of seeing Howard. "Just because you love me doesn't mean that other men do—silly darling."

His good arm was drawing her closer, his hand caressing her body. "Two months without my lovely Katje," he murmured as he moved to kiss her breasts and she sank her fingers into his golden hair. Then all the old excitement of his love-making drove everything but Van Riebeck from her mind. They had not made love like this since before their quarrel in Lydenburg and she knew how she was going to miss him when she was in Europe.

For the first week aboard the *Lancaster Castle*, Katie was fully occupied in trying to lift Mary from her slough of misery over Sannie.

Repeatedly, using almost the same words, she told Katie, "You've no idea, Mother, what a wonderful person Sannie is. I've never known anyone so kind and sweet. I believe I've loved him since we were small children and used to play together. I only realized it when one day we were riding our horses in the surf and my horse slipped and threw me. Sannie was off his horse in a second and picked me up. We clung to each other and I kissed him. He didn't kiss *me* first—*I* was the one. That's how we started." She began to sob. "I'm sorry—it was impossible not to love him."

"Try not to dwell on the past, darling. Come on, let's get dressed for dinner and tonight you've just got to dance. Those young officers are all quite besotted with you and you keep refusing to dance. Now tonight you simply *must* dance with them."

By the end of the second week of the voyage, it was no longer necessary for Katie to force Mary to dance. She was just naturally beginning to enjoy being admired and sought after by the good-looking men on board and Katie decided it would be best to delay the news of Sannie's death. Time enough when Mary was well established in new surroundings in Italy, immersed in music, when Abend Bloem and Sannie belonged to an almost misty past.

Katie too was enjoying all the attention she was getting from the attractive men on board. She enjoyed the rest, the freedom from problems, excepting Mary, who was fast recovering.

When the *Lancaster Castle* was a few days out of Southampton, Katie became as excited as Mary about seeing England.

"Do you think Nancy and Cousin Marie will come to the docks with Grandmama to meet us?" Mary asked.

"Oh, I should think so, although Southampton is a long way from Windsor."

Then came the last night's dinner and dance when everyone exchanged addresses and promises to meet in London. It came as a relief to Katie when she noticed Mary giving her grandmother's address to several eligible young men.

The next day the *Lancaster Castle* neared England and everyone rushed on deck to get the first view of the country, which was disappointing, flat and small after the grandeur that they had left of Table Mountain and the sparkling blue waters of Table Bay.

Then the ship moved into position alongside the docks and minutes later the gangplanks were lowered; then officials started coming aboard whilst the passengers waited impatiently and the air was filled with jubilant cries as people on board recognised friends and relatives waiting for them.

"Oh dear, how disappointing, Mother, I can't see Nancy or Marie." Mary caught at Katie's arm. "What a shame! I wonder if they've come to meet us and where's Grandmama?"

"Well—I don't know, darling, but. . . ."

"Katie! Katie! I've found you!"

She knew that voice as from behind her strong hands clasped her shoulders and she twisted around to look up into a man's gay brown eyes and a handsome, smiling face with black curling hair stirred by the sea breeze.

"Howard!" she cried in delight. "Oh, Howard!"

Then he was kissing her full on the lips and she was returning his kiss as he held her close in a tight embrace. Several seconds later she made herself pull back, laughing nervously whilst her hands flew to straighten her bonnet as she said, "What a surprise, Howard! We never expected *you* would meet us."

"Excuse me, your Grace," an officer said. "I take it that you've found your passengers?"

"I have! Thank you very much for your help." Then Howard turned to Mary and kissed her cheek saying, "I obtained permission to come aboard with the officials. Just couldn't wait for you to land."

"Cousin Howard, it's just lovely to see you," Mary cried, "but where are Grandmama and Nancy and Marie?"

"Ah, Nancy is staying with French friends of mine in Paris." He exchanged an amused glance with Katie and immediately the warm rapport of six years ago was re-established between them. "She considers she is in love again—with the family's heir."

Relieved laughter bubbled out of Katie. "Oh dear, how like Nancy, but what's important—is he nice? And suitable?"

"I think you'll approve of him, if you like Frenchmen—it's a fine family. Marie and my aunt await you in my carriage. I didn't bring my aunt to the docks in this crowd, she's getting old and Marie stayed with her."

"Dear Lady Eaton. I'm longing to see her."

"And she's longing to see you, Katie." He settled his grey top hat a little aslant on his thick dark hair. "Thank God you're as beautiful as always, but I knew you would be and how lovely Mary has grown." He smiled at the girl. "I've arranged for you both and my aunt and Marie to be my guests at my London house—I do hope you'll accept and tonight, I've a box for us at the Opera at Covent Garden—Adelina Patti is singing."

"Cousin Howard! How wonderful!" Mary clapped her mittened hands together with joy.

"Ah, my little cousin, my future little opera star, your real musical education begins tonight."

The barrier on the passenger gangplank was now lifted and excited people started to stream down to the docks. Katie said, "Should we go, too?"

"We'll do everything you desire." The Duke stood back and waved Mary forward then in a low voice told Katie so Mary could not hear, "I haven't changed, as always I'm your devoted slave. I adore you."

"Howard—really—how absurd you are." But looking up at him, her eyes were wide with pleasure, then she warned herself that her looks must be nothing more than friendly yet her entire being was excited by his presence, by the meaning it brought to her—it meant that once more she was an attractive, desirable woman, that he spread civilization at her feet. No wrongdoing if she enjoyed it and his company for a short while.

THE END

The Publisher will be pleased to send you free of charge, upon request a complete and up-to-date list of all titles available.

Ulverscroft Large Print Books Ltd.
The Green, Bradgate Road,
Anstey,
Leicestershire.
LE7 7FU
England.

GUIDE
TO THE COLOUR CODING
OF
ULVERSCROFT BOOKS

Many of our readers have written to us expressing their appreciation for the way in which our colour coding has assisted them in selecting the Ulverscroft books of their choice.

To remind everyone of our colour coding—this is as follows:

BLACK COVERS
Mysteries

★

BLUE COVERS
Romances

★

RED COVERS
Adventure Suspense and General Fiction

★

ORANGE COVERS
Westerns

★

GREEN COVERS
Non-Fiction

ROMANCE TITLES
in the
Ulverscroft Large Print Series

FICTION TITLES
in the
Ulverscroft Large Print Series

Enquiry	*Dick Francis*
Flying Finish	*Dick Francis*
Forfeit	*Dick Francis*
High Stakes	*Dick Francis*
In The Frame	*Dick Francis*
Knock Down	*Dick Francis*
Risk	*Dick Francis*
Band of Brothers	*Ernest K. Gann*
Twilight For The Gods	*Ernest K. Gann*
Army of Shadows	*John Harris*
The Claws of Mercy	*John Harris*
Getaway	*John Harris*
Winter Quarry	*Paul Henissart*
East of Desolation	*Jack Higgins*
In the Hour Before Midnight	*Jack Higgins*
Night Judgement at Sinos	*Jack Higgins*
Wrath of the Lion	*Jack Higgins*
Air Bridge	*Hammond Innes*
A Cleft of Stars	*Geoffrey Jenkins*
A Grue of Ice	*Geoffrey Jenkins*
Beloved Exiles	*Agnes Newton Keith*
Passport to Peril	*James Leasor*
Goodbye California	*Alistair MacLean*
South By Java Head	*Alistair MacLean*
All Other Perils	*Robert MacLeod*
Dragonship	*Robert MacLeod*
A Killing in Malta	*Robert MacLeod*
A Property in Cyprus	*Robert MacLeod*